ISBN: (978-1-911761-08-2)

**Published by arrangement with
Noble Legacy Publishing Ltd.**

About the Author

A descendant of William Wallace, **Stuart R. Fleming** is a storyteller shaped by legacy, land, and the subtle power of second chances.

The Fifteenth great-grandson of William Wallace, Stuart, carries a heritage of resilience and voice, not through battles, but through stories. Raised in Paisley, Scotland, his early life was steeped in the grit and grace of a family rooted in truth-telling and tenacity.

After a long and meaningful career in health and social care in London, Stuart turned to writing, not as an escape, but as a return. His work is deeply human, weaving memory with myth, and always seeking the place where brokenness meets beauty.

That place, for him, is Greece.

What began as a sailing adventure with his partner, navigating the waters around Poros with a dictionary in one hand and the helm in the other, turned into something far richer. Over time, the sea gave way to soil, and they built a life on the island of Kythera, among fig trees, stray cats, and friends who became family. The island's wild heart and layered stillness echo through every page of his work.

Stuart writes with warmth, clarity, and an emotional honesty that lingers. His characters, like their creator, are seekers, standing on thresholds, carrying pasts they cannot discard but choosing, always, to move toward light.

Greek Odyssey of the Heart is his most personal book yet, a love letter to courage, to reinvention, and to the spaces that help us remember who we are.

Dedication Page

*For all those who left not in anger, but in search of
something quieter. To Catherine, who first whispered,
"Just come." To the sea, for keeping its promises. And to
the readers, may you find your own Poros, in your way,
when the time is right.*

Greek Odyssey of the Heart

By

Stuart R. Fleming

Noble Legacy Publishing

"A deeply charming and evocative book. Be prepared to fall in love with the characters and the islands. A brilliant well written first novel."

— **Dame Marianne Griffiths**

Contents

Foreword

I never planned to write this book.

At least, not consciously. But as with all meaningful journeys, something deeper was at work, a longing, a quiet ache, a question I hadn't yet dared to speak aloud.

Greek Odyssey of the Heart began not with a plot, but with a feeling. The feeling of salt on skin, of standing in a place that knows you even before you remember yourself. The feeling of being seen, not through performance, but through presence. And the realisation that healing doesn't always roar in with the wind. Sometimes, it grows slowly, like thyme between stones.

This is a novel, yes. But it is also a letter. A thank you. A truth I couldn't write until the sea had softened me enough to speak it.

Wherever you are as you open these pages, whether broken, brave, or somewhere in between, I hope you find a reflection here. Not of answers, but of gentle invitations.

Because some books aren't written to impress. They're written to reach.

And this, dear reader, is one of them.

— **Stuart R. Fleming**
Kythera, 2025

Introduction

Sometimes, you have to leave everything you know to remember who you are.

This story follows Aimee, a woman who walks away from a life that looks fine on paper but feels hollow in the bones. Her journey is not about dramatic reinvention or picture-perfect recovery. It's about quiet bravery—the kind that says *yes* to uncertainty. The kind that finds joy in olive oil and sea glass. The kind that learns to live again, not louder, but truer.

Set among the islands of Greece, *Greek Odyssey of the Heart* invites you to breathe slower, to listen deeper, and to believe, if only for a moment, that beauty can meet you where you least expect it.

This isn't a story about escape.

It's a story about return.

Prologue

Aimee closed the door to the flat in Soho without looking back. The key turned with a finality that surprised her — not the flippant slam of a decision made in anger, but the quiet seal of something that had simply run its course. She stood at the top of the stairs for a moment, suitcase handle clenched in one hand, tote bag slung over her shoulder. Below, a taxi idled with its hazard lights blinking patiently against the grey of a late London morning.

The flat, now silent, still held traces of him — Richard. The antique mirror he'd insisted they hang in the hallway. The flickering gallery invitation cards pinned to the corkboard, some from exhibitions he'd pretended to enjoy. And the faint smell of his cologne, like dried pine and ambition.

She didn't hate him. Not exactly. But loving him had felt like dancing on a cliff edge — thrilling, disorienting, and eventually exhausting. Every gesture had been performative, every conversation a stage. There had been no room to breathe, let alone belong.

Her phone buzzed in her coat pocket.

Catherine: Taxi? Airport? You've remembered your passport this time, yes?

Aimee smiled despite herself.

Two nights earlier, her sister's voice had come through the line with that familiar blend of warmth and provocation.

"Just come," Catherine had said. **"The house I've found is old but solid — a place with stories. I could use your help, too. I'm trying to renovate, and I need your real artistic eye. Come stay. Get over Richard. Or don't. Just eat lemons and swim and remember what it feels like to laugh without checking the room."**

Aimee had laughed then, thinly, but the invitation had struck deep. Poros. The very name stirred old affections — an island that smelled of sun and thyme, where they had holidayed as children. There were photos somewhere of the two of them with salt-stiff hair and skinned knees, feeding stray kittens beneath taverna tables and collecting sea glass in old jam jars. It was the last place Aimee remembered feeling entirely herself.

And then there was the gallery.

She hesitated only once that week — not over Richard, but over leaving the gallery behind. It had taken her years to build that space. Small, sunlit, hidden just off Greek Street. It had once been a failing florist. Now it was Lysistrata — named with a wink, curated with intention, and one of the only places she had ever felt entirely in control.

On Monday, she'd met Sam — her gallery manager — in the back office, the air thick with the scent of bubble wrap and eucalyptus oil.

15

"**You're going?**" Sam had asked, not unkindly. "**Properly going?**"

"**For a while,**" Aimee replied. "**Maybe longer than that.**"

Sam had nodded. "**Good. London's eating you. You haven't painted in months. You need salt air and non-English men.**"

Aimee had laughed and then cried and then handed over the keys.

Now, as she slid into the back of the cab and gave the address for Heathrow, she felt the weight of it all: the loss, the relief, the delicate wire of hope that something unknown might grow from this pause.

Poros wasn't a plan. It was a direction.

A place to be, not to become.

She looked out at the streets of Soho one last time as they turned onto Charing Cross Road. A cyclist shot past, a woman walked briskly with a spaniel in a tartan coat, and the theatre signs flickered their usual morning yawn.

She didn't know if she was running from or toward.

But she was moving.

And sometimes, that was enough.

Chapter 1:
The Arrival

The ferry wheezed into Poros with all the grace of a hungover giant. Aimee stood at the rail, a battered leather bag by her side, her hair knotted by the wind, and uncertainty fluttered beneath her ribs. She watched the island materialise with whitewashed houses stacked like a theatre set, water catching the sun like shards of glass. This wasn't a holiday. It was a flight. Retreat. Defiance.

She hadn't told many people she was leaving London. There had been whispers in the gallery world, speculative texts from former lovers, a stilted phone call from her agent. But she'd kept her plans folded small, private, like an old letter read under your breath. Catherine had offered the villa without conditions. She couldn't face her partner, Richard. His retributions, texts, unanswered calls waiting like a bad diagnosis. She would find the time and strength to deal with him later. For now, it had been a curt goodbye on the London doorstep.

Her sister Catherine's call had prompted her departure.

"just come," *she'd said* **"There's time here. Time to breath. Marco and Serge are on the Yacht Samantha. It'll be old times and new."**

Time. What a strange gift. What a frightening one.

Marco and Serge met her at the dock with a sign that read: **Aimee – Welcome Back**. Marco wore sunglasses as oversized as his grin and a shirt that looked as though it had been tailored from a Mykonos sunset. Serge waved like they were long-lost cousins reunited by fate. Marco and Serge were the two sisters' best friends for many years in the countryside of West Sussex. They'd shared joys and sorrows, their bond something outsiders often found hard to name.

She laughed. The first real laugh in weeks.

Marco enveloped her in a hug smelling of salt, citrus, and some homemade cologne best described as **"enthusiastic"**. Serge followed with a kiss on each cheek and a murmur of *"Καλώς ήρθες,"* You are welcome, as if blessing her with the entire island.

The car they ushered her into was the colour of egg yolk and slightly smaller than her London wardrobe. It coughed reluctantly into gear and bounced through the narrow streets of Poros like a goat with opinions. Marco drove with one hand and narrated with the other, pointing out everything from the bakery that made **"the only koulouri worth waking up for"** to the butcher who sang arias on Thursdays.

Serge passed her a Koulouris wrapped in paper. **"For your nerves,"** he said, **"and your good health."**

Aimee chewed slowly, staring out the window as the sea played hide-and-seek between houses. Her heart felt strangely full and hollow at once, like a

18

balloon tied to a rock. The arguments with Richard slipped behind her like a silk scarf unravelling.

As they turned up a hill lined with olive trees, the town fell away behind them, replaced by silence and shimmer. Villa Petrouni revealed itself in pieces: a crumbling gate, a winding path, a bougainvillea-draped porch with chipped blue shutters. It looked like something forgotten and forgiving. The front terrace revealed itself with an explosion of hot pink bougainvillea and the sea below of a completely improbable blue. Catherine and her partner Lawrence had bought it the previous autumn and spent a few months fixing up its faded visage.

Just below Poros Town, nestled on the edge of the Aegean Sea, is a delightful maze of winding narrow streets that seem to whisper secrets of the past. At the heart of the town stands the old clock tower, a silent sentinel that has watched over generations of fishermen, artists, and travellers. Its timeworn stone face, weathered by the salty breeze, marks the passage of time with a steady, yet unhurried, tick-tock. The clock tower rises above the town like a reminder that the rhythms of life here are timeless, dictated by the pulse of the waves and the sun, not the clock.

The streets of Poros are a maze of cobblestones, their rough surfaces worn smooth by centuries of footsteps. As you meander through the alleys, you'll find yourself ducking under vine-draped archways, turning corners that lead to hidden courtyards, and discovering secluded corners where the scent of jasmine and rosemary mingles with the salty air. Here and there, a flickering lantern or an open window invites a glimpse into the quiet life within a family gathered around a table, a pot of strong coffee brewing, or the soft murmur of a conversation in the cool evening air.

Lemon and orange trees line the streets, their vibrant fruits offering splashes of colour against the pale stone walls. In the spring, the trees are heavy with blossoms, filling the air with a heady perfume that seems to cling to the skin long after you've left the streets behind. The sight of the sun filtering through the branches, casting dappled shadows on the ground, creates a timeless atmosphere, as though the world has paused for a moment to savour the simple joys of life.

The town itself is a blend of old and new, with modern cafes and shops nestled alongside ancient stone houses. The architecture, a testament to the island's rich history, is a mix of Venetian and neoclassical influences, with whitewashed walls, blue shutters, and wrought iron balconies that seem to lean toward the sea. Everywhere you look, there are small details that make the town feel alive perhaps a patch of vibrant bougainvillea climbing up a wall, or a cat lounging lazily on a sun-drenched windowsill.

They rounded the last bend, and there it was, Villa Petrouni. Blush walls softened by bougainvillea, shutters weathered like old postcards. The sea shimmered below like a secret. It looked like something forgotten and forgiving, waiting for someone to come home to it, its vibrant purple flowers spilling over the edges of the balcony like a riot of colour against the Mediterranean sky. The terracotta rooftops, faded by years of sun and salt, offer a warm contrast to the cool blue of the sea that stretches out before them. From the villa's large windows and expansive terrace, you can see the endless horizon where the sea meets the sky, the gentle ebb and flow of the waves below soothing the soul.

The shutters were worn and flaking, a quiet reminder of the years gone by. Yet, there is a beauty in their weathered state, each flake of paint tells a story, each crack in the wood a testament to the villa's endurance against the elements. The villa stands as a symbol of resilience, a home that has witnessed countless sunsets and storms, yet still offers a haven for those seeking peace and tranquillity.

The garden was a sanctuary, a lush oasis of lemon and olive trees, herbs, and flowers that bloom in the warmth of the Greek sun. The scent of the garden mingled with the sea breeze, creating an intoxicating atmosphere that draws visitors back again and again. A stone path winds through the garden, leading to a small courtyard where the sound of a distant church bell chimes in the air.

From this vantage point, the town of Poros stretches out below, its narrow streets winding down to the harbour, where the boats bob gently in the water. In the distance, the old clock tower stands tall against the sky, its clock faces a constant reminder that time, like the waves, moves ever onward, but in this quiet corner of the world, it moves slowly, as if savouring every moment. The view is not just a snapshot of the island, but a living, breathing portrait of life in Poros, a place where the past and present exist side by side, where time feels like a distant memory, and where the beauty of the land and sea becomes a part of you.

Catherine's note was pinned to the front door, the instinctive sister

"Welcome home. The kettle is on. The past is not invited."

Inside, the house smelled of rosemary, dust, and lemon polish. The kind of scent that suggested ghosts were welcome as long as they helped with the dishes. The furniture was a mismatched choir of old Greek wood and English comfort. Aimee ran her hand over the carved table in the hallway and exhaled a breath she hadn't known she was holding.

"Your room overlooks the orchard," Serge said. **"It has unreasonable floral curtains and extremely reasonable silence."**

Marco added, **"And no Wi-Fi until Tuesday, which is either a tragedy or a blessing."**

They helped her with her bag, showed her the quirks of the shutters, the cupboard that stuck, the tap that coughed when startled. Then they left her with the key, a bowl of fresh apricots, and a dinner invitation **"when your soul has unpacked."**

She sat on the edge of the bed and stared at her suitcase. It was filled with clothes that had never belonged here, shoes that expected pavements, and sketchbooks that had witnessed too much or not enough.

The silence of the villa pressed in not oppressively, but curiously. A listening silence. Had she done the right thing, could she put Richard behind her? His tantrums had become legendary. Friends stopped calling, and dinner invitations dwindled. Aimee had sought help for him, medical and psychological. She had partnered with a true narcissist, finally, after some therapy herself, she knew that to allow either of them to move forward, something had to give.

The giving could only be hers to gift, leaving with as much of her battered self-esteem as she could muster.

That evening, after a shower and a long nap that seemed to stretch into past lives, Aimee stood on the terrace with a glass of wine. The sky turned lavender and the air smelled of thyme and tide. Somewhere in the orchard, a goat complained about something existential. Bells rang from the village below like a conversation between centuries.

She opened her sketchbook. Not because she felt inspired, she didn't. She felt untethered, as if her edges had been smudged. But the blank page stared at her gently, asking nothing.

She drew a single olive branch.

Then a lemon.

Then a line that curved into a woman's face, she didn't recognise but somehow missed.

It wasn't art. Not yet. But it was a beginning.

The next morning, she awoke to birds arguing in the lemon tree and sunlight crawling across the floor like a cat that had lived there for years. She brewed coffee the way Serge had shown her: strong, stove-top, unforgiving. And drank it barefoot on the steps, watching the light change the colour of the sea.

Later, she walked into town, sandals slapping against warm stone, nodding at old women who stared without malice, just curiosity. She bought tomatoes that tasted of the sun and bread that felt like an apology for every supermarket baguette she'd ever endured.

She saw a man sitting outside a shuttered shop, carving into olive wood with the focus of a monk. She almost asked him what it was. Instead, she drew him later from memory, catching only the curve of his spine and the tilt of his hat.

Each day softened something in her. The ache in her jaw was from clenching. The hum behind her eyes. The restlessness that had once been mistaken for ambition.

Marco and Serge invited her to the harbour for dinner on the third evening. They sat by the water, grilled fish on the table, a bottle of retsina sweating between them. Serge talked about a man he once loved who stole a typewriter and moved to Vienna.

Marco reenacted an argument with the ship's electrician using a spoon and a sardine.

Aimee laughed so hard she cried.

Later, walking back up the hill, she realised she hadn't thought about her gallery, her ex, or the reviews in *Art Now* for nearly six hours. She considered that a victory.

Back at the villa, she lit a candle and wrote in the margin of her sketchbook:

"I think I am becoming someone I might be able to love again."

Chapter 2:
New Beginnings

The villa woke to the sounds of the island: shutters creaking open, doves shuffling across the tiled roof, the gentle clatter of crockery below. Aimee stood barefoot in the kitchen, wrapped in the unfamiliar quiet. It wasn't silent like in London, restless, expectant, stitched with sirens, but something softer. More generous. It gave her space to breathe.

Sunlight bled through the wooden shutters in wide golden bands. A breeze unhooked a dish towel with casual mischief. Somewhere beyond the orchard, a goat bleated like an eccentric opera singer, and a dog barked once in mild protest. She poured herself strong Greek coffee from the little Bialetti moka Serge had left on the counter with a cheerful note: **"For courage. And digestion."**

The lemon tree outside the kitchen window was heavy with fruit. She studied it as if it might reveal something. Then, without ceremony, she opened her sketchbook and drew the shadow of its branches curling across the stone sill.

Later that morning, Catherine padded in wearing her dressing gown, curls a soft halo, and took her coffee black. She had gotten in late from a wedding on Hydra last night and crept in quietly. **"You're drawing before breakfast,"** she said, not surprised but quietly pleased. **"That's usually a sign something's in the air."**

Aimee shrugged. **"It was either that or start repainting the shutters."**

Catherine smiled. **"You say that like it's a bad thing. This place could use a woman with a brush. I've missed you more than I can say."**

They took their breakfast: fresh bread, figs, and thick honey from Crete on the terrace. The sea blinked in the sunlight. Boats nudged one another at their moorings far below.

"It feels like time's moving differently here," Aimee said. **"Slower. But not stuck."**

"It is," Catherine replied. **"That's the thing about islands. They're like suspended sentences, and let's not start on the slow cogs of Greek bureaucracy."**

The conversation drifted into a quiet. Catherine reached for her notebook as if it were inevitable.

"Now. Let's talk about this place."

"Bathroom three has a drip," Aimee announced, **taking the seat opposite. "More like a tap with commitment issues on, off, on again. Let's just call it Richard."**

Catherine chuckled, then sighed. **"That's on the list. Along with the cracked cistern in the attic loo, the leaking pipe under the sink in the east bedroom,** and the fact that the downstairs shower hisses like a sea monster every time you turn it on."

"The kitchen, too," Aimee said, stretching. "It has charm, but the oven door won't close, the fridge makes that awful clunking sound, and the tiles are... slipping away from the wall, slowly and tragically."

"It's all fixable," Catherine said. She turned the page in her notebook, revealing a sketch of the floor plan. "I've been thinking. Mum left me just enough to do this properly. Not grand, but enough to turn this into something special. Six rooms, not too many. A rustic, creative retreat. A place for artists, writers, those who just need space and time. No corporate blandness, just real soul."

Aimee looked around the old villa, imagining the rooms with clean lines, soft linens, bursts of colour, and character. Lemon trees in the courtyard, sea breeze filtering through mosquito nets, pots of geraniums baking in the sun.

"I think it's exactly what this house wants to be," she said. It's waited long enough. Let's make it sing. I've thought about it long enough. If we get it to a lovely standard, there's a good chance it will be a success. When I was on Hydra for the wedding and the yoga retreat, I was inspired by the simple aesthetic and laid-back vibe. Just the sort of place that could fly here with the short connection to Athens. "Can you stay and help?"

Aimee hesitated. She glanced toward the orchard, where the wind stirred the lemon leaves. Part of her wanted to run; she always ran. But this time, something in her stayed still. **"Of course. I can't think of anything better,"** Aimee said.

Catherine smiled, relieved. **"You're sure? I don't want you to feel pressured into anything. I know you're still settling after everything. Richard, the house, your gallery."**

Aimee reached across and placed her hand on her sister's. **"I'm not pressured. I'm grateful. This place saved me in a way. You did too. And yes, I have some money from Mum's estate as well. Not much, but if it comes to it, if we need a new septic tank or a better water system, I'll pitch in."**

"You always pitch in."

"It'll need plumbing, rewiring, and probably roofing in places."

"And heart," Catherine added. **"It needs a sense of welcome. Noisy dinners under the pergola. Late-night conversations with strangers who become friends. That sort of thing."**

They sat in silence for a moment, the kind that didn't need filling. The cicadas were already singing in the olive trees beyond the open window.

"Let's start with the plumbing," Aimee said at last, grinning. **"Before someone else gets surprised by that sea monster shower."**

They both laughed. Outside, a breeze stirred the bougainvillea, and for the first time in years, the old villa felt like it was listening.

There was comfort in Catherine's presence, her dry wit, her unspoken understanding, her way of never asking too much and never offering too little. Aimee was acutely aware that not everyone had a sister who could simply appear at the right moment bearing lemons and no expectations.

"You haven't mentioned Richard, and what's next Catherine said after a while."

"I haven't thought about Richard."

"Even better."

They spent the morning pottering: Catherine repotted a sprawling basil plant, Aimee cleaned out the cupboards in the guest room, finding ancient teacups and a terrifying collection of souvenir plates. At midday, they wandered down into the village to the bakers, then on to the harbour.

The Lemoni Gallery sat quietly on a corner, its windows clean, its walls white and welcoming. Aimee slowed her pace.

"You going in?" Catherine asked casually.

"Not yet."

They kept walking.

Later that afternoon, while Catherine napped, Aimee took a long walk into the hills behind the villa. Aimee carried her sketchbook like a shield, though from what, she couldn't say. The path twisted between olive groves and low stone walls. At the top of the hill, the view opened wide, the village below like a painting in miniature.

She sat. Drew the rooftops. A cat on a ledge. A child kicking a ball against a shutter. The curve of the shoreline. Each pencil stroke was a quiet defiance. A refusal to disappear.

By the time she returned to the villa, her skin was warm, her hands smudged with charcoal. Catherine handed her a glass of cold white wine and nodded approvingly. **"Now that's the look of a woman who's told the world to wait."**

The next day, Catherine left for Athens to meet Lawrence. Her parting gift was a wink and a note taped to the kettle: *Don't forget who you are just because the water's calmed down."*

Aimee spent the first day alone wandering. The village revealed itself slowly, shuttered doors painted in sea-washed hues, old women in black watching her pass with gentle suspicion, a tiny shop selling only olive oil and gossip steeped in vinegar. She passed the Lemoni Gallery again. This time, the woman inside was dusting a sculpture shaped like a fish with too many fins. The courtyard was a work of art in itself, potted lemon trees leading the eye to the white neoclassical front doors.

Aimee hovered, unsure.

The woman caught her eye, smiled, and nodded once. Not an invitation. But not a dismissal either.

She didn't go in. Not yet.

Instead, she found a bench by the water, pulled out her sketchbook, and began again. She drew hands her own, imagined others, hands holding lemons, hands wringing towels, hands open and unsure. She felt a chink of joy, a rush of warmth unfamiliar but so welcome. She tried to remember when this last happened to her. A successful opening for a big artist, a wonderful afternoon with her mother in West Sussex driving through a poppy field. Certainly not in her personal life. The barbed words the apologies to friends after a tense dinner party, with Richard oblivious to the damage he was causing.

Back at the villa, she opened her portfolio for the first time in months. The older pieces stared up at her works from London, from exhibitions past, from nights when Richard had stood beside her like a sponsor, not a partner. Some were technically perfect but lifeless. Others bled anguish but had no soul. She sifted. Selected. Started forming a new shape to her work

The next morning, she returned to the Lemoni Gallery.

This time, Elena was outside arranging small ceramic bowls on a table that looked like it had once been part of a church.

"Back again," Elena said without looking up.

Aimee gave a soft laugh. **"Was I that obvious?"**

Elena straightened. **"Not at all. Just... memorable. Would you like to come in?"**

32

Aimee hesitated, then nodded.

Inside, the space was quiet, cool, smelling faintly of plaster, sea salt, and lemon oil. The gallery walls were covered in a thoughtful arrangement of pieces some restrained, some riotous with colour. Nothing screamed for attention. Everything asked you to listen.

Aimee paused in front of a charcoal sketch of a fisherman's hands pulling in a net.

"Elena," she said softly. **"Do you choose all of this?"**

"I try to," Elena replied. **"I like art that doesn't perform. It confesses instead."**

They talked briefly. About form. Light. Silence. Elena asked if Aimee painted, though it wasn't really a question.

"I used to show," Aimee said. **"Before I forgot why I started."**

"Maybe it's time to remember."

That night, Aimee couldn't sleep. She lit a candle, made tea she didn't drink, and laid her portfolio out on the floor like a prayer. She pulled out seven pieces none grand, none statement work, but each quietly urgent. A half-peeled lemon. A child's shadow cast on a beach. A faceless woman drawn from the back, one hand on a suitcase, the other clutching an olive branch.

She set them aside. She would bring them to Elena. Not to exhibit. Just to see what happened.

When she arrived the next day, Elena greeted her with the easy grace of someone who understood nerves.

They sat in the back room. Elena looked through the pieces slowly. She said nothing for several minutes.

Finally, she looked up.

"These are lovely. They don't pretend. They just are. That's rare."

Aimee exhaled.

"We're doing a small group exhibition in two weeks," Elena said. **"Three local artists. Two from abroad. Would you join?"**

"I'm not sure I'm ready."

"No one ever is. That's what makes it honest."

Aimee left holding a folded paper frame sizes, delivery dates, a quiet miracle. She walked home in a daze. It felt like something inside her had clicked back into place like a shoulder socket, painful and necessary.

Over the next days, she worked. Not feverishly. Not in a trance. Just consistently. She reworked some older drawings, gave them air. She painted new pieces, quietly, like whispering secrets to the paper.

She remembered how to love the making. Not the showing. Not the praise. The texture of graphite. The smell of fixative. The ache in her shoulder after hours bent over a page.

Catherine returned from the trip to Athens in search of fabric and taps, the day before the exhibition. She brought a bottle of sparkling wine and two ridiculous sunhats.

"You look... grounded," she said.

Aimee laughed. **"Still floating. But anchored somewhere, somehow."**

That evening, they walked to the harbour. The gallery was lit softly. Aimee's five pieces were displayed on the side wall, under a small sign that read: *New Work – Aimee Fellows.* No biography. No fanfare.

People wandered. Paused. One woman stood for a long time in front of the lemon.

Aimee stood to the side, wine in hand, Catherine next to her.

"How do you feel?" Catherine asked.

"Strangely calm."

Later, back at the villa, Aimee sat alone on the terrace. The stars were out in force, the air heavy with jasmine and the promise of another still, golden morning.

She opened her sketchbook and began again.

Not because she had to, but because, finally, she wanted to

Chapter 3:
Ripples and Encounters

In the days after the exhibition, the island settled back into its rhythm, slow and sun-warmed, like the second half of a Sunday afternoon. Aimee wasn't elated. She wasn't deflated either. Just subtly rewired like a painting that had been turned ever so slightly on the wall.

Now, the sketches in the back studio didn't explain themselves or excuse her. They just existed, hers, without footnotes.

Elena had sold three pieces. Quietly. Without ceremony. Aimee only found out because one of them had been taken down and replaced with a new work by someone else. The little lemon, the impulsive sketch she'd made after spilling her coffee, now hung in an Athenian flat. Bought by a woman who'd said, barely audibly, **"It reminds me of someone I almost became."**

Aimee didn't know what to do with that, so she watered the rosemary instead.

Catherine had gone back to Athens for a few days, on the critical matter of toilets and basins. She left behind a fridge full of leftovers and a half-read detective novel on the sofa. The house felt wider without her, but not emptier.

She spent one morning sketching the clock tower, another crouched over a chair she used to loathe, now willing to see its shape again. She tried a self-portrait and ended up with a woman who looked like she was waiting for a boat. Maybe she was.

On Wednesday, the air changed.

It wasn't weather, exactly, just a sense that something was about to shift. The light had a different angle. The sea sounded further away. Even the cats seemed mildly confused.

Aimee took her sketchbook down to the harbour, which had become a sort of chapel to her a place of movement and stillness in equal parts. She sat near the edge, back against a sun-warmed bollard, drawing the silhouettes of masts in the water. The boats bobbed in a rhythm she was starting to understand.

Then, a splash loud, messy, and entirely unseasonal.

Not the polite kind, not a child dipping a toe or a fish breaching. This was a full-bodied, theatrical splash followed by a shout and a chorus of startled Greek.

Aimee looked up.

A man had fallen into the harbour.

No. Correction. A man had *tumbled* into the harbour, perhaps chasing something or possibly saving face. Hard to tell. His arms flailed briefly before he righted himself, saltwater streaming from his hair.

Then he laughed.

The laugh was full-throated and shameless, and it bounced off the stone and glass like an invitation.

People gathered. A woman with a shopping bag scolded him gently. A teenager offered a towel. But the man waved them off, still treading water, still grinning.

Aimee stood slowly. She wasn't sure why.

He caught her eye.

Their eyes locked for only a second, long enough for her to register that he had strong shoulders, sun-browned skin, and the kind of expression that made you feel like you were already in on the joke.

Then he swam toward the steps.

She walked down without thinking, a towel from her beach bag in hand.

He surfaced like something out of a folktale more soaked poetry than Poseidon, with a grin that said he'd flirted with sea gods and gotten away with it. His hair dripped into his eyes. His shirt clung to his chest. His grin did not waver.

"You dropped something?" she asked.

"My balance. Possibly my dignity."

"Well, you've got your audience."

"Then I hope they clapped."

Aimee handed him the towel. Their fingers brushed. It felt like something small and electric, a detail that would be sketched later, or remembered.

"I'm Aimee," she said, unsure why she was offering it.

"Michalis," he replied. **"Apparently not as nimble as I used to be."**

He took the towel, rubbed the back of his neck, and sat heavily on the stone ledge beside her.

"Usually I'm more graceful," he said.

"Is falling into harbours your usual opener?" Aimee asked, her posture suddenly alert.

"Only when trying to impress strangers."

She raised an eyebrow. **"How's that working for you?"**

"Still breathing. Still charming. So far, so good."

A pause. The sea knocked softly against the quay. The moment hung there, not awkward, but tentative.

"Thank you," he said, quieter now.

"For the towel?"

"For not making it a story to tell your friends over wine."

"I might still do that," she said, but smiled to take the sting from it.

Michalis wrung water from his shirt. It formed a perfect arc before splattering onto the stones. "You're not from here."

"**No. But I'm not exactly a tourist either.**"

"**Somewhere in between?**"

"**Trying to be.**"

He nodded. "**That's a good place to be. Most of us live there without realising it.**"

He stood. The shirt clung stubbornly to him, so he pulled it off with a shrug. Aimee turned her gaze toward the sea, but not before noticing the faint tan lines, the scar across his shoulder, the ease with which he stood in his own skin.

"**I run a taverna,**" he said. "**Well ran. It's complicated.**"

"**How so?**"

"**It's a long story, and I'm not sure you've earned it yet.**"

She looked at him. "**Do I look like I'm in a hurry?**"

He considered that. "**No. You look like someone who listens.**"

They walked slowly back along the harbour's edge, Michalis barefoot, shirt over his shoulder. The small crowd had dispersed. Just another island moment folded into the day.

At a corner near the bakery, he stopped. "**This is me.**"

"You live above the bakery?"

"I live near the smell of good bread. Don't judge me."

She laughed.

"Would you..." He hesitated. **"Would you like to have a coffee sometime? Or something stronger, if you're the dangerous type."**

She didn't answer right away. The last time someone had asked her out, it had been over a gallery wine bar, with an eye on her name more than her face.

But this was someone who had just fallen into the sea and didn't seem to care. Who had thanked her for kindness and offered no explanations.

"Yes," she said. **"Coffee sounds nice."**

He smiled. **"Then it's a date."**

As he disappeared up the stairs, she caught herself still smiling. Not a big, swooning smile. Just one that felt like it belonged to her and no one else.

She wandered through the market afterward, picking up tomatoes and a new pencil set she didn't need. Everything felt a little lighter.

That afternoon, she sketched the moment, not his face, but the shape of him in water. The blur of movement. The curve of a smile. She left the space where their hands touched empty, unshaded.

She wasn't trying to capture him—just the feeling.

When Catherine returned the next day, windblown and glowing, Aimee didn't mention Michalis straight away. They made dinner, opened a bottle of wine, argued about basil, and watched the light fade across the garden.

But later, as they sat beneath the stars, Aimee told her.

"There's someone."

Catherine blinked. **"Already?"**

"He fell into the harbour."

"Romantic."

"He laughed the whole time."

Catherine smiled. **"Is that what did it?"**

"No," Aimee said, surprising herself. **"It was that he didn't seem to care who saw him do it."**

They met for coffee two days later at a small café tucked behind the town hall. Aimee had passed it often. Its blue chairs were always half-filled with people who looked like they belonged to the scenery.

Michalis was already there when she arrived, sitting in the sun with his elbows on the table and a small glass of water untouched beside his espresso. He looked up, smiled without standing, and shaded his eyes with one hand.

"You came," he said.

"You doubted me?"

42

"I hoped. I always prefer to be pleasantly surprised."

She sat. The café owner, a woman with a braid like a rope, appeared silently and offered Aimee a menu. She waved it away with a smile.

"Whatever he's having," she said. "Unless it's awful."

"It's excellent," Michalis replied. "But you'll hate it if you like anything too polite."

"I'm not really in a polite mood."

He grinned.

They talked for over an hour, not about the things you'd expect, not about work or family or politics. Instead, they circled oddities: favourite smells, why some people hated aubergine, the exact right time of day to swim in saltwater. He told her a story about a pelican that used to steal cutlery from his taverna. She confessed that she sometimes gave names to trees if she sat under them long enough.

He didn't ask her what she did. She didn't ask him who he used to love.

There was something in the way he listened, not leaning forward, not nodding performativity, just *there*, present, like it mattered.

Eventually, she asked, "So, the taverna?"

He tilted his head. "It's closed for now. Might not reopen."

"Why?"

He looked at his espresso cup like it might answer for him. "My sister and I ran it. Family place. Long story. Our lease came up. The building's being sold. Or it was. Still complicated."

"I'm sorry."

He shrugged. **"It's a season, like anything else. You get used to them changing. Doesn't mean it doesn't sting."**

"And now?"

"I'm figuring it out."

She nodded. **"That makes two of us."**

A pause.

Then, softly, he asked, **"Did you leave something? Or someone?"**

"Both," she said. **"But I'm not sure what I've found yet."**

They parted with an awkwardness that wasn't unpleasant, the kind that lingers when something has begun and no one's sure what to name it yet.

As Aimee walked home, she passed the bakery where Michalis had stopped to speak with the owner, an older man with wild eyebrows and a scowl that softened the moment Michalis greeted him. She watched as he gestured with both hands, made the man laugh, and accepted a warm koulouri with a humble little bow.

She turned the corner before he saw her, not out of fear but preservation.

That evening, Catherine cornered her on the terrace with a glass of wine and a grin. **"So, the fisherman."**

"He's not a fisherman."

"What is he?"

"I don't know yet."

Catherine raised her glass. **"Even better."**

That weekend, the weather turned. The sky bruised at the edges, the air heavier than usual, and the sea darkened to the colour of polished stone. Aimee stayed in most of the day, sketching in broad, loose strokes. Her thoughts drifted toward Michalis more than she meant them to. There was no denying it now he had lodged somewhere between curiosity and longing.

That evening, just as the rain began to tap on the shutters like an impatient aunt, there was a knock at the door.

She opened it to find Michalis, hair damp, shirt half-unbuttoned, his face alight with something urgent.

"Do you have five minutes?" he asked.

"For you? Maybe six."

He grinned. **"Put on shoes."**

They walked quickly, umbrellas forgotten, rain curling in their hair. He led her not to the harbour café, nor the bakery or the gallery, but to a shuttered stone building set just off the waterfront.

The sign above the door read *To Kima,* the taverna she'd heard mentioned in passing, once a staple of the village before it mysteriously closed.

Inside, it smelled of memory. Wood smoke. Sea salt. Distant joy.

Michalis lit a lantern.

"This was ours," he said. **"My sister and I. My father, before that."**

Aimee took in the curved walls, the heavy chairs stacked neatly in a corner, and the ancient till that looked as though it belonged in a museum.

"It's beautiful."

"It was home."

"What happened?"

He hesitated. "Eleni, my sister, she's proud. Fierce. After our parents died, this was her way of keeping them close. But the lease was always a point of friction. The building belongs to someone else or did. Now he wants to sell. And here's the twist..."

He looked at her, his eyes bright.

"He's offering it to us. First. At a price we can manage."

Aimee blinked. **"That's... amazing."**

"It is. Terrifying. But amazing."

"Do you want it?"

He laughed. **"What I want and what I fear are often the same thing."**

They stood in silence for a moment. The rain tapped louder now, as if asking for an answer.

"You came to tell me?" she asked**.**

"I don't know why, but yes."

"I'm glad you did."

"I don't know if I can do it again," he said. **"Start over. But Eleni... she's already drawing up menus."**

"Then maybe you already are doing it."

He looked at her, and something quiet passed between them, a warmth that didn't ask anything yet, but promised it might one day.

Outside, the rain eased.

He offered to walk her back, but she declined. **"I want to remember this walk alone,"** she said.

He didn't push. Just nodded once. **"Fair."**

She watched him turn the key in the old wooden door, then disappear into the mist.

Back at the villa, Catherine was curled on the sofa, reading.

"That was a long milk run," she said without looking up.

Aimee smiled. **"Not milk. More like a lightning bolt in the shape of a man."**

Chapter 4:
Foundations

Aimee had expected to see Michalis again in the casual, incidental way of island life, a nod across a market stall, a wave from a passing scooter. But instead, three days passed. The wind shifted. The village settled into the hush of early spring fatigue, and life returned to its usual rhythm.

She spent her mornings sketching boats at the harbour, her afternoons rearranging the studio aimlessly in the face of the tug of uncertainty. Michalis didn't appear. No call. No message. Just an absence that hummed with possibility.

And then, on the fourth day, she saw him. Not alone.

He was on the back of a pickup, unloading crates of olive oil outside a grocery shop. Next to him stood a tall, lean woman, arms crossed. She said something in rapid Greek, sharp as a switch, and Michalis laughed. Not the bright laugh he'd shared with Aimee, but something worn-in. Familial. Familiar. He turned, saw Aimee across the square, lifted a hand, and hesitated.

The woman turned too.

Eleni.

Aimee didn't need introductions to know who she was. There was something in her stance, protective, appraising, like someone who had spent years holding things together by sheer force of will. Her gaze lingered on Aimee for a moment too long. Not unkind. But not welcoming either.

Aimee smiled. Eleni didn't return it.

The moment lingered, then passed. Michalis raised his hand again apologetically this time, and turned back to the crates.

Aimee walked on, trying not to assign meaning. She was good at that; years of gallery shows and critics' reviews had trained her to separate the art from the noise.

That evening, Catherine and Lawrence arrived.

Their ferry docked late, just as the sun was melting into the sea and the first lights flickered on in the old town. Aimee met them at the harbour, Lawrence wheeling a comically overstuffed suitcase and Catherine already talking about wine and paint colours.

They embraced like people who knew what time could take and chose to protect the bones of love anyway.

Back at the villa, they opened a bottle of Agiorgitiko and settled on the terrace. Catherine took one look at Aimee and narrowed her eyes.

"You've got that look like you're holding back the juicy bit," she said

"You know I met someone," Aimee said.

"I know it."

49

Lawrence raised his glass. **"Do we like him?"**

"I think I do," Aimee said. **"But I also think I might be one sibling short of approval."**

Catherine tilted her head. **"Ah. The sister."**

"She saw me. She saw *me*," Aimee said. **"And I've never felt so transparent in my life."**

Lawrence chuckled. **"Older sibling?"**

"Hard to tell. It could be either. Could be both."

Catherine grew thoughtful. **"Give her time. Women like that don't open the door just because you knocked once."**

As the stars came out, the conversation turned to the villa and what it could become.

"We've been thinking," Lawrence said, swirling his wine. **"You remember the little hotel next door?"**

"The one with the green shutters and the massive, stubborn jasmine? Of course."

"It's for sale."

Aimee blinked. **"You're buying a second house?"**

Catherine shook her head. **"We can't commit now; this place is a money pit."**

"We're not buying it. Just dreaming it aloud. Let's keep it on the radar." Catherine repeated, eyes bright with something more than wine.

Lawrence leaned forward, elbows on the table, the bottle between them like a lantern. "We've got the ideas; it could be like an extension of this place. I have bargained with work to see if I can work remotely, maybe with a once-a-month trip if needed."

"You got it?" Aimee asked.

He nodded. "As of next month, I'll be working part-time from here. Sussex can survive without me."

"And the rest of the time?" Aimee asked, though she already knew.

"I prune bougainvillaea and perfect my hummus," Lawrence said solemnly.

Catherine grinned. **"We want to turn the villa into something more... deliberate. A place for art, and writing, and maybe a bit of cooking if you're feeling Greek."**

"A retreat?" Aimee asked, cautious.

"A living, breathing space for creativity. For people like you. And not just you."

"I'm flattered."

"You're invited," Catherine said. **"Not as a guest. As part of it."**

Aimee hesitated. The idea tugged at her like tidewater, equal parts awe and unease. It certainly would cut some ties that bind.

Lawrence refilled their glasses. **"We know it's sudden."**

"It's not," Aimee said. "Not really. Just... bold."

Catherine took her hand. "You were bold once. You still are. We're just giving you a place to be again."

The silence that followed wasn't heavy. It was full.

Aimee looked at the villa shutters still cracked blue, walls dappled by the sea-salt wind, and imagined it humming with voices, with paint, with music, with *possibility*.

"I'll need a decent kettle, and a toilet that doesn't make a noise like a plane taking off," she said at last.

Catherine laughed. "And a fridge that doesn't sigh in despair."

They stayed up late. Talked through names. Ideas. What they would offer. How would they keep it grounded? How would it stay honest?

They reminisced over childhood memories. The sun had dipped just low enough to throw golden threads through the bougainvillea that framed the terrace. Aimee leaned back in the old wooden chair, its paint chipped, its joints loose but still faithful, like a well-worn friend. Catherine sat beside her, knees curled up, cradling a glass of white wine. Below them, the village exhaled slowly into the evening a rustle of laundry, the clink of cutlery, and the occasional echo of a radio drifting up from somewhere unseen.

"I'd forgotten," Aimee said quietly, **"how the light can do this. Turn everything to memory."**

Catherine tilted her head. **"What memory are you chasing now?"**

Aimee smiled, eyes far away. "The house called Sunnydale is on Wickham Park. Do you remember the smell of the seaweed flats at low tide? That sharp, briny air? It used to rush up from the Ouseburn like it was trying to tell us something."

Catherine laughed, warm and unguarded. "And Mum shouting out the window, 'You two better not come back smelling like the estuary!'"

They both dissolved into laughter that easy, rolling kind that comes only from shared history.

"There was that one summer," Aimee said, **"when we convinced ourselves the apple tree in Mrs. Jamieson's garden was magic."**

"Oh God, yes, because it blossomed twice!"

"And we tried to cast spells by burying toffee wrappers under it."

"It did make the apples sweeter," Catherine replied, mock-serious.

They fell into silence again, not awkwardly, but like they'd reached a clear still pool and both wanted to linger.

Newcastle in the 1980s had not always been kind its skies often grey, its buildings soot-streaked and bruised by time but inside their small, loving house, it had been golden. Their mother had made it so with her laughter, her lemon-scented ironing, her hands that moved constantly sewing, cooking, calming. Their father, quiet and bookish, had taught them the names of stars and Greek islands long before they ever imagined sailing to one.

"Remember when Dad made that papier-mâché volcano?" Catherine said, nudging her foot against Aimee's. "We turned the living room into Pompeii for the science project."

"He ruined your new ballet shoes with vinegar and bicarbonate of soda."

"And you cried harder than I did," Catherine said, amused.

"I just knew we'd never find another pair with bows like that again. Not in Fenwick's, not anywhere."

They sipped their wine in the hush that followed. The kind of hush where crickets begin their song and jasmine begins to breathe.

"I sometimes wonder," Aimee said slowly, "how we ended up so far from that life."

Catherine turned. "We didn't end up far. We just went looking for things. You with your art, me with my books and Lawrence and everything. But when you strip it back we're still those girls playing archaeologist in the back garden. You painting fossils onto broken roof tiles. Me lecturing the rose bush about the Ptolemies."

Aimee let out a breath, part laughter, part ache. "Do you ever miss it?"

"Every single day," Catherine said without pause. "But I wouldn't go back. I'd just bring more of it forward. We often compare notes on this with Marco and Serge, how lucky we all were to have loving parents. The grounding the confidence it can bring."

The next morning, the sun returned with a golden vengeance, and Aimee awoke to the scent of fresh coffee and the sound of Catherine bickering with Lawrence over the optimal window angle for a future studio.

She wandered into the kitchen to find Eleni there.

Eleni.

Standing with arms crossed, watching Catherine point a wooden spoon at a blueprint on the table.

Aimee froze. Not from fear. From awareness.

Eleni turned.

"You're the artist," she said.

It wasn't a question.

"I am," Aimee said, lifting her chin slightly.

Eleni said nothing. Just observed her, like a curator inspecting a piece with too much praise attached.

Catherine looked up, oblivious. "Oh, good, you've met! Eleni popped in to talk about some work being done on the garden wall between the two properties. Apparently, it's been crumbling since 1987."

"Longer," Eleni said.

The moment stretched.

Aimee walked forward, slowly. "Can I offer you some coffee?"

Eleni studied her. **"I've had mine."**

A beat.

"Well, if you change your mind," Aimee said. "We also have some… excellent figs."

"They're not from Poros," Eleni said. "Imported from Crete."

"I won't hold it against them."

A pause. Then was that the slightest twitch of Eleni's mouth?

Not a smile. But something that had once been one, and maybe could be again.

She nodded once to Catherine, then left with a kind of measured grace that made it clear nothing surprised her, and everything was filed away.

The door clicked shut.

"She's tough," Aimee said.

"She's loyal," Catherine replied. "To Michalis. To the past. And to what she thinks safety looks like."

"I can respect that," Aimee murmured.

And she did.

But it didn't make her breath easier when Eleni was in the room.

The next evening, the villa smelled of garlic and ambition. Catherine was making something, unfortunately, experimental with octopus and red wine. Lawrence had been sent to the market twice, once for herbs and once to retrieve a forgotten bottle of wine.

Aimee stood at the sink, washing dishes she hadn't touched, listening to the voices echo between the kitchen and the garden. She felt steadier than she had in years. Still uncertain, still slightly afloat but anchored by something new.

They chatted over Villa Petrouni plans and searched for information on similar retreat-type small hotels. A visit to the ancient town of Corinth seemed like a good opportunity to meet a French couple who had set up a couple of years ago. Catherine emailed them and her friend Linda for advice. Leaving an open invitation for Linda to visit.

A knock at the back door.

She turned, towel in hand.

Michalis stood there.

He looked like he'd run or almost changed his mind. Shirt damp at the collar, hair tousled, smile caught between relief and apology.

"Hello," he said.

"Hello yourself."

"I was nearby. Thought I might…"

"Come in."

He stepped inside. The light caught the side of his face tired, but open.

"You've been busy," he said, nodding toward the blueprints on the table.

"So I've heard."

"And Eleni?"

"She stopped by."

A pause.

"She's… complicated," he said.

"I'm learning."

"She's not trying to make things difficult."

"I know. She's trying to protect you."

He looked at her, really looked. "And you?"

"I don't need a shield. Just… a little understanding."

He nodded slowly. "Then we're halfway there."

From the garden, Catherine called out, "Is that a guest? Bring them wine or shame yourself sister!"

Michalis grinned. "That's your sister?"

Aimee rolled her eyes. "You have no idea."

They walked out together. Catherine waved a ladle like a sceptre, Lawrence offered a seat, and within moments, Michalis was folded into the table like he'd always been meant to be there.

He talked about the taverna. The offer. His hesitation. Eleni's drive.

"She says if we do it, we do it *our* way," he said. **"Simple. Honest. No pretence."**

"Sounds familiar," Aimee said, smiling.

After dinner, as the candles burned low and the wine deepened, Eleni appeared at the gate.

She didn't come in.

She stood, arms crossed, expression unreadable.

Michalis went to her. They spoke in quiet Greek. Aimee watched from the porch, not intruding, not retreating.

Eventually, Eleni's gaze found hers.

She didn't smile.

But she nodded.

Just once.

It was enough, it was Greek αποδοχή acceptance, to a certain point.

Later, as the guests drifted home and the stars returned to their vigil above the hills, Michalis and Aimee stood in the orchard, the grass still warm from the day's heat.

The lemon trees whispered overhead. From the terrace, the soft clink of glasses being cleared, the echo of Lawrence's laughter.

"I'd like to see you again," Michalis said, voice low.

"You see me now."

"Then let's not stop."

She looked up at him, not searching, not questioning, just *there*.

He reached for her hand. She took it.

For a moment, they said nothing. It wasn't needed.

Then he leaned in slowly, as if asking permission not with words, but breath.

And she met him.

The kiss was not urgent. It was not fireworks or declarations. It was warmth. It was a door opening. It was the breath between endings and beginnings.

When they parted, their foreheads touched, and Aimee smiled not out of giddiness, but relief.

"I thought you might taste like the sea," she whispered.

"I was hoping for wine and wild thyme," he said.

She kissed him again, just once, more softly.

Then they stood quietly, hands entwined, while the orchard and the stars bore witness.

Chapter 5:
Tides and Tethers

The yacht *Samantha* swept into the Poros strait like a woman late to a party but too glamorous for anyone to mind. Her white hull bore the salt-smacked marks of a long sail, and her genoa, the forward sail, hung in tatters, flapping like a pirate's flag. It should have looked tragic. It looked heroic.

At the helm stood Marco, one foot perched dramatically on the bench like he was posing for a regatta calendar. Serge, barefoot and sun-browned, was coiling a line with theatrical scorn.

"They'll never believe what the Dokos Strait did to us," Serge muttered, tossing the rope into a locker as they glided toward their mooring.

"I plan to embellish with conviction," Marco replied. "That wind was biblical."

The town of Poros shimmered in the late afternoon sun. Red roofs stacked likeliness of a sonnet. Church bells in the distance, barely audible over the sputter of mopeds and gulls. For Marco and Serge, this was not an arrival. This was a return.

As the yacht slipped into her berth, Catherine and Aimee appeared at the edge of the quay. Aimee waved with both hands. Catherine had a bottle of wine tucked under her arm and two glasses clinking from a basket.

Marco was the first to leap off the boat, arms open wide, nearly taking out a German tourist with a selfie stick.

"Darlings!" he cried. "We are wrecked gloriously! Ruined! Heroic"

Serge followed with slightly more dignity and two enormous bags of lemons from Ermione.

Aimee hugged Serge first, nearly toppling him. He smelled of sea and saffron. "You smell like you've sailed through a spice rack," she said.

"We sailed through a storm," Serge corrected, pointing to the ragged sail.

"And yet, here we are," Marco said, wrapping Catherine in a hug that nearly dislocated her shoulder. "Four hours of shrieking winds, one near-divorce over the chart plotter, and I am *still* the better helmsman."

"You overshot the channel by a nautical mile," Serge said mildly.

"Details."

They walked up toward the Villa Petrouni together, Marco insisting on dragging one of the lemon sacks "as penance," while Serge updated them on the trip.

"We started in Napoli, perfect weather. Then spent a night in Ermione. Gorgeous food. Horrid plumbing. Then the straits. A gust from the gods' *whoosh* rips the genoa clean off. We nearly lost the coffee pot."

"Then Marco nearly flung the compass overboard," Serge added.

"I was channelling Odysseus."

"You were channelling Poseidon on a bad day."

They laughed the whole way up the hill, Aimee carrying the wine, Catherine carrying their news, both buoyed by the familiar energy of these two theatrical, grounding, always a little sunburned.

At the villa, dinner was spread beneath the olive trees, grilled aubergines, stuffed peppers, bowls of tzatziki and warm bread. The lemon tree cast shadows across the table, and the cicadas struck up their usual busy chorus.

"To the survivors of the Aegean," Catherine toasted.

"To *Samantha*, who never gave up," Marco replied, patting the yacht as if she could hear.

"To wine," Serge added. "Our truest navigational aid."

They ate until the sun dropped behind the ridge and the plates were scattered with crumbs and seeds, sparrows pecking with gusto. Stories spilt like olive oil of an old fisherman who'd blessed their hull with a sprig of basil, of a taverna in Ermione where the waiter proposed to Serge (mistaking him for a French travel writer), of a tiny bay where they swam in phosphorescent light.

But beneath the laughter, something flickered. A sense of change.

"Alright," Aimee said, narrowing her eyes. "You're hiding something."

Serge and Marco exchanged glances.

Marco leaned back, dramatically folding his napkin. "We're putting down roots."

"You're buying a house?" Catherine asked, eyebrows raised.

"We're buying a base," Serge said. "A little place in Poros town. Near the bakery with the scandalous koulouri."

"Just a modest little townhouse but with a terrace made for poetry and wine," Marco added. "But it's ours. After twelve years of summers, we thought... why not, and with you two settling here at Villa Petrouni."

A silence fell not of shock, but of recognition.

"You're staying," Aimee said softly.

"Not full-time," Serge said. "But more than before. Certainly more than a sailing season."

"And when we're not here," Marco said, "you'll have a key. A base. A bolthole."

Aimee looked at Catherine. Catherine looked at the stars.

Something was brewing.

Something was beginning alright.

The next morning, the sea stretched out smooth and silver, as if it had slept well. The island hummed with early light, mopeds growling, shutters opening, coffee pots clattering to life. Marco and Serge appeared with conspiratorial grins and sunglasses too large for the hour.

"Come," Marco said, tapping his watch. "It's time for the unveiling."

Catherine blinked. "Unveiling of what?"

"Our modest little dream," Serge said. "Prepare yourselves. Wear sensible shoes and an open heart."

Aimee looked at Catherine. Catherine looked at her sandals. "We'll try."

They walked down through the lanes of Poros town, past the bakery that smelled like sugar and history, past laundry lines strung like flags of everyday life. The streets grew narrower, steeper, until the houses pressed in like gossiping relatives.

Finally, Serge stopped before a vivid blue door tucked between two larger buildings.

"This is it."

Aimee tilted her head. "It looks like it's hiding something."

"It's perfect," Marco said, unlocking the door with a flourish.

Inside, the house was calm and bright. Whitewashed walls, arched doorways, and floors tiled in mismatched patterns that felt accidental and magical all at once. The downstairs was small, a sitting room, a kitchen barely wide enough to stir tea in, but every inch of it felt like it had been loved into being. Dust pervaded every nook and cranny.

They climbed a narrow staircase, the kind you had to take sideways if you were carrying groceries or ambition. At the top, Marco paused dramatically.

"Ready?"

"Always," said Catherine.

He opened the door.

The terrace opened like a secret too beautiful to keep.

It stretched the full width of the house, edged with terracotta pots bursting with rather wild basil, mint, and a bougainvillea that had no intention of staying put. And beyond the low wall, the Poros Strait. Samantha is standing proudly like a best friend at a wedding. The water was broad, glittering, flecked with the white trails of boats slipping past like whispered secrets.

Aimee stepped forward, hand to her chest. "It's... ridiculous."

"In the best way," Catherine breathed.

"You see why we couldn't resist," Serge said, quieter now.

They stood there in silence, each absorbing the view, the scent of salt and jasmine, the soft creak of a boat's mast somewhere down the hill.

"This is the kind of place," Marco murmured, "where sending a postcard feels unnecessary because you're already living the wish."

Catherine turned. "You'll keep this for good?"

"That's the plan," Serge said. "We'll still sail, of course. But this... this is the anchor."

Aimee nodded. "It feels like you've found something that holds everything gently. Movement and stillness."

Marco smiled. "That's the goal."

They spent the next hour on the terrace with Greek coffee and biscuits Serge insisted had been imported from a tiny bakery near Galaxidi. They made plans for the furniture. They debated which neighbour had the best laundry etiquette. They took turns imagining who'd be first to write a novel here and who would just read one luxuriously.

And all the while, the sea went on sparkling like it knew exactly what it meant to be permanent and fluid all at once.

Later that evening, after the wine had mellowed and the view had turned to shadow and silver, they lit candles on the terrace of the townhouse. No agenda. Just the slow ease of old friends sinking into silence and memory.

Aimee sat cross-legged on a faded cushion, sketchbook beside her, untouched. Catherine leaned against the wall, a shawl around her shoulders. Marco and Serge shared the bench they'd always gravitated to, an old habit from Sussex days, when they'd hold hands under blankets as the rain hit the conservatory roof.

Lawrence had once called those winters "soul seasons." The time when nothing was performed, and everything was true. Nights of long stews and wood-burning fires, of flickering candlelight and the kind of companionship that never needed narration.

They had gone through so much in those years. Parents fading gently, sometimes not at all. An illness that refused to be brave. Goodbyes that caught in the throat. They had taken turns delivering quiet strength, a soup left at the door, car rides offered without reason, a silence shared beside a fire when words would have shattered something fragile.

The griefs had not broken them. They had bonded them.

And then, the sailing began. It was just a trip that first summer, Marco and Serge inviting Samantha aboard, promising dolphins and simplicity. It became their ritual. Year after year, they met in small harbours and taverna jetties, bearing local olives and news from England, watching the sun bounce off different seas and letting laughter return like birds to spring trees.

It had been on one of those long, wine-soft evenings, anchored off Hydra with goats bleating in the cliffs above, that Catherine had turned to Aimee and said, "I want a place here. Not just a house. A purpose."

And Villa Petrouni had followed.

Now, here they were years later, with lives weathered and softened, but never diluted. Aimee looked around at the others, her chosen family, and felt something ease inside her, like a door left ajar on a summer night.

"I used to think you had to *say* everything," she murmured. "Now I think... it just has to be true."

Serge nodded, his hand resting lightly on Marco's knee. "Truth speaks. Even in silence."

Below them, the strait whispered in the late afternoon, boats rocking gently, lights bobbing like prayers in glass jars.

And on that terrace, nothing had to be spoken.

Everything was understood.

Part 1.
Terrace Reflections: Serge and Marco's Relationship

Later that evening, after the wine had mellowed and the view had turned to shadow and silver, they lit candles on the terrace of the townhouse. No agenda. Just the slow ease of old friends sinking into silence and memory.

The candles flickered in jam jars and small ceramic bowls, casting shadows that danced along the bougainvillea like passing thoughts. Aimee sat cross-legged on a faded cushion, sketchbook beside her, untouched. Catherine leaned against the wall, a shawl around her shoulders. Marco and Serge shared the bench they'd always gravitated to the same one they used to curl into back in Sussex winters, when they'd hold hands beneath old woollen blankets while the conservatory roof rattled with rain.

Serge's fingers now absentmindedly traced patterns on Marco's knee. Not performative, not even intentional. Just a gesture of knowing the kind that only decades together can craft. Marco, eyes half-lidded, raised his glass lazily toward Serge's bare ankle. bare and tucked beneath him like a boy.

Catherine watched them, chin resting in her palm, and exhaled a soft sigh, one that came not from envy, but from recognition.

70

"**They've always had that,**" she said quietly to Aimee. "**That invisible current.**"

Aimee nodded slowly. "**Strong. True. Steady.**"

She looked across at the two of them, Serge with his quiet humour and the kind of gentleness that came from surviving storms without needing to talk about them; Marco, fierce with love, directness, and impossible charm, but always softened by Serge's stillness.

"**I've chased men who only liked the chase. Who mistook devotion for drama?**" Aimee said. "**But what they have... It's not about conquest. It's about anchoring each other.**"

Serge looked up and smiled. "**We learned that one the hard way.**"

Marco chuckled. "**We once tried to build an Ikea wardrobe together in 2008. Nearly divorced on principle.**"

"**It was the Allen key that broke us**," Serge added. "**And then remade us.**"

Laughter rustled through the terrace like wind through dry leaves.

"**But it was when we stopped trying to be ideal for each other,**" Marco said, more thoughtfully now, "**that things got real. When we could say, 'This is me messy, tired, wrong about most things, but here.' That's when it worked.**"

Aimee let the words settle. **"I need that. I want that. Not perfection. Just truth and presence, a man who gives more than he takes."**

Catherine reached for her hand and squeezed it. **"You've earned it and then some."**

Marco raised his glass, voice low. **"To endurance not surviving, but remaining. Through storms and seasons. But of being with someone long enough to know their seasons. Their habits. Their quietest fears."**

Serge clinked his glass against his. **"To be known."**

"And still loved," Catherine added.

They toasted without ceremony, the glasses singing a quiet note into the night.

And on that terrace, nothing had to be spoken.

Everything was understood.

Part 2.
Morning Walk – Aimee and Serge

The next morning, Aimee rose early, earlier than usual, drawn not by alarm but by a tug behind her ribs, something like homesickness for a future you can feel. She pulled on a light jumper, slid her feet into sandals, and crept out without waking the others.

Poros was still stretching itself awake. The scent of bread, that beautiful perfume of crust and warmth, drifted from the bakery below. A tabby cat meandered down the lane, tail flicking like punctuation. The air was cooler than she'd expected, still blue from the last trace of night.

She walked without a plan, letting her feet choose the path. Past the cracked plaster walls where lemon trees leaned into courtyards, past a shuttered bookshop with hand-painted signs, past a low archway where someone had written in chalk: το φως μέσα σου είναι αληθινό, the light within you is real.

She sat down on the low wall, just opposite the archway, and watched the island blink itself into life.

When footsteps approached, she half expected a stranger, a baker, or a yawning child sent to fetch milk. But it was Serge, barefoot in espadrilles, carrying two small cups of thick Greek coffee and a paper bag twisted shut.

"You read my mind," she said.

"No," he smiled. "I just always know where you'll be when you're thinking too hard."

"I was watching you and Marco," she said. "And thinking... I want what you have. Not the showy bits. The anchoring. The... quiet honesty. It's like you've learned how to hold each other without needing to hold on."

Serge smiled faintly. "It wasn't always like that. We tried too hard, then not enough. We fought about small things, big things, and unspeakable things. There were times we thought we wouldn't make it."

"And yet you did."

"We realised love isn't a feeling you chase. It's a choice you return to. Even on the worst days."

"I used to think love meant drama. That it had to shake you. But now I wonder if the real thing... steadies you."

"It does. Eventually. After the shaking."

"Do you think that kind of love can still find you," she asked, "if you've made all the wrong choices first?"

Serge turned to her, eyes soft. "I think it usually only finds you after."

Part 3.
Sisterhood in the Square –
Aimee and Catherine

Then came the sound of sandals scuffing. Catherine.

She emerged from the narrow alley wrapped in a cardigan three sizes too big probably Marco's with her hair in a loose knot and a determined look that softened when she saw them.

"I was looking for you two," she said. "Then I realised I wasn't. But here you are anyway."

Serge stood and kissed her cheek. "We're only ever one thought ahead of you."

"I hope not," she said, accepting the last of the coffee. "My thoughts are chaos this morning."

She lowered herself onto the wall. "Do you remember that first summer here? When we came with a list of all the things we were going to fix?"

Aimee laughed. "And ended up fixing none of them."

"Except maybe ourselves," Catherine murmured.

"You were right," Aimee said quietly.

"About what?"

"About what I deserved. About the life I thought I had to settle for."

Catherine smiled. "You were right too. When you said this island does something to you. I didn't believe it. But now I think it's a place that strips you back to what matters. There's no room here for pretending."

"Or for hiding," Serge added. "Poros is too small for secrets."

"Do you think we'll keep choosing this?" Aimee asked.

Catherine didn't answer at once. "I think we did, somewhere between last summer and this sunrise."

4. Morning at the Villa Petrouni – Shared Intentions

Back at the villa, Marco was already out under the olive tree, scarf around his neck, coffee cup held like a philosopher.

"I see the morning council has convened," he said. "Do we begin with gossip, philosophy, or plans?"

"Forgiveness," Serge said. "You forgot the one you need most."

Lawrence brought juice and figs. "I vote plans. We're on this rock together now. Let's make it a good one."

They gathered at the table, still littered with candle stubs. "What are we planning?" Aimee asked.

"What we're building next," Catherine said. "Not just the villa. The life."

"It's the first time in years we're all in one place at the beginning of something."

"I keep thinking about that terrace," Aimee said. "What it means to put something down. A tether, not a trap."

"I want to grow something here," Catherine added. "Not just the villa, but something rooted in us."

Aimee smiled. "It's like sailing. You don't always control the wind, but you can choose your course."

"Or your crew," Marco said.

Chapter 6:
(Opening section: Villa Petrouni,)

The sun was just beginning to surrender when Michalis arrived at Villa Petrouni, his steps light but deliberate across the path to the weathered blue door. He carried a bottle of deep red Agiorgitiko, and tucked into his jacket pocket was a small velvet pouch frayed at the edges, precious beyond measure.

Aimee had arranged a table beneath the pergola. The vines above were catching their autumn colours, blushes of amber, threads of red curling into gold. A candle flickered beside a bowl of olives and torn bread. There was something in the air that evening, a hush beneath the island sounds, as if even the sea and sky had paused to take notice.

She greeted him with a kiss on the cheek. Her eyes, tired from a day of painting shutters and canvas alike still shone. Michalis stepped into the courtyard as if it were a sacred space and in many ways, it was. The place had changed since his first visit. Or perhaps, it was he who had changed.

They ate slowly roasted vegetables, lemon potatoes, simple fare sanctified by hunger and affection. They started with small things a neighbour's goat that had escaped its pen and become a local celebrity. A young couple at the retreat in matching caftans and matching contempt. Laughter rose easily between them, a dance that neither had to lead.

As dusk deepened, Michalis reached for his jacket. "I brought you something," he said.

Aimee looked up, surprised. "You did?"

He drew out the velvet pouch and placed it on the table with reverent care. "This belonged to my mother," he said. "Eleni kept it safe all these years. We both did."

Aimee opened the pouch with careful, almost hesitant fingers. Inside was a bracelet silver, delicate, slightly tarnished with age. It was simple, yet unmistakably beautiful. A narrow filigree band encircling a single, tiny blue stone.

"She wore it every Easter," Michalis said softly. "It's the last thing I remember her wearing before she passed."

Aimee sat in silence, fingers slowly tracing the curves of the metal. "Why are you giving this to me?"

"Because you're part of me now," he said. "Because you see me, not just the part I show to the world, but the ones I've spent years trying to protect."

Her breath caught. "This is... I don't even know what to say."

"You don't have to," he said. "Not tonight"

But Aimee's eyes brimmed with tears not joy, not sorrow, but something older. Something tangled deep in the quiet, protected spaces of her chest. It had been years since she'd allowed herself to feel this kind of safety. London had taught her to doubt everything, every compliment, every gift, even the engagement ring Richard had withdrawn "for cleaning." The dull realisation: every moment of warmth came with a price.

"This is too much," she whispered. "I don't know if I'm capable of..."

"Of what?" Michalis asked gently.

"Of deserving this."

He reached for her hand. "You already are. I never asked you to be anyone else.

Aimee looked down at the bracelet in her palm, then back at him. "I've been so scared," she admitted. "Scared of losing myself again. Of giving everything.... and being left with nothing."

Michalis nodded, his thumb brushing over her wrist. "We've both been broken by people who couldn't see us. But that doesn't mean we can't build something stronger."

She closed her fingers around the bracelet, then leaned forward and kissed him not with the heat of newness, but the quiet trust of being truly seen. The candle guttered softly between them.

That night, after the dishes were cleared and the stars had taken their places, Aimee wore the bracelet to bed. She fell asleep with Michalis beside her, their passion wonderfully spent, the window opens to the sound of waves and the whisper of something just beginning to bloom.

Part 1:
A Quiet Understanding

The kitchen at Villa Petrouni was washed in late-afternoon light liquid gold that spilled through the shutters and settled over everything like a benediction. Outside, cicadas stitched the silence with their rhythm as steady as the sea beyond the olive trees.

Aimee stood at the stone sink, rinsing bunches of wild thyme and flat-leaf parsley. Her sleeves were rolled to her elbows, her hair caught loosely in a clip that had mainly surrendered. The silver bracelet on her wrist caught the light with each movement, a glint, a flicker, like sunlight on the sea through almond leaves.

Eleni entered quietly, drying her hands on a linen cloth, her eyes resting briefly on the bracelet, then shifted away. She crossed to the counter with a bowl of ripe tomatoes, setting them down with more force than necessary.

"I was thinking salad," she said, avoiding Aimee's eyes.

"Perfect." Aimee smiled gently. "Shall I slice or crush?"

Eleni paused, reaching for the knife. "I'll slice. You're the crusher."

They worked in near silence, not uncomfortable, just careful. Knife scraping on wood. Basil leaves rustling. A dog barked once outside, then stopped, as if embarrassed.

After a pause, Eleni's voice cut through, low and dry. "That bracelet... it was our mother's."

Aimee glanced down at her wrist. "Michalis told me."

"She never took it off except for kneading dough. She said it held blessings from her mother... and hers. A chain of protection."

Aimee stilled her hands in the parsley. "It's beautiful."

Eleni's voice caught. "Every Easter. Even in hospital. Even at the end."

Aimee turned, leaning against the counter. "I didn't realise. I didn't know it meant... that much."

Eleni exhaled, her hand tightening on the knife handle. "Before she died, I promised I'd protect Michalis. From harm. From heartbreak. I don't think she ever believed he was strong enough to bear it."

Aimee nodded, quietly receiving the weight of the promise. "You've done your best. "

"I don't know if it was enough," Eleni said, finally meeting her eyes. "He's been hurt. Twice. Each time, he thought it was real. And each time... he broke."

Aimee didn't blink. "I know."

"You're different," Eleni said, softer now. "But I didn't let myself see it. I didn't want to risk hope."

"I understand."

"No," Eleni said. "Truly. I didn't want to like you."

That made Aimee smile a small, sad smile. "I've been a risk before. And someone's possession."

Eleni's eyebrows rose.

"Richard," Aimee said. "He didn't break me in one blow. It was inch by inch, in ways that made me question my instincts, myself. "For years, I thought the world had gone sepia. My abnormal became my normal."

Eleni set down her knife.

"And then I came here," Aimee continued, "and the colour returned. Sketching again. Laughing. And Michalis, he didn't ask for anything. He simply made space."

A pause followed. Not awkward, just full.

"I thought I was protecting him," Eleni said, her voice catching. "But maybe I was just scared."

"We all are, sometimes."

Eleni looked at the bracelet again. "And he gave it to you. Voluntarily."

"Yes," Aimee said, her eyes softening. "No conditions."

"I don't know if I can forgive myself. For doubting him. For how I treated you."

Aimee reached across the counter and gently touched Eleni's hand. "You don't need to apologise. You loved him first. And hardest, with instinct"

85

Eleni blinked, the glimmer of tears catching her off guard. "It's just... love is hard."

"But living without it is harder," Aimee said quietly.

Eleni nodded. "Our mother used to say 'If it's real, it will weather storms. If it's not, the breeze will take it.'"

"Well," Aimee said, glancing out the window, "I've had a few storms."

"And still," Eleni said, "here we are."

They stood for a moment in the stillness of the kitchen, the sun low now, shadows lengthening across the worn tile floor. Aimee resumed chopping, but slower this time, more mindful. Eleni wiped her eyes, muttering something about onions in the air, and reached for the olives.

When Serge and Marco returned with a basket of fresh bread and too many lemons, they found the two women laughing softly over how Aimee had tried to add cinnamon to tzatziki once, convinced it was cumin.

"Peace in the kitchen at last?" Marco asked, peeking in theatrically.

"Peace," Eleni confirmed, surprising even herself.

Aimee turned, holding up a spoonful. "Try this. It may just be the best salad in Greece."

"And the most emotional," Serge whispered to Marco, who raised his eyebrows and smiled.

Later that evening, when the meal was served under lanterns strung between olive trees, and the table glowed with wine, wax, and warmth, Eleni handed Aimee the bread. Their fingers touched no flinch, no pause.

From then on, they were no longer strangers orbiting a shared star.

They were sisters not by blood, but by choice.

Morning arrived with unnerving perfection.

The sea lay flat as glass, the sky brushed in every shade of blue, and the island moved at its usual unhurried pace boats bobbing gently, cats sunning themselves on warm stones, and the scent of fresh bread and freesia floating through the narrow streets.

Aimee was seated outside the little café near the harbour sketching the curve of a fishing boat's bow. She wore the bracelet. It had become habit not a statement, not a symbol, just part of her now. Her pencil moved slowly. The day felt weightless, like it was holding its breath.

Fishermen busied themselves with nets and gossip. A flotilla from a local sailing company breezed by like expensive ducks on the water. Each flying the flags of their respective county of origin, and all with a Greek flag as a mark of respect for the host nation. The colours blurring in the morning sky as all nations passed on their way down the straight.

Boys played football nearby, their ball splashing into the water more often than not.

Down at the quay, Serge stood at the helm of *Samantha*, his sunglasses glinting, his grin wild. Marco was adjusting the lines, humming something operatic under his breath as he tucked a final knot in place. The sail had been replaced new, proud, and eager to catch the light. Michalis on the prow was nervous slightly sick and at the same time a little euphoria was creeping in.

From the topmast behind them, a banner began to unfurl coaxed by the wind. as *Samantha* turned the bend into the Poros strait.

AIMEE, WILL YOU MARRY ME?

It flapped once, caught the wind then soared like a blessing from the gods.

Gasps and murmurs rose from the café terrace. Tourists pointed, locals smiled knowingly. Aimee shaded her eyes, blinking against the sun. Phones were brought out for quick pictures.

First the yacht. Then the banner. Then the breath she forgot to take.

For one suspended heartbeat, Aimee didn't move as she read the banner flapping above *Samantha's* mainsail "AIMEE, WILL YOU MARRY ME?" blue and gold, bold and unmistakable. Her breath caught in her throat. What undid her wasn't the drama it was the quiet certainty beneath it, the unmistakable *truth* in it. This was Michalis rooted, tender, funny, entirely himself. At the

**quay's edge now, his chest rose and fell eyes
locked on hers, love unhidden.**

.

The island sounds faded Poros itself seemed to hold
its breath. The clink of cutlery, the chatter of tourists,
the cicadas in the pines and all she could hear was the
sea lapping against stone and the pounding of her
own heart. Sandals off, heart first, she ran. A cheer
rose like a wave from the harbour as she leapt from
the edge, her dress floating behind her, and hit the
water with a splash that made Michalis laugh aloud.

They collided somewhere mid-channel arms
around shoulders, lips brushing, salt and tears and
sunlight all tangled together. Around them, boats
bobbed, and strangers clapped, …but the world had
narrowed to one wild, clear truth: yes. Yes.

Their bodies met in the sea, arms tangled, eyes wide
and laughing. Foreheads touching, they caught their
breath together.

"You're insane," she laughed, breathless.

"I was worried it might be too soon," he said,
breathless too.

"Ask me for real," she whispered, eyes gleaming,
waves lapping around them.

Treading water, he took her hand, the one with the
bracelet. "Aimee, will you-"

"Yes," she said, cutting him off. "A thousand times,
yes."

From the dock, Serge blew a kiss. Marco dabbed his eyes dramatically with a lemon-patterned napkin. Somewhere, a fisherman raised his glass.

Eleni stood quietly by the quayside, the slight smile tracing her lips as she watched Aimee leap into the sea. Tears welled in her eyes, not of sadness, but of something older, a letting go, …like a knot finally loosening at the centre of her chest. For all her doubts, for all the quiet guarding of her brother's heart, she saw it then Aimee *loved* him, honestly, not with drama, but with depth. As they embraced in the water, Eleni pressed her hand to her chest in a Greek gesture. Their joy was undeniable, and at last, she felt ready to welcome it and herself fully, completely, home.

The bells of Poros rang out mass or miracle, no one could say., it didn't matter. The boys forgot their football at least for a time. A group of ladies leaving the church started to clap, many had known Michalis since a small boy.

Aimee and Michalis kissed, soaked in saltwater, sunlight, and the kind of love that stilled the Aegean and made time kneel.

Chapter 7:
The Wedding

Aimee awoke to the hush of first light seeping through the shutters of Villa Petrouni. The room glowed soft and gold; beyond the window, the sea gleamed like poured mercury. For a moment, she didn't move lay still and quiet, wrapped in the hush of the morning and the rhythm of her heartbeat. Then it returned, soft but certain: this was her wedding day.

The reality of it was both electric and surreal. She sat up, gathered the sheet around her, breath catching in her chest. The usual tangle of thoughts wasn't there. No panic. no doubts. Just a calm certainty like standing on the shore of a long held dream.

There was a knock at the door.

Catherine stepped in, carrying Aimee's favourite blue porcelain cup and a plate of honey biscuits. Hair damp from the shower, robe loose, she smiled with quiet certainty.

"You didn't run," she murmured, placing the cup on the bedside table

"I thought about it," Aimee replied, taking the coffee. "But then I remembered he makes better moussaka than I do."

They laughed, the kind of sisterly laughter that echoes softly from shared childhoods. Catherine sat beside her, brushing a stray hair from Aimee's face.

"First, Aimee Mother's pearl necklace. You must have it" Catherine pulled out a classic strand of natural pearls with a small sapphire and diamond clasp. "These must be yours now, my darling." Aimee dabbed furiously at her eyes and kissed Catherine.

"You're ready," she said. "You've never been more ready for anything."

Downstairs, the villa had already begun to hum with movement and purpose. Serge and Marco were orchestrating floral arrangements with the flair of Roman generals. The scent of rosemary and myrtle filled the air as they tied garlands along the bannister and fanned out eucalyptus on the breakfast table.

"Less pink, more blush!" Serge called out.

"Blush is pink, you madman," Marco replied.

In the courtyard, Pippi was methodically laying out koufeta, sugar-coated almonds in tiny linen pouches. She placed five in each: for health, wealth, happiness, fertility, and long life. She whispered a blessing into everyone. A dear friend, she was taking no chances that Aimee's day would be without a hitch.

Caroline, one of the girls' most trusted friends from London, burst out of her room in a flowing satin kimono and oversized sunglasses. "Darlings!" she sang. "I am ready to bless this wedding with sequins and scandal." She twirled and nearly knocked over a vase.

Aimee appeared at the top of the stairs, barefoot, wearing an aquamarine robe trimmed with lace. The room quieted for a second. She looked radiant, not because of anything she wore, but because she looked utterly at peace.

Eleni arrived moments later, holding a small, battered tin box. She crossed the room in silence and handed it to Aimee.

"These were our mother's," she said. "She wore them on her wedding day."

Inside were silver hairpins, worn smooth with age, each one shaped like an olive leaf or a tiny flower. Aimee blinked back tears.

"Thank you," she whispered.

Eleni nodded. "It's time I began to love you. I think she would have loved you. I have never known Michalis like this. He is yours."

Together, they pinned Aimee's hair in quiet companionship, no more words needed. The tension that had once existed between them had softened into something new not quite sisterhood yet, but the beginnings of it.

By late morning, the sun hung high and bright over Poros Town. Olive branches adorned the railings, and petals carpeted the steps.

Michalis stood at the entrance in a crisp blue linen suit, waiting. A sprig of rosemary peeked from his lapel, a quiet symbol of remembrance and fidelity. His shoes gleamed, his hair was neatly brushed, but his eyes kept scanning the crowd. At his side stood

Yiorgos, his koumparos, the childhood friend who once pushed him off a fishing dock and later helped him build his first boat. Yiorgos beamed with the quiet pride of a man who knew this moment had been a long time coming.

Inside, the ceremony room had been softly transformed. Olive branches stood in tall glass vases beside each window. At the front, a small table held two golden wedding crowns, *stefana* joined by a white ribbon, and two simple rings. The air was scented with wax and bay leaves.

As the guests took their seats, a soft instrumental melody began, played by a young woman on a lyra. The doors opened, and Aimee stepped inside, escorted by Catherine. A collective gasp swept through the room. She wore a gown of aquamarine silk that shimmered like water. Her hair was swept up and pinned with Eleni's silver leaves, a single sprig of lavender tucked behind her ear.

Father Antonis greeted them with a warm smile and began the ceremony.

He lifted the rings high, blessing them three times in the name of the Holy Trinity. Then he placed the rings on Aimee's and Michalis's right hands and guided them through three exchanges, a silent choreography of unity, the unbroken circle passed from hand to hand.

Next came the stefana, presented on a silver tray. Yiorgos stepped forward and gently placed the crowns on their heads, one for Michalis, one for

Aimee, linking them with the ribbon. He crossed the crowns between them three times, a symbol of sacred bond, equality, and shared responsibility.

Aimee's heart pounded. Her hand trembled slightly in Michalis's. He gave it a firm squeeze.

The priest led them in a ceremonial walk around the table, a Dance of Isaiah as the lyra played again: three circles symbolising the journey of life, guided by God and upheld by community.

When Father Antonis finally declared them husband and wife, the room erupted in joyful applause. Catherine's eyes shimmered, Serge dabbed at his cheeks with a handkerchief, and Caroline shouted, "About bloody time!"

Part 1-Candles on the Tide

Outside the town hall, the sun had risen higher, casting sharp shadows across the square. Heat shimmered on the cobblestones, the harbour glistening just beyond. As Aimee and Michalis stepped outside, a cheer erupted from the gathered friends and townsfolk. Someone tossed handfuls of rice into the air joyfully, where it flew like tiny white birds.

A cluster of elderly women scattered almonds and petals, calling out blessings in Greek. "Na zisete!" May you live long! "Kali tychi!" Good luck!

"Ptou! Ptou! Ptou!" rang out the traditional mock spitting, as old ladies crossed themselves and pretended to spit three times to ward off evil and jealousy. Caroline joined in with gusto, puckering up and pretending to spit dramatically into the breeze, prompting laughter and gasps from startled tourists.

Michalis kissed Aimee's forehead, then her lips, and took her hand. "Ready?"

"Born ready," she said with a radiant smile.

The walk from the town hall to the beachside taverna took just a few minutes, but a local violinist and drummer serenaded them all the way, their joyful folk tune coaxing even the slowest walkers to dance. Serge waved a white linen napkin overhead, twirling with Marco. Catherine walked barefoot along the sun-warmed stone, her heels dangling from one hand.

The taverna was transformed. Tables lined the sand beneath garlands of olive and lemon leaves, white lanterns floating overhead like small moons. The sea lapped softly just meters away. Glassware sparkled in the afternoon light. A long table near the front bore a handwritten sign: *For the Newlyweds and Their Dearest Troublemakers.*

As they arrived, plates appeared moussaka with nutmeg and cinnamon, chargrilled lamb skewers, roasted potatoes with lemon and oregano, bowls of tzatziki and caper dip, heaps of golden fried calamari. Towers of crusty bread, baskets of briny olives. It was a feast in waves, and just when you thought it was over, another course arrived.

The band picked up their instruments again: a lyra, a bouzouki, and a guitar, weaving a lilting, rhythmic version of a classic island tune. The music curled through the air like incense.

Michalis stood first, extending his hand to Aimee. She took it, and they began the sirtaki, tentative at first, then bolder with each step. Slowly, others joined Catherine, then Serge, then Marco until the whole crowd rose like a tide, pouring onto the sand, arms linked, swaying in time to the music.

Pippi clapped from the sidelines, her camera slung loose around her neck. Linda and James stood nearby, smiling with wine glasses in hand.

After the second song, Yiorgos tapped his glass with a fork and rose for a toast.

"I've known Michalis since he was eight," he began, voice rough with emotion. "I watched him fall out of olive trees, scrape his knees in the harbour and once, yes, once, cry because his sister took the last piece of baklava." Laughter followed.

"But today," he said, raising his glass, "I see a man who's found his home. Not just a person, though what a person! but a harbour for his heart. Aimee, welcome to the family you've already been part of in spirit. May your lives be long, your sorrows light, and your wine never watered down."

Glasses clinked. Retsina flowed like sunlight. Caroline handed out shots of tsipouro and limoncello to unsuspecting guests, warning, "It's rocket fuel but romantic."

Then came the *money dance*. Aimee and Michalis stood in the centre of the dancing circle as guests approached, one by one, pinning money to their clothing with safety pins and clothespins. Some pinned bills to Aimee's hem, others to Michalis's jacket, and soon they were covered in fluttering paper wings.

"For the olive harvest!" someone shouted.

"For the plumbing repairs!" another added.

"For the honeymoon and the next one after that!" Serge winked.

Even the children got involved, shyly offering folded euros and old notes their grandparents had saved. It was joyful, messy, deeply moving.

Then the plates came out. Now a thing of the past in Greece, but sneaked into the proceedings.

Not dinner plates, but cracked old ceramics Marco had found in the back of a local shop. The first one shattered against the stone courtyard with a glorious *crack*, and the crowd cheered.

Yiorgos took his turn next, spinning on the spot before tossing his plate with an exaggerated flourish. "To love!"

"TO LOVE!" they shouted in reply.

Dozens more followed, shattered on purpose to ward off evil and bless the couple with luck. The clatter echoed against the tavern walls like percussion, each crack punctuated with cheers.

Serge pretended to shield Marco with his jacket. "I can't watch!"

"I'm Greek now," Marco announced, tossing one with gusto and barely missing Caroline's foot.

Even Father Antonis broke one, much to everyone's delight.

Later in the evening, when the music slowed and candles burned low, Catherine rose to give her speech. She stood in front of the long table, the sea behind her, and placed her hand gently on Aimee's shoulder.

"My sister has always been light," she said. "But London, and life, dimmed her for a while. When she first came to Poros, she didn't know she'd find her way back to herself. But she did, and Michalis, that's no accident. You saw her. You cherished her. You let her be everything she is."

Aimee looked down, blinking away tears. Catherine went on.

"And now, here we are. Witnessing what happens when two people come together not because they have to but because they choose to, with eyes open and hearts whole."

The applause was long and heartfelt. Michalis reached for Aimee's hand under the table. Caroline blew her nose noisily. Eleni stood, slowly, and raised her glass, eyes meeting Aimee's across the table.

"To joy," she said.

Part 2- After the Last Song

The dancing resumed after the speeches, wilder and more exuberant than before. The stars were out, a net of silver flung across the indigo sky, and the music pulsed like a heartbeat. Children darted between tables, hands sticky with honey. Elders clapped in time from their chairs. The whole beach seemed to sway in celebration.

Caroline found herself dancing with Thanassis, the tall, quiet Cretan gardener who spoke more to plants than people. They laughed as she attempted a hasapiko, misstepping wildly but keeping her dignity by spinning into a dramatic bow. Thanassis grinned, clearly charmed, and offered his hand for another dance.

At the bar, Linda stood immersed in her thoughts, her marriage, her crazy divorce still not finished. Seeing her friend so happy and hopeful, she wasn't sure if her quiet tears were joy or regret, only that new beginnings were possible.

Catherine and Pippi took over the makeshift "guest book", a stack of handmade cards and coloured pencils. Guests were invited to draw something for the couple instead of writing. Some drew boats. Others sketched lemons, cats, or olive trees. Marco sketched Michalis and Aimee as ancient gods overlooking the bay. Serge drew a wine bottle with wings.

Meanwhile, in the small galley kitchen of the good yacht Samantha, Eleni oversaw the final preparations for the bridal bed.

A Greek tradition centuries old, the bridal bed was not just symbolic, it was sacred. The sheets had been freshly ironed. Almonds, rice, and coins were thrown onto it by the women of the family, blessing the couple with sweetness, fertility, and prosperity. A few dried rose petals from Eleni's garden were sprinkled in, and a bottle of perfume was uncorked to scent the air.

"I remember doing this for my cousin," Eleni said, smoothing the final sheet. "We argued the whole time about which side the bed should face."

Linda laughed. "And who won?"

Eleni gave her a sly look "The bed," she said, with a wicked smile.

Back at the taverna, Caroline grabbed the microphone and began to announce the cake-cutting with the flair of a game-show host. "Ladies, gentlemen, and all sea nymphs in attendance! Gather your spoons and brace your stomachs."

The cake was a towering creation of pistachio and orange blossom cream, built by a local baker who'd spent three days perfecting it. Aimee and Michalis cut the first slice together, their hands clasped on the knife, and fed each other with laughter and a smear of cream on the nose.

Children were handed tiny boxes of *loukoumia* while adults sipped sweet geranium liqueur and leaned back in their chairs, full and content. Conversations drifted from politics to poetry, from family gossip to plans.

Aimee and Eleni stood side by side for a few quiet minutes. The music softened into a gentle waltz.

"I didn't think it would be this beautiful," Aimee said softly.

"Neither did I," Eleni replied.

Aimee looked over at the crowd. "You did this."

"We all did," Eleni corrected her. "That's how it works. No one builds a life by themselves."

Aimee touched her wrist, the bracelet Michalis had given her warm from the day's sun

---

As the hour crept past midnight, the dancing slowed, and couples began their goodbyes. Candles burned low, flickering in the breeze. Sandals dangled from fingers, heels forgotten.

Serge and Marco embraced each guest with the warmth of men who'd thrown their hearts into a celebration and come out proud. Caroline handed out baklava wrapped in napkins. Pippi hummed a tune as she gently packed away the drawings from the guest book.

Aimee entered the living room alone and paused at its edge. This was hers. Not just the wedding. The life. The island. The joy.

Catherine joined her quietly, barefoot and holding two glasses of wine.

"Today has been so beautiful," she said.

"Do you think Mum would have liked it?" Aimee asked.

"She would have cried before breakfast," Catherine smiled, touching the glowing pearl necklace.

They toasted, clinked glasses gently, and Catherine slipped out again, leaving Aimee to breathe in the moment.

Down at the harbour, the yacht *Samantha* bobbed gently in the moonlight. Lanterns strung across the mast glowed amber against the velvet-dark sea. Serge and Marco stood on the dock, arms around each other, pointing at their work with approval.

Michalis was already aboard, barefoot, his jacket gone, shirt sleeves rolled up. He held a bottle of wine and two glasses.

When Aimee arrived, a soft cheer rose from the guests still lingering at the waterfront. Catherine waved both arms. Caroline howled like a wolf. Someone threw a handful of flower petals into the air.

Michalis helped Aimee aboard, steadying her as she crossed from land to sea.

"Ready to leave your wedding?" he teased.

"Ready to take me away?" she replied.

They kissed slow and sure, the kind that says everything words never could.

Part 3- Towards Everything

As the yacht *Samantha* eased away from the dock, the crowd onshore waved and whistled. Lanterns swayed in the breeze, casting warm golden ripples across the water. Poros twinkled behind them, the soft lights of tavernas, the clock tower glowing on the hill, and the last flickers of candles on the beach.

The town had opened its arms to them, embraced their story, and offered its blessing.

Michalis wrapped an arm around Aimee's waist and handed her a glass of wine. They stood at the stern, watching the shoreline recede. Music still drifted across the water, faint, unmistakable, already becoming memory.

"I've never seen Eleni laugh like that," Michalis said. "Not since we were children."

"She's full of surprises," Aimee smiled.

"She's full of love. It just takes her time to trust where to put it."

They leaned into each other, barefoot on the teak deck, breathing in the salt and the jasmine that clung to Aimee's skin. The waves parted softly, and the island behind them faded not with loss, but with promise.

They sailed for an hour, not speaking much, letting the quiet settle. The moon rose silver and perfect over the Saronic Gulf, lighting their way like a lantern hung just for them.

"I want us to always remember this," Aimee said eventually, "Not just the music, or the wine, or the dancing, but this. This calm. This knowing."

"We will," Michalis replied. "Because we made it."

In the morning, Poros would stir again, fishermen hauling in their nets, children laughing on the quay, goats clambering along stone paths. But for now, the whole island seemed to sleep with them, wrapped in a spell of celebration and sea air.

Aimee changed into a soft white dress, something simple for the night air. She removed the silver pins from her hair and tucked them into a velvet pouch. As she stepped back onto the deck, she saw Michalis at the helm, adjusting the sails to catch just enough wind to glide them silently through the sea.

They passed a small uninhabited island, a rocky outcrop ringed with pines, and Aimee reached for his hand.

"Let's never stop sailing," she whispered.

"Let's never stop choosing this," he replied. "Even when it's hard," he said. "Especially then."

They sat in silence for a long while, just watching the horizon. Eventually, Aimee leaned her head on his shoulder and closed her eyes.

Back onshore, the remnants of the celebration were being quietly tidied. Serge and Marco walked the beach with lanterns, collecting napkins and empty wine glasses, their arms still looped around each other. Catherine and Pippi returned to the villa, barefoot and exhausted but glowing.

Eleni stood at the garden gate, watching the distant lights of Samantha disappear around the island's curve. She didn't cry. But she smiled that rare, full smile that belonged to a woman who had seen her brother happy at last.

She whispered something into the night in Greek, a wish, a blessing, perhaps even a thank you.

Aimee and Michalis spread a woven blanket across the deck and uncorked a bottle of wine between them. They toasted once more, this time not to the crowd, but to each other.

"To beginning," she said.

"To everything," he replied.

And then they lay back under the open sky, surrounded by sea, stars, and silence.

There were no more words that night. Just the creak of wood, the rustle of sails, the steady rhythm of a boat and people who knew where they were going.

They weren't sailing away.

They were sailing toward everything.

Chapter 8:
James

James arrived on the evening ferry, quiet as a question mark. The kind of arrival that didn't ask for attention but drew it anyway, a tall man in a slate-grey jacket, his overnight bag worn at the handles ...his expression calmer than the sea behind him. He stepped off the ramp with measured care, like someone relearning how to walk after too long in one position. His polished but worn shoes made soft sounds on the dock.

Catherine waited with a straw hat in hand and a cardigan draped over her shoulders though the warmth made both unnecessary. She smiled and stepped forward.

You look just the same," she said then instantly regretted it. He didn't. His hair had greyed at the temples. His shoulders stooped just a little more. His eyes hadn't dimmed, but their reach had shrunk.

James let out a half-laugh. "Better than hearing I've aged like a president."

James was one of Lawrence's oldest friends. They'd studied law together in Guildford. They graduated together, were best men at each other's weddings, played cricket on Sundays, and shared long business lunches that yielded little business but strengthened their bond. Lawrence had long been divorced. James's wife, however, had died of cancer after a

109

year-long battle. Now, two years later still not quite ready for life James had accepted Lawrence's invitation, hoping something might help him open again.

She reached for his bag. He let her. Together, they walked slowly toward the car.

The road to Villa Petrouni wound upward through pine and lemon trees. The late light thick and golden, pooling over the hillside like melted butter. Catherine drove one-handed, narrating small landmarks: the ruined windmill, the bakery with the argumentative brothers, the shortcut through the olive grove no one ever used.

James listened in the grateful silence of someone unburdened from speaking. Occasionally, he nodded. He asked no questions.

The villa appeared through a curtain of bougainvillea, shy and sun-drenched. Catherine pulled into the gravel drive and switched off the engine. "You'll have the blue room," she said. "It's quiet. Faces east." He paused at the threshold, not hesitating, just adjusting. Sensing.

Inside, Villa Petrouni smelled of lemons, sea air, and something older, polished wood, perhaps, or memory. James followed Catherine down the cool hallway, past stone floors and faded rugs, into the guest room where the shutters had been cracked open just enough to let the light stripe the bedspread.

"I'll leave you to settle," she said, and placed his bag at the foot of the bed. Dinner's in an hour only if you're up to it."

He gave her a look, maybe gratitude, maybe just a look.

When the door closed, James stood in the centre of the room, not moving. The blue of the walls was gentle, not the blue of sadness, but the blue of distance. He sat on the edge of the bed, then stood again. His fingers touched the wooden frame of the mirror, traced the edge of the bedside table, hovered over the spine of a book he didn't open.

It was his first time alone in weeks. Real alone. Not administrative. Not condolence-filled. Not "let us know if you need anything" alone.

His hand went to his coat pocket, where a worn letter still lived. He didn't take it out. Just touched it as if to confirm that it hadn't vanished with the change of country.

Downstairs, Catherine moved through the kitchen like someone rehearsing calm. She checked the rice twice. Stirred the lentils three times. She had seen James only occasionally since the funeral, each time more withdrawn, more see-through. Grief sat on him not like a storm, but like fog. Thick and patient.

Lawrence came in, wine bottle in hand, kissed her cheek. "He settled?"

She nodded. "He's here. That's something."

They ate on the terrace. James joined them after a long shower, dressed neatly, but not trying. He accepted a glass of wine. Ate slowly. He answered questions in short, civil sentences. Not cold, just... suspended. Like a man wrapped in gauze.

Serge and Marco arrived halfway through the meal, boisterous and sun-pinked from a supply run. Marco carried a bunch of herbs like a discovery.

"New face!" Serge said, and reached to shake James' hand with both of his.

James stood barely and managed a smile.

After dessert, the sky bled slowly into darkness. Cicadas struck up their relentless chorus. Catherine lit candles. No one rushed. The night moved around them, gentle as water around stones.

James excused himself early, retreating to the blue room with the quiet grace of someone who'd learned to leave before the ache arrived.

James rose early, long before the villa stirred. The air held that sweet, briny stillness of Greek mornings, when even the cicadas paused. He stood on the terrace with a cup of strong, bitter coffee Catherine had left brewing. The olive trees shifted in slow conversation with the wind. He didn't move for a long time.

When Catherine appeared, barefoot, holding her sandals in one hand, she didn't speak at first. She joined him, watching the sea.

"There's someone I'd like you to meet," she said eventually, "His name's Takis, local counsellor. Retired teacher. Almost entirely unflappable. Spends most of his time drinking herbal tea and waiting for people to find the words they've misplaced."

James didn't reply. He took another sip of coffee.

"I think he could help," she added.

He didn't say no. That was enough.

Takis lived in a small whitewashed house above the town, reachable by a path that twisted like a goat trail through dry sage and lavender. By the time they arrived, the door was already open. A breeze stirred the curtain gently.

Takis greeted them with a quiet smile and two mismatched mugs of tea. He was barefoot, in a linen shirt the colour of dust, with the gaze of someone who'd read too many books and buried too many friends.

James took the chair by the window, arms folded, gaze drifting somewhere between Takis and the olive grove beyond.

Catherine gave Takis a glance. Her work here was done, and she slipped out.

For the first ten minutes, Takis didn't ask anything. He spoke of his garden, the tomatoes that refused to ripen, a neighbour's rooster who crowed not at dawn but whenever he damn well pleased. He told James the chair he was sitting on had belonged to his grandmother, its leg once mended with a violin bow and a prayer. James said nothing, but something in his shoulders softened.

Finally, Takis looked at him directly "Grief's like fog, isn't it? You can breathe, just not clearly."

James looked away. "It doesn't lift," he said.

"No," Takis agreed. "But you start walking in it. And you notice things. The sound of your feet. The slope of the hill. The smell of basil."

They stayed for nearly an hour. Or rather, Takis spoke. James listened. Occasionally nodded. By the end, James had taken a second cup of tea and forgotten to check his watch.

When he stepped outside, the light had shifted. Somehow, the town felt closer.

Back at the villa, the late morning hummed with gentle disorder. Catherine had organised an impromptu art session under the pergola. Serge handed out paper and charcoal like a maître d' with menus. Marco stood at an easel, sketching the lemon tree, brow furrowed in concentration.

At the far end of the table, Linda quietly sketched her wine glass. She hadn't meant to stay long at the villa, but something in the air or maybe in the quiet had asked her to. The presence of the sisters and of her friend Caroline lifted her.

James returned from his walk with the quiet daze of someone who'd left part of himself behind. He passed the table, nodded at Serge, who offered a cheerful wave and then his gaze caught Linda's.

Brief. A flicker. But it lingered just enough.

Later, when the sun had mellowed into the honeyed light of late afternoon, Linda found herself in the kitchen, refilling her glass. James was already there, setting washed mugs on a towel.

"Catherine's obsessed with that fennel tea," he said, with a faint smile. "It tastes like regret," Linda said, smiling at her own boldness.

James let out a small, surprised laugh. "I'm James."

"I know," she said. "I'm Linda."

They stood in silence for a moment that didn't feel uncomfortable.

"Did you draw that wine glass?" he asked.

"I did."

"Did it look like the real thing?"

"Not at all."

"Good," he said. "Accuracy's overrated."

She nodded. "Especially in art," she said.

And with that, they parted, not quite strangers anymore.

It arrived tucked between yoga flyers and a postcard from Caroline that read simply: *"Still dangerous. Don't wait for me to behave."*

The solicitor's letter was pale cream, official, and unsigned, the kind of impersonal that felt both dismissive and explosive. Linda read it twice on the terrace, making no sound. Her fingers curled slightly at the paper's edge, but her face stayed composed, too composed.

The numbers were precise now: offshore trusts. Undeclared investments. Her ex-husband hadn't just been unfaithful; he'd been a coward in every currency that mattered. But here, nestled among the legalese, was the outcome of the forensic audit: recovery likely. Partial settlement confirmed—estimated award: £4.2 million, plus costs.

She set the letter beside her espresso and stared at the olive tree, as if it had spoken out of turn. She set the letter beside her espresso and stared at the olive tree, as if it had spoken out of turn. It wasn't joy she felt, nor relief. Not yet.

"What's the verdict?" came James's voice from behind.

She didn't turn at first. "Justice," she said. "A very late arrival, though."

He stepped onto the terrace and sat down opposite her. The table between them felt like neutral ground.

"I overheard Serge say you looked like you'd just seen a ghost," he said. "Or an accountant."

Linda gave a small laugh. "Same thing. This one's just sent news that might change everything. Or nothing."

She pushed the letter slightly toward him. He didn't pick it up, just glanced, respectfully, at the contents. Then he looked back at her.

"Does it feel like vindication?"

No," she said. "It feels like math."

James nodded. James nodded. "But also?"

She exhaled slowly. "Also, like I wasn't as stupid as I feared." He hid everything in offshore accounts, shell companies, the works. I thought I'd walked away with scraps. Turns out I just hadn't found the rest of the cupboard."

James was quiet for a moment. Then: "That takes a special kind of cruelty."

Yes," she said. "And a particular kind of paperwork."

Yes," she said. "And a particular kind of paperwork."

"You're probably wondering why I stayed so long," she said at last.

"I'm not," James said. "We all stay too long in something."

She studied him then not with idle curiosity, but with the slow unfurling of empathy. "And what did you stay too long in?"

"A world that moved too fast," he said. "And a love that was already halfway gone… before I saw it. The worst part? She died before we got to have one last fight."

Linda blinked. "You wanted a fight?"

"I wanted the truth," he said. "But grief's a master at leaving questions hanging."

Then, she reached across the table, not far, not dramatically, and touched the edge of his sleeve. It wasn't romantic. It wasn't maternal. It was human.

"I used to write him letters," she said. "During the divorce. But I never sent them." Just folded them away. I thought if I said it all out loud, put it down, the pain might behave."

"Did it?"

"Some days. Other days, I just got better at folding the pain."

James leaned back. "I haven't written a word since she died. Not even a postcard."

Linda looked toward the sea. "Maybe it's time you wrote something that doesn't need to be sent."

They let that linger.

Inside the villa, Marco laughed too loudly at something Serge said about scandalous aubergines.

Catherine's voice drifted through the hallway, trailing classical guitar.

James rose. "Walk?"

She nodded.

They strolled to the orchard, where fig trees sagged with ripeness. The sunlight caught her hair. His step steadied. They didn't speak much, but they didn't need to.

It was not a beginning, exactly. But it was a gesture toward one.

Pippi arrived with little fanfare but undeniable effect. He stepped off the ferry in a beautifully faded sundress, canvas satchel slung over one shoulder, and a notebook already half-filled with notes about the crossing, which, she said, "had all the rhythm of a drunk accordionist."

She hugged Catherine first, tightly and without ceremony.

"I brought you fig jam," she said. "And the truth, if you want it."

"I'll take both," Catherine replied.

Pippi was the kind of woman whose laughter felt like warm honey, slow, golden, and good for everything. Her stories wandered through logic but always found their landing. She noticed what people dropped behind their eyes and offered it back gently, like a friend returning a forgotten glove.

She'd met Linda years ago through Caroline, "the only woman who could make a broken heel look like a battle scar," and they'd remained fond companions. Linda liked that Pippi didn't prod. Pippi liked that Linda listened with the kind of silence that meant something. Both adored Caroline for her outspokenness.

It didn't take Pippi long to spot James.

She didn't say much. Just a raised brow over morning coffee and a soft, "Oh. That one."

"What?" Linda asked.

"Nothing," Pippi replied. "Only that some ghosts wear suits and others wear healing like a borrowed coat. Yours wears both."

That evening, dinner was light: roasted vegetables, tzatziki, and a salad so bright it felt like eating sunlight. The conversation ebbed and flowed. Pippi regaled them with a tale of a lost sandal and a narrow escape involving a disapproving goat. Pippi regaled them with stories of a nudist beach on Crete where she said it was possible to pick out the most "outstanding husband." Caroline laughed so much he snorted wine.

James mainly stayed quiet but present, the set of his shoulders looser, the pinch around his eyes less defined.

After the meal, Linda found him by the fig tree. He was watching the sky turn to ink.

She handed him a glass of water. "You look like someone who's just agreed to live."

"I might have," he said.

She smiled. "Good. It suits you."

They walked a little, side by side, without purpose. Past the herb garden. Past the low stone wall that framed the orchard.

"Something is calming about all this," he said. "Even the mess of it."

"It's not a mess," she said. "It's life with the volume turned down."

At the gate, they stopped.

"Thank you," he said, though he didn't specify what for.

"For what?" she asked, her voice light but steady.

"For not asking me to be anything."

She didn't reply. Just reached out, took his hand gently, not in romance, not in declaration, but in simple human truth.

The stars blinked awake.

From the villa, Pippi's voice carried faintly: "...and that's when I realised the man wasn't a priest at all, just a particularly persuasive lothario..."

They smiled.

And for a moment, under the quiet Greek sky, nothing more was needed.

Chapter 9:
New Currents

The ferry from Hydra slipped into Poros harbour with little ceremony. Still, Marco insisted it felt "like a royal procession," waving from the quayside with a French linen scarf that caught the wind and fluttered with theatrical enthusiasm.

Aimee and Michalis stepped off the gangway hand in hand, tanned, barefoot in their sandals, wearing that softened look couples acquire after nights of salt air and shared silence. Michalis carried a small wooden crate of wine from a taverna in Spetses. Aimee had her sketchbook tucked under one arm and a scarf tied around her hair, like she'd belonged here all along.

Serge pulled them both into an embrace that nearly toppled a luggage trolley. "The lovers return!" he shouted. "And still in love, I hope?"

Michalis grinned. "More than ever. But also hungry."

"We've got that covered," Marco said. "Tonight: the terrace, music, too much food, possibly a Greek dancing lesson

"And possibly not," Serge muttered, rubbing his ankle.

By the time they reached Marco and Serge's townhouse, the late afternoon light had turned everything to gold. Their terrace, high above the

Poros strait, offered a sweep of blue and the sound of boat masts clinking like wind chimes. Lanterns swung gently between olive branches. A long table had been set with ceramic plates, mismatched napkins, and two jugs of cold rosé already sweating through their sides.

The guests gathered slowly. Pippi brought a tomato tart she claimed had been "improvised by a recipe and divine intervention." James arrived with Linda, the two of them sharing a companionable silence and a small bowl of stuffed olives. Catherine floated between conversations like a born hostess, offering wine refills and stories about a new potter from Spetses who made "mugs that looked like small, sad amphorae."

Caroline arrived late, as if by design. She wore a wrap dress that moved like water and sunglasses that concealed everything but the slight smirk on her lips.

"I had to change twice," she said, air-kissing Catherine. "It's exhausting being this effortlessly compelling."

"And so humble," Pippi added dryly, handing her a drink.

"I live to slay and to serve," retorted Caroline.

She took a seat with a view of the strait, legs crossed, a glass in one hand, scanning the horizon like a queen awaiting tribute.

Which was precisely when Ettiene arrived.

He was, as Caroline later put it, "too French for anyone's safety," tall, lean, with a shock of white hair and a linen shirt unbuttoned just enough to signal self-awareness without preening. He'd come at Marco's invitation, a friend of a friend who'd moored his small yacht near Serge and Marco's *Samantha* and was "between voyages, between jobs, and possibly between great loves."

Caroline didn't rise when he was introduced. She simply looked up from her glass and said, "Ah. The sailor."

Ettiene smiled. "Guilty."

"Of what?" she asked.

"We'll find out," he replied, taking the seat beside her.

It was less a spark and more a flare, and everyone felt it.

Marco raised a brow. Serge whispered, "Danger."

Dinner unfolded with laughter and the kind of chaos that only friends or old film scripts can choreograph so well. Plates of grilled lamb, roasted aubergines, and salads overflowing with mint and citrus were passed back and forth. Aimee and Michalis shared glances that spoke volumes. Catherine and Lawrence plotted retreat schedules with Pippi. And James found himself laughing unguarded and warm at one of Caroline's outrageous tales about a New York banker and a tragically misjudged tattoo.

Marco appeared with a huge plate artfully arranged with halved lemons, filled with lemon posset, pistachio, and violet flowers on each. A spontaneous round of applause and much clinking of cutlery ensued.

As dusk melted into darkness, candles were lit, wine flowed faster, and the strait below shimmered like silver.

Aimee rose at one point, barefoot and flushed from sun and wine. "We're so lucky," she said, to no one in particular, "to find each other in a world this strange."

Michalis took her hand and kissed it, the warm breeze in her hair. Catherine welled up at the sight of her sister glowing after years of numbness and relationship insecurity.

Etienne leaned closer to Caroline. "Do you believe in luck?"

She turned to him, her eyes just catching the candlelight. "I believe in timing. And timing, my dear sailor, just walked through the door."

He blinked, caught off guard, then laughed low and soft, as though surprised to find himself doing it. He was, indeed, mesmerised.

Chapter 9

The following morning was slow, silken, and sweet with the scent of last night's laughter. The air was already warming, cicadas tuning up somewhere deep in the pines, and the sea beyond the strait looked polished.

126

Michalis and Aimee walked hand in hand down the back lane behind the villa. They weren't going anywhere in particular, not yet, but Michalis had paused twice, glancing sideways toward the low stone building just across from the garden wall.

"The little hotel," Aimee said, noticing. "You've been thinking about it."

He nodded slowly. "It's been empty a long while. There's something... honest about it. The bones are good."

Aimee studied the building. Shutters closed, tiles cracked but not unloved. "You want to look into it?"

"I want to ask if it's possible," he replied. "But I wasn't sure if... it would seem like too much. After the wedding. After all this."

She smiled, brushing her fingers against his wrist. "Michalis, nothing about life here feels like too much. If anything, it feels like we're only just starting."

He looked at her, then really looked, and saw not the woman who had jumped into a harbour to kiss him, but the one who now moved through Poros as if she'd always been stitched into its story.

"We should ask Eleni," he said. "She might know who owns it. I think we had some connection."

Back up at the villa, Catherine and Pippi sat with coffee and a notebook on the veranda, sunlight catching in the steam rising from their cups.

"What if we structured the retreat around the idea of place?" Pippi was saying. "Not just geography but personal place. Emotional place. Where are you, and how did you arrive there?"

Catherine nodded, scribbling a line. "I like it. We could pair painting with journaling. Cooking workshops in the evening. Something soulful, not twee."

"Exactly," said Pippi. "I don't want dreamcatchers and forced bonding. I want olive oil and breakthroughs."

Marco walked past with a crate of lemons. "Put that on a T-shirt."

James had set up a small work area in the corner of the orchard: a folding table, a pencil roll, and a few legal files stacked beside a sketchbook. Linda sat not far off, under the shade of a fig tree, her pad balanced on one knee, drawing the curve of a terracotta pot that refused to stay symmetrical.

"You've made it your office," she said, nodding toward his setup.

"I'm experimenting with the idea of balance on this rickety table and in life," he replied.

She raised an eyebrow. "Between things that pay the bills and things that repair the rest," he clarified.

She smiled and returned to shading the pot.

There was something between them now, not romance, not expectation. Just the comfort of being seen without having to explain anything. It was more than enough. Both had their demons to tame.

Eleni arrived late in the afternoon, walking up the gravel drive with a bag of tomatoes and a faint look of curiosity.

"I brought the good ones," she said, holding them up. "Michalis will insist otherwise, but these are sweeter."

Aimee met her at the gate with a quiet smile. "He says that about everything you grow. As he should."

They shared a small hug, less stiff than before.

Over lemonade, the conversation drifted: old neighbours, changing weather, a recipe for lemon cake that didn't use eggs. It was Aimee who finally brought it up.

"There's a hotel next door," she said gently. "It's been empty a while. We wondered if anyone we know might still own it."

Eleni went still for a beat. Then: "The *Mikro Xenodocheio?*"

Michalis, across the table, looked up. "That's its name?"

"It was, years ago." Eleni set her glass down. "It belonged to an Irini, an aunt of my late husband, Demitris. I haven't seen her in years. We talked about Easter and Christmas. She moved to Athens and put someone in charge of the few guests. But I don't think it's been open in a few years now. But... I could make a call."

"Would you?" Aimee asked.

Eleni nodded slowly. "It may come to nothing. But it may not. And if something beautiful could grow there again..." she glanced at them both "perhaps it's time."

Kosmas, the real estate agent, arrived at precisely ten o'clock, sunbeam energy and rolled shirt sleeves, his leather satchel swinging with purpose. He looked barely twenty-five but carried himself with the confidence of a man who'd memorised every topographical map of Poros, along with its house plumbing histories.

"Ah, the dreamers," he chirped, greeting them with a quick bow. "Shall we go and meet your next chapter?"

Linda blinked. "He's been rereading brochures," she whispered to James, who gave a rare smile.

They followed him down a narrow path that curved beneath Villa Petrouni's sun-washed terraces, where the pines thinned and the breeze grew sweeter. And then, there it was.

Tucked discreetly against the hillside, the *mikro xenodocheio* looked like something conjured from a half-remembered dream. Whitewashed walls, softened by years of sun and salt, bore the patina of

130

time in their flaking edges. Their chalky brilliance caught the morning light and reflected it with a kind of faded pride, as if recalling decades of laughter, arguments, arrivals, and departures. Shutters the colour of pomegranate and sun-faded teal; some hung crooked, others tied back with rope. Letting the breeze tumble through uninvited.

"There are six rooms," Kosmas explained, as they stepped beneath a vine-draped lintel. "None large. But each with something... distinct."

Inside, the rooms whispered stories. Ceilings of local pine, beams darkened to honey. Lime-plastered walls kept bare, save for black-and-white photographs: fishermen, barefoot children, a donkey with two amphorae, and a tilt of the head that suggested world-weariness.

The beds were old wrought iron rust-blushed but solid, dressed in white cotton and folded blankets. Each room held a writing desk, a jug for wildflowers, and a lantern for when the power failed, as it still sometimes did.

Aimee trailed her fingers along a window frame. "This place breathes," she said.

Kosmas grinned. "That's not a crack, that's ventilation with character."

They laughed, but there was a hush underneath it, the hush of people falling a little in love with a place.

In one of the rooms, Linda stood silently beside a chair shaped like a question mark. She wasn't imagining luxury or profit. She was imagining light

131

through the shutters, someone pouring tea, the peace of stillness that people forgot to want.

James moved to stand beside her.

"It's not glamorous," she said.

"No," he replied. "It's honest."

She nodded. "That's rarer."

Back outside, Kosmas led them down the side garden, where fig trees leaned in like gossiping old men.

"The original owner," he said, "was a carpenter from Galatas. It was built for artists in the 1950s. His goddaughter, Irini, owns it now. She's in Athens quite privately, but she keeps it running through the summers, just about."

Michalis turned to Eleni, who had joined them a few minutes earlier, and nodded toward the grapevine-draped door. "This was Demitris's aunt's, wasn't it?"

"Yes," Eleni said. "Irini inherited it. She always said this house healed people."

Kosmas continued, "She's not eager to sell, but she's older now. Might consider it with the right intention. Not someone trying to turn it into a boutique hellscape, if you'll forgive me."

"We would forgive you twice," said Catherine.

Aimee glanced around at the trees, the steps, the cracked tiles with thyme pushing through. "I could paint here," she murmured. "Not for galleries. Just for… truth."

Kosmas smiled, as if sealing a promise. "I'll make contact."

Later, over lemonade and apricots on the Petrouni veranda, the talk turned real.

"Irini, she would sell to us," Eleni said, after a long call on the balcony. "But she wants to know it won't be gutted. She's sentimental, stubborn, and has dear memories invested there."

"I know we could make this happen, but that garden is immense," Linda said.

They looked at her.

"I've been thinking," she continued. "I don't want to go back to London. Not to my old life. And I have… options now. I could help buy it. Invest, I mean."

James said nothing, just looked at her with steady, unflinching approval.

"You're sure?" Catherine asked.

"No," Linda said. "But I'm ready to find out."

It was just after the heat had broken that blissful lull between day and dusk, when the sun seemed to sigh rather than blaze, and shadows took on the colour of old honey. Aimee and Catherine sat beneath the pergola at Villa Petrouni, sandals kicked off, glasses of chilled rosé in hand. The fig trees whispered above them.

The villa had quieted into a rhythm, not silence, but peace. The latest retreat guests had returned from an afternoon sketching along the Monastery ridge. Pippi was somewhere in the kitchen, experimenting with a recipe that involved too many herbs and no measuring spoons. Marco and Serge could be heard on the upper terrace, arguing fondly over the best material for shower tiles in the soon-to-be-renovated rooms of the *xenodocheio*.

Aimee leaned back, her head tipped against the chair. "I didn't know this kind of life existed," she said.

Catherine smiled. "It didn't. We built it."

There was a stillness between them, the kind only sisters can share. Not needing to fill the silence, only to rest inside it.

"I think I'm falling more in love every day," Aimee said softly. "Not just with Michalis. With all of it. The sea, the garden, the people who come here and leave lighter."

Catherine's gaze softened. "You seem lighter too."

Aimee turned to her. "Do you ever think about who we were back then? Back in London?"

Catherine made a sound that was part laugh, part sigh. "I think about how much noise there was. Inside and out. I used to think being busy meant being important."

"I used to think being loved meant being chosen by someone. Even if they didn't see me."

There was a long pause. A cicada started up in the olive tree. Then Catherine reached out and covered her sister's hand with her own.

"You're seen now."

They sat like that for a moment until footsteps broke the quiet.

It was Takis, the local postman and unofficial bringer of wisdom. He held a slim envelope in his hand.

"From Athens," he said. "Looks important. Thought I'd better walk it up myself."

He handed it to Aimee with a smile and a wink, then disappeared down the steps like a man vanishing into a fable.

Aimee turned it over. Handwritten. Elegant.

She broke the seal and unfolded the page. Read it once. Then again.

Catherine leaned in. "What is it?"

Aimee looked up, eyes wide with a kind of surprised serenity. "It's from Irini's lawyer. She's agreed to sell."

Catherine sat up straighter. "Truly?"

"She'll send her power of attorney to meet with Kosmas next month. It's official."

There was a long, delicious pause before Catherine let out a small whoop of joy. "Oh, Aimee! This is happening."

Aimee laughed, light and clear. "It's happening."

They stood together, wine forgotten, the hills echoing with a joy that wasn't loud, but deep. The sisters held hands and held hope. Life, in all its odd ways, had found them and they it.

They called Marco and Serge to share the news and the moment. "Linda and Michalis, we must get them here quickly," Aimee shouted.

From the kitchen came a yell: "Who's shouting before the herbs have blended?" and Pippi's head appeared around the corner. "Is someone getting married again?"

"No," Catherine called back. "Just falling further into the life we didn't know we needed."

"About time," Pippi said, and vanished again.

The long table was set beneath the whispering olive trees of Villa Petrouni's upper terrace, where vines curled like question marks above strings of lights ready for a celebration of the small hotel-to-be. The scent of rosemary and lemon drifted through the warm air. Catherine had laid out her mother's old linen, starched and white, against the wood, while Lawrence presided over a clutch of local wines with quiet satisfaction. The evening sun spilled gold across the tiled rooftops and made the glasses glow.

Linda arrived on James's arm, her laughter light, her eyes brighter than anyone had seen in months. She wore a deep blue wrap dress that caught the breeze just so, and James, ever gentle, offered her a seat like a man who knew how lucky he was. Their closeness was unforced now, companionable, the flicker of something precious beginning to take root. Catherine caught Lawrence's eye across the table and gave a tiny nod. He had seen it too.

Aimee and Michalis came up the path a few minutes later, hand in hand, cheeks sun-kissed from the last days of their honeymoon sail. Michalis carried a bottle of tsipouro; Aimee, a basket of figs and almonds she had gathered herself from the trees at the edge of the villa plot. There was a new ease in the way they moved, a softness born of shared silences and laughter echoing off a cabin wall, of waking to the same breath on the same pillow for days without end.

Caroline swept in with Etienne close behind, the two of them a flurry of glances and unmistakable tension, the kind that wraps itself around a room like warm silk. Her laugh was loud, her lipstick unapologetic. Etienne, all Gallic charm and soft linen, pulled out her chair with a theatrical bow that made her roll her eyes and blush like a teenager. Their dance was a dance of sparks and fuses, all edges, all invitation.

Serge and Marco arrived last, arm in arm like the finale of a cabaret show. Marco wore a bright coral shirt he had picked up in Ermioni and had already spilt wine down one sleeve. Serge looked around with mock gravity and declared, "This, my darlings, is the family we get to choose." Everyone clapped. They took their seats as self-appointed uncles, proud and tender, offering kisses and sharp asides in equal measure.

Pippi, radiant in a kaftan the colour of summer storm clouds, had brought a pot of slow-cooked lamb and a dish of roasted aubergines that smelled like heaven. She moved quietly but with purpose, her stories unspooling between bites of her grandmother's Yorkshire kitchen, of missed trains in Palermo, of a chance encounter in Delhi that had changed everything. She had a way of listening that made people want to speak, and by the end of the night, even Etienne had confessed that he once trained as a dancer before life took him elsewhere.

"Of course you did," Caroline said, amused. "You've got legs like a flamingo in heat."

"Merci," he replied, kissing her hand. "I shall take that as affection."

As the stars came out and the sky turned navy blue, the mood softened. Lawrence lit a few candles along the table, their flames bobbing in the breeze. Someone started humming a tune, maybe Serge, and within moments, Michalis had brought out a small laouto and began to play. Catherine sang softly at first, her voice low and sure, then louder, until they were all singing with her.

Aimee looked around the table at Catherine with a flower tucked behind her ear, at Marco grinning over his wine glass, at Linda's fingers grazing James's hand, and Caroline dancing barefoot with Etienne on the stone path, and felt, for the first time in a very long while, that something lasting was forming. Not just a holiday. Not just a house. But a life that might be shared, tested, and built upon. A real kind of home.

She squeezed Michalis's hand. He turned and smiled, his eyes full of knowing.

"Χαρά μου," he whispered. *My joy.*

"To surprises," she said. "And to what happens when you stop pretending not to want them." To surprises," they echoed.

And the wind rustled the olives like an old woman chuckling to herself, delighted by the foolishness and bravery of those still daring to love.

Chapter 10:
The Path Through Jasmine

By October, the first rains returned to Poros, not torrential, not yet, but enough to soften the earth, coax thyme into bloom again, and stir the soil around old roots that had long forgotten movement. The air changed. The brittle high summer gave way to something fragrant, fertile, expectant.

Behind the micro xenodocheio, the garden began to breathe.

It started slowly. A few hours here, a morning there. James and Lawrence, both methodical in temperament though different in background, took to the space with shared reverence. They cleared beds, uncovered forgotten stone paths, pruned where they dared, and gently encouraged what wanted to grow. The cypress trees, once drowned in wild olive suckers and blown seed, now stood like quiet sentinels, their dark fingers drawing the eye along the path that curved toward the sea.

A bougainvillea untamed, vulgar in colour, magnificent in presence burst into fuchsia bloom along the western wall, its blossoms spilling over like silk scarves from an overturned trunk. They didn't dare trim it yet. It had something to say, something blousy and bold.

And then there was the jasmine. Unapologetically rampant, it had taken possession of an entire corner. It had scaled the pergola, spilt across a collapsed trellis, and, as Lawrence declared with mock solemnity, attempted "a slow but effective coup." Behind it, James discovered something not at first, not obviously. But one morning, hacking gently through its dense green lace, he uncovered the rough bark of an olive tree.

It wasn't just any tree. This one was old, perhaps 80 years, maybe more. Its trunk was twisted like a cathedral column, hollowed in places, and silvered with lichen. But it was alive. Its leaves trembled as if blinking awake. It had been smothered, yes, but not defeated. James called Lawrence. Together, they cleared it slowly, quietly, without ceremony, as though unearthing something sacred.

"This," James said softly, brushing a palm across the bark, "is the heart of the place."

Lawrence nodded, placing a hand on James's shoulder. "Then we build around it."

They didn't know then how right they were.

Word spread that Irini, the previous owner, would be visiting. Catherine mentioned it one evening over supper at Villa Petrouni.

"She called me from Piraeus. She's catching the Flying Dolphin over. Said she wants to see what we've done with her 'darling disaster.' I think she's half curious, half furious."

"She sold it," Caroline said, swirling her wine. "She doesn't get to be furious."

"She does, actually," Catherine replied, smiling. "Irini gets to feel however she wants. That woman raised three children in that house and ran the guesthouse when it was considered scandalous for a woman to host foreigners without a husband present."

"Then I love her already," Caroline said. "Shall I wear something respectful or ridiculous?"

"Both," said Aimee. "That seems safest."

Irini arrived the following afternoon, tall, straight-backed despite the stiffness in her knees, carrying a handbag that looked like it could survive a war, and wearing a scarf knotted so tightly beneath her chin that Catherine feared for her circulation. She refused help up the hill, pausing only twice to curse the cobblestones in deeply imaginative Greek.

By the time she reached the garden gate, she was breathless and pink with effort.

"Water," she commanded. "And then tsipouro. Possibly in reverse order."

She sat heavily on the old stone bench, fanned herself with a napkin, and looked around with narrowed eyes.

No one dared speak. Even Caroline, dressed in a linen kaftan that shimmered over her charms like champagne, held her tongue.

Irini drank her water, nodded once, and said flatly, "I hope you've replaced the plumbing. It's all 1960s

142

rubbish. The water heater wheezes like a dying mule."

Michalis brought her the tsipouro himself, bowing low. "We're working on it."

Irini sipped and sighed. "Good. You may live."

Relief broke over the group like a breeze. Chairs were pulled up. Conversation resumed.

"You've uncovered her," Irini said later, eyes fixed on the olive tree.

"She was waiting," James replied.

Irini's face softened. "My godfather planted that tree. He was a carpenter in Galatas. Made every beam in the house with his own hands. Left it to me in his will. I was just a girl then, helped with the linens, and served coffee. People laughed at him for setting up a guesthouse here. Said no one would climb this hill for a bed and a basin. But he said, 'The view is payment enough.'"

She paused. "He loved that tree." A gasp escaped her lips, and a tear followed.

There was a long silence, broken only by the call of a dove in the pine above.

"I feel ashamed," Irini said, more quietly now. "I let it all go. After he died, after the tourists stopped coming, we had the military junta. Then the cats took over the pantry. I just stopped coming up the hill. My life took me away on its path."

Aimee touched her hand. "But you kept it. And now it's here and you're here. That's not failure, Irini. That's trust."

Irini blinked, looked down, and nodded. "And stubbornness," she added. "I'm very good at that."

That night, they all gathered at Michalis and Eleni's restaurant. The long table under the vine trellis overflowed with grilled lamb, roasted chickpeas, caper salad, and homemade wine. The air was thick with music; a bouzouki trio had settled in unannounced, their strings running wild with old songs and half-remembered folk rhythms.

Caroline and Irini sat side by side, laughing like old conspirators.

"My first love," Irini said, "was a French painter with a drinking problem and a stolen passport."

Caroline gasped. "Mine was a Welsh sculptor who lived on a boat and stole my best silk underwear."

"Did you marry him?" Irini asked.

"God, no. I first married an Irish barrister. Even worse, but more lucrative."

They toasted to poor decisions with raki, under the raised eyebrows of Michalis, who watched in quiet delight.

At the far end, Serge and Marco taught everyone a clumsy kalamatianos. Catherine danced like a joyful fool. Aimee whirled until she lost a shoe. Linda, serene and steady, clapped along beside James, who smiled more that night than he had in months.

Eleni allowed herself one quiet sway in the kitchen before disappearing to fetch more figs.

At one point, Irini rose slowly, glass in hand.

"I was afraid," she said, "that I'd come back and feel nothing but ghosts. But I see now it's not a ruin. It's a rhythm. The place is alive again, as it should be. As it must be."

They raised their glasses. Even the bougainvillea seemed to nod.

Michalis stepped forward. "One more thing. The old donkey path behind the lower terrace? It still exists. The municipality agreed to let us clear it. So, Irini, next time you visit, no more steps."

Irini's eyes glistened. "Well," she said, "I suppose I'll have to live long enough to try it, won't I?"

Irini didn't sleep much that night. The guest room was simple, comfortable, but her mind was too busy unbraiding itself from the past. She lay in the dark, listening to the sounds of the house, not the noises of age and decay she had grown used to, but the creaks of restoration, of memory returning. The wood of the shutters breathed. The pipes didn't groan quite so much. Somewhere near the kitchen, a clock ticked with the patient pulse of time resuming its rhythm.

She thought of her godfather, his hands, nimble-fingered and sure, measuring beams with nothing more than a glance and a carpenter's pencil nub. He had believed in building things that lasted. Not just furniture or staircases, but dignity. Presence. She remembered him on the day they opened the guesthouse nervous, proud, hiding his wine breath behind a sprig of mint. The first guest had been a Belgian woman with two dogs and a great many questions about plumbing. She'd stayed a week and sent postcards for ten years.

Irini smiled in the dark. The house had known love. That mattered.

They rose before dawn.

Michalis, Lawrence, and James took tools and a thermos of strong coffee to the rear of the hotel, where the footpath began or had once begun before being swallowed by pine and bramble. It was slow work, but not hard. The stones still held their line, and thyme scented the air each time it was disturbed.

By the time the first bell tolled across the strait, the path was clear. A soft wind stirred the pines. The way was open.

In the morning, Irini dressed early. The scarf she tied now was a softer one, yellow, with a faded border. She moved slowly but with purpose, her joints stiff but determined. At the back door, she paused not from pain, but from something else—a kind of awe.

Irini breakfasted under the pergola, walnut bread, honey, and coffee in a white enamel mug. Linda sat with her, not speaking. Some mornings are too full for words.

Irini made her way slowly, first to the olive tree, placing a palm on the bark. Then to the pomegranate tree by the gate, where she closed her eyes, lost in private thought.

"That one, the pomegranate," she said. "Please keep it. My husband proposed beneath it right after burning the lamb and dropping a jug of wine. He was so nervous, I said yes out of love and pity. And perhaps..." she winked, "because other things happened under there."

Caroline laughed. "You are an old seductress."

Irini grinned. "I've earned the title."

The garden had changed overnight. Not physically that had happened weeks ago, but in my mood. It no longer looked like a garden being rescued. It looked like a garden in use. There were signs of breakfast preparations, footprints in the dew, pruning snips left on the bench as if someone had just stepped inside for coffee. It had been adopted and loved again.

She found Linda by the kitchen, arranging figs into a shallow dish.

"I woke up early," Linda said, "and found the pomegranate had dropped a few fruits. I thought it might be a good omen."

Irini took one, turned it in her palm. "It always is. That tree never lied."

They sat in companionable silence as the sun crept higher and the scent of coffee curled into the garden.

Catherine joined them, hair still damp from her shower, wrapped in one of Aimee's scarves. "You were quite the star last night," she said to Irini. "I think Caroline wants to kidnap you."

"She wouldn't cope," Irini said, smirking. "I snore, and I have opinions on most men. Etienne is very nice, but not for her long-term. Sailors all the bloody same"

"She'd adore that, and I would think she would agree"

Irini looked at her. "You've done something good here. This isn't just a project it's a home."

"We're trying," Catherine said. "We're still figuring it out."

"You're listening to the place. That's more than most do."

She looked toward the far edge of the garden. The new path the old path curved just beyond the line of cypress. Beyond it, pine trees shaded the way, and the sun fell dappled through branches.

"I'd like to walk it now," Irini said.

James and Lawrence came to help, but she waved them away.

"I want to feel it. Just me. Just for the first time."

She took the cane Serge had offered her earlier *"Italian hardwood, darling, nothing less for you"* and placed each step carefully. The stones were uneven but forgiving, their edges softened by time. She walked slowly, pausing once to catch her breath beneath the pine.

Along the way, she passed the olive tree and touched its trunk lightly with her fingertips. "You waited," she whispered. "Well done, old girl."

The path narrowed slightly before it opened again at the small terrace near the road, where the taxi waited. The driver, a young man with a forehead already damp from the morning heat, stepped forward, bowing respectfully. Irini was a creature of Poros myth.

The others were gathered there James, Lawrence, Aimee, Catherine, Michalis, Linda, Marco, Serge, even Eleni, who stood half in shadow, her arms folded and the ghost of a smile on her lips.

"I have something to say," Irini announced, straightening her back.

No one spoke.

"I thought I'd come and hate what you'd done. Not because it wasn't right, but because it wasn't mine anymore." She paused. "But I don't. I don't hate it. I love it. You've made it live again. You've made it better, even and I don't say that lightly."

She gestured to the pomegranate tree behind her.

149

"You've honoured what matters. That tree, that olive, the stones, the silence between rooms. You've left room for the past to breathe and still made space for something new."

Catherine stepped forward, quietly emotional. "You'll always be welcome, Irini. Irini kissed her cheek.

"To be honest," she added, "I just wanted to be sure you weren't serving instant coffee and margarine. That would've been a deal-breaker."

There was laughter, then embraces.

Back in the garden, Lawrence poured more coffee and sat beside James on the mosaic bench. The sunlight filtered through the pergola, dappled on their arms.

"She's a force," James said.

"She is," Lawrence replied. "The kind of force that makes you do things better."

"She reminds me of someone," James added.

Lawrence looked over. "You?"

James smiled faintly. "Maybe."

They watched a butterfly settle on the rosemary hedge, its wings twitching with life.

"I think this is going to work," Lawrence said. "The retreats, the house, all of it."

"I know it is," said James. "It already has."

By midday, the garden was quiet again. The pomegranate tree cast a long shadow across the path. Beneath the olive, a pair of shears rested, forgotten, glinting faintly in the sun. The jasmine now trimmed, now respectful framed the doorway like a memory softened by time.

And somewhere within it all, the house held its breath not waiting, not mourning, but alive in the fullest sense. Full of laughter, footsteps, scent, and promise.

It had found its rhythm again.

She walked the new path slowly, cane tapping, shoulders straight. The others waited at the bottom by the road, where the taxi idled in the sun.

She turned once before entering the car, looked back at the house, the hillside, the tree.

"I see you. I love you," she said softly.

As she stepped into the taxi, she looked up at the house one last time the pink walls, no longer flaking but still imperfect; the bougainvillea, a cascade of riotous colour; the shutters open, catching light and wind alike.

"I see you," she whispered. Then, to the driver: "Go slowly. I've earned the view, young man."

And then she was gone the taxi winding down through lemon groves and tiled roofs toward the port.

Above, the pomegranate tree rustled part farewell, part promise and the garden, now reborn, turned its face to the sea.

Chapter 11:
Walls and Wonders

If Villa Petrouni had been a dream conjured into reality, then To *Mikro Xenodocheio* was its groaning, glorious sibling born of stone, sweat, and a great deal of swearing in three languages.

Renovations began not with a bang, but with a clipboard Linda's clipboard, to be precise which she carried like a sceptre. She had made her peace with Aimee's floating scarves, Marco's gesturing hands, and Serge's exclamations about "the mood of a cornflower." But she would not, under any circumstances, make peace with chaos. Not while ordering tiles and plumbing supplies.

"I will not preside over decorative indecision," she declared one morning, red pen poised. "Not while there are invoices outstanding."

Serge bowed deeply. "We are not worthy."

Marco added, "But if I may just imagine the entrance in ochre and light. Terracotta floor restored and polished. Perhaps a Murano glass cloche light?"

They'd barely started, and already two walls were marked for demolition, a floor had revealed its secrets (three layers of tile and what appeared to be the remnants of a goat shed), and the old plumbing had staged a final act of protest. A cupboard door off the hallway long boarded over with a mural was taken down to reuse as a wall hanging. Behind it, a long-forgotten ante-room: perfect for a small library off the reception. Lawrence and James appeared, covered in dust but triumphant.

Over lunch, the plans were poured over again to see if any more surprises lurked in the topological diagram. Two bedrooms had deep fireplaces, long breeze-blocked over. A well in the garden. And a strange outbuilding currently invisible beneath a sea of plumbago.

The boiler, installed sometime during the 1960s (possibly by a man with a hammer and a cigarette in his mouth), let out a sigh, a whine, and a majestic bang in the middle of the night. Catherine, half-asleep, had mistaken it for an earthquake.

By morning, there were buckets beneath every pipe and a plumber named Giorgos, who refused to speak until his coffee was, in his words, "the temperature of lava." He also worked much better in the presence of Pippi

Kosmas, as ever, was the calm in the storm. He and Michalis handled the building permissions like two diplomats negotiating a trade agreement papers filed, neighbours appeased, inspectors charmed with coffee and orange cake.

"The good news," Kosmas said one afternoon, looking slightly less cheerful than usual, "is that you now have provisional approval for the extended terrace pergola and the ensuites."

"And the bad news?" Michalis asked.

"That it's conditional upon you not painting anything turquoise."

"Done," said Marco, crestfallen.

Linda made lists. She priced every tile twice, sourced reclaimed wood from a salvage yard in Nafplio, and somehow managed to negotiate delivery costs down by quoting a shipping firm's own policy back at them.

Catherine and Aimee, sleeves rolled up and ponytails high, took to sanding furniture with the same vigour they once applied to structuring legal contracts and gallery openings. They repainted wardrobes, replaced handles, and debated whether *seafoam* was a real colour or a marketing myth.

"I think it's a feeling," Aimee said.

"It's a paint chip," Catherine replied. "But let's use it anyway."

And then there was Caroline.

Caroline, who arrived each morning in a linen jumpsuit, hair swept up, lips the colour of rebellion. She could charm the dust off beams. The electricians offered to rewire twice as much as quoted for the same price. The tiler extended his stay by a week. And the carpenter a quiet man from Galatas with strong forearms and very few words began bringing fresh bread and wine to the site each morning.

"I don't know what you do," Pippi said one afternoon, watching Caroline talk a grumpy mason into redoing a doorway. "But you do it very, very well."

Caroline winked. "Darling, I give them attention. Men are like sad plants just need some attention and encouragement."

Thanassis had been sent by Kosmas, who claimed him to be "the best plantsman in the Peloponnese and possibly part tree." He was to advise on landscaping, soil restoration, and how to prevent the bougainvillea from swallowing the shutters. He lived just at the top of the ridge beyond Villa Petrouni and had Greek danced at Aimee and Michalis' wedding.

He didn't talk much. But he did listen to the soil, to the light, and, most unsettlingly for Caroline, to her.

He watched her carefully. Without the usual hunger or games. Just... attention. The kind that made her feel briefly transparent.

By the second day, she found herself dressing in colours that matched the blooms he'd planted.

By the third day, she offered him lemon water without being asked. By the fourth, she caught him smelling the air beside her after she passed. "Lime and basil," he said quietly. "Jo Malone. Heathrow duty free," Caroline replied, with a wink.

Meanwhile, the renovation continued its wild symphony.

Linda now operated like a small import-export firm, receiving deliveries with the precision of a naval officer. Catherine handled interior detailing "No, that vase does *not* evoke serenity, it evokes gout." Serge and Marco were covered in plaster dust and creative fervour Aimee sketched colour washes for the hallways that somehow made people stop, stare, and breathe Marco continued to insist on ochre.

Linda had been wandering through the narrow backstreets of Poros when she stumbled upon it a small, sun-drenched pottery studio tucked between a lemon grove and a crumbling wall draped in ivy. The scent of warm clay and pigment drew her in like a spell.

Later, she returned with Aimee, who instantly fell in love. It was as if the micro xenodocheio had been waiting for this moment for colour, craft, and soul to infuse its rooms.

Maria, the ceramic painter, greeted them with a smile painted in honey and warmth. Her fingers were stained with turquoise and lapis proof of her morning's work. Her brother Tasos, the potter, appeared from behind a beaded curtain, hands still grey with slip. Together, they were the latest in a long, quietly proud line of island artisans each generation shaping not just vessels, but the very essence of Greek domestic beauty.

Each room of the xenodocheio had begun to speak to them not in words, but in hues and moods.

The soft green room, with its seagrass linens and brass fixtures, would hold celadon vases and speckled platters like mossy river stones.

The blue room, facing the Aegean, would gleam with indigo mugs and sky-hued washbasins. For the sun-drenched southern suite, they chose ochre and burnt orange joyful tones like sunsets over Nafplio. The pink room received blush-toned pitchers and tiles patterned with fig leaves. Even the yellow room cheerful as a canary at breakfast would glow with dappled lemon-green sconces and hand-painted knobs on the wardrobe doors.

Maria and Tasos listened, asked questions, and understood without needing too many words. They sketched, they laughed, they served tiny clay coffees in thimble-sized cups. Aimee, watching the way Tasos turned a lump of clay into something both ancient and new, felt a tug of time as if the island itself were quietly blessing their endeavour.

By the time they left, a full commission had been agreed each room to be graced with pieces as unique as the guests who would one day sleep within them.

Meanwhile, Michalis sleeves rolled up, pencil behind his ear had become the de facto foreman. Calm. Assured. Always one step ahead of the next small disaster.

One night, as they gathered on the upper terrace, feet aching and hearts full, James raised his glass.

"To the madness," he said.

"To the miracle," added Aimee.

"To the man who made the bougainvillea behave," Caroline said, casting a glance toward Thanassis that lingered far too long across the terrace.

By the sixth week, *To Mikro Xenodocheio* began to resemble less a building site and more a place preparing to welcome life again. The dust had primarily settled. The electricians had finished their rewiring ballet, and the plumbing, now mercifully modern, no longer hissed like a vengeful serpent at the turn of every tap.

The group had fallen into a kind of rhythm: morning coffees taken at the same uneven wooden table, Linda assigning tasks with resolve but surprising gentleness, Marco humming opera while painting shutters, Serge insisting on testing bed frames "with dramatic horizontal leaps."

Thanassis had started leaving sprigs of rosemary by the villa steps. No one asked why. Everyone appreciated it. "Rosemary for remembrance and the heart," observed Linda.

One afternoon, Aimee returned from the art supply shop in Galatas with a parcel of new brushes and found Caroline on her knees in the entryway, laying out mosaic tiles with the kind of precision usually reserved for heart surgery.

"You're up early," Aimee said.

"I couldn't sleep," Caroline replied without looking up. "I kept dreaming the hallway had the wrong energy."

Aimee sat beside her, cross-legged.

"And what's the right energy?"

"Something that says: come in, take off your expectations, and sit down."

Aimee nodded. "That's exactly what it feels like."

They worked quietly for an hour, side by side, until Thanassis arrived with a small potted fig. He placed it by the door, said nothing, and left.

Caroline watched him go.

"I don't know if he's testing me or teasing me," she murmured.

"Maybe he's just seeing if you'll stop performing."

Caroline laughed. "Impossible."

Pippi, in her usual sidelong but focused fashion, had begun interviewing the team one by one. Not formally, just over tea or tomatoes. But she was collecting something: stories, feelings, a sense of place.

"It's for the retreat brochure," she told Catherine. "It's a novel," Catherine replied.

"Well," Pippi said, "what's the difference?"

The brochure, when it appeared, was beautiful, filled with Pippi's vivid sketches and prose that read like memory wearing its best dress.

James had taken to sketching the building in phases: foundation, frame, and furnishing. He said it helped him understand things that weren't linear. That healing, like construction, didn't go floor by floor.

Sometimes, you needed to return to the base before painting the eaves.

Linda joined him some afternoons. Not to draw just to sit. She had never thought of herself as someone who needed quiet. But now, she realised, it had simply never been offered.

"You don't always have to be the strong one," James said one day, almost offhand.

She smiled. "Don't tell anyone. I've got a reputation."

He handed her a sketch of the hotel's side window, open, curtain blowing, nothing and everything visible.

"It's you," he said.

She blinked. "That's a window."

"Yes," he said. "And you're letting something in. It's time."

The first completed room at *To Mikro Xenodocheio* felt like a secret whispered between stone walls.

Its sea-glass green walls shifted tone with the light, soft and barely there in the morning, deepening to olive dusk by late afternoon. The finish was imperfect by design; Catherine had insisted that the brush marks remain visible, so the walls "breathed like memory." Cream linen curtains moved gently in the breeze from the balcony doors, which opened to a glimpse of the sea framed by fig leaves and terracotta rooftops.

The bed was the centrepiece restored with care by Serge, its wrought iron frame burnished to a warm patina. The brass fixings caught the sunlight with a muted gleam, like old jewellery rediscovered in a drawer. The mattress was firm but forgiving. Layers of fine cotton sheets were topped with a honeycomb blanket and two hand-embroidered pillows Aimee had found in a shop in Ermioni. On the bedside table sat a carafe of water and a small ceramic lamp shaped like a pomegranate.

Aimee's framed print, a watercolour of a sleeping cat nestled beside a half-read book, hung above the writing desk. The desk itself, a narrow antique with one stubborn drawer, had been sanded and oiled to a warm glow. Fresh flowers wild fennel and thyme stood in a recycled marmalade jar.

The bathroom, though modern in convenience, wore its history proudly. The mirror was a piece of driftwood, found by Caroline and shaped lovingly by Thanassis. It hung above a shallow stone basin carved from local marble. The tap fittings were brushed brass, a respectful echo of the bedroom's accents, and the walls were lined with handmade tiles in soft creams and sage. The shower walk-in and perfectly sealed offered intense water pressure, a victory Linda had won after two weeks of negotiations with Giorgos, the local plumber.

On the shelf beside the basin sat two beeswax candles, a dish of rosemary soap, and a rolled cotton towel tied with twine.

A pair of armchairs, zingy green and blue linen, patterned with lily pads and cranes, gave a cheerful corner to sit and relax, or simply throw your clothes. Under the small east-facing window sat an old bamboo desk and chair: enough space for a computer, or the books that needed to be read or ignored as the mood dictated.

It wasn't flashy.

It wasn't slick.

It was simply beautiful, the kind of space that made people feel instantly at home.

They stood in the doorway, Catherine, Aimee, Linda, Serge, Marco, James, and Pippi, all in varying states of dust and disbelief.

"It looks like it's always been this way," Aimee said.

"That's how you know it's right," Linda replied.

Pippi ran a finger along the old wardrobe's edge. "I'd sleep here," she said. "And I'm the pickiest guest you'll ever meet."

From the hallway came Thanassis' voice: "Only one room done?" Caroline appeared behind him, smirking. "Careful. That's blasphemy around here". Thanassis shrugged. "Then bless me". "Mmmm, I might just do that," replied Caroline.

Thanassis didn't smile. But he did raise his glass.

And that, as it turned out, was more than enough.

That night, they lit candles on the terrace. Catherine made lemon chicken. Marco decanted the rosé with theatrical flair. The sea turned from gold to indigo as stars winked into the sky one by one like secrets being revealed.

"I had a thought," Catherine said quietly, turning to Lawrence beside her. "Oh dear." She nudged him. "No, listen. When this is ready fully ready I think we could offer a retreat for grief, along with the other areas."

He looked over at James and Linda, seated side by side beneath a fig tree, sipping something warm, their conversation easy and slow.

"For people who don't know how to start again," she added. "This place... it helps.". Lawrence nodded. "It does. It really does."

They sat together, hand in hand, the garden surrounding them in a hush of jasmine and olive.

Lawrence, after years, feels content and with renewed purpose.

Linda, daring to dream again.

In the morning, an email arrived.

A woman from Berlin. She'd heard through a friend of a friend about a place in Poros where something good was happening. She was recently widowed. She wanted to paint. She didn't want pity.

She asked, Simply, do you have a room for me for all of May?

Catherine read it twice. Then again.

Then she replied: ***Yes. We've been waiting for you***.

Chapter 12:
5 Shared Labour – The Final Morning Scene

Later that morning, the group slipped into a rhythm of doing. Serge painted the gate. Marco produced a suspiciously long list. Catherine and Lawrence sorted pantry jars. Aimee coaxed a lavender plant back to life.

"I used to dread quiet days like this," she said. "They made me feel guilty."

"Capitalism's last curse," Lawrence muttered.

"But now," she continued, "I'm finally learning how to be still without apology."

"That deserves a banner," Marco declared, pinning bunting to a fig tree.

They laughed a laughter with roots, born of seasons weathered together.

From the terrace, Serge called out. "Lunch in twenty. Bread, olives, something with artichokes. And possibly the last of the feta."

"Last of the feta?" Catherine gasped. "Why were we not informed earlier?"

Aimee lingered by the lavender, brushing soil from her knees. The plant was bent, brittle, but not broken. It only needed light. And time. All things she finally had.

She looked toward the villa and felt something loosen like breath held too long.

Not an ending. Not quite a start. But something is ready to root.

Part 1:
Back to the Blue

Poros emerged like a memory sharpened by absence the clock tower pale and unmoved above rooftops the colour of lemon sherbet. The yacht *Samantha* eased forward under Marco's guidance, gliding across the strait with graceful inevitability. They'd spent a week in sea-silvered mornings, swimming in sky-mirrored coves, and dining beneath stars that outnumbered words. But now the voyage was folding gently to a close.

Aimee leaned over the rail, her hand twined with Michalis's beneath the sun-warmed wood. The wind was modest, catching her hair and stirring the last of the salt-kissed days they'd stored up between Hermione and Hydra.

"I think I love returning more than leaving," she said.

Michalis smiled. "Then we must make sure our home is always a place worth returning to."

Behind them, Serge emerged from below deck in loose white linen, humming something gloriously off-key in French. Catherine sat aft beside Lawrence, the crossword of a Greek-English newspaper opens between them like a bilingual riddle of the Sphinx.

The harbour sharpened into view: stone quayside, heat shimmering on sun-bleached facades, a fisherman's call across the water all familiar, yet haloed by the magic of return. They were back, but altered. The kind of change only salt, sunlight, and the sacred promise of chosen friendship could bring.

At the harbour, Eleni was waiting, not with fanfare or flourishes, but with a subtle nod and a small bouquet of thyme and bay. She handed it to Aimee without a word. Their hands touched briefly, and Aimee met her eyes. Something unspoken passed, not quite approval, but acceptance. The kind that mattered.

"You've both gone a little brown," Eleni said dryly. "Too much love and not enough shade."

Michalis laughed and kissed her cheek. "We brought back a few ideas for the kitchen."

She arched a brow. "That better not include that fig-and-chilli monstrosity from Hydra."

Aimee grinned. "Only if you're brave enough."

They walked together toward Villa Petrouni, which gleamed like a painting on a canvas of olive trees. A banner, likely Marco's work, hung cheerfully across the stone arch: Κ α λ ώς ή ρ θ α τ ε π ί σ ω, *Welcome Back.*

Inside, the villa was a flurry of anticipation. Linda was arranging a trio of ceramic swallows she'd bought in Athens, each painted in the soft palette of dawn. Caroline had clearly taken it upon herself to overhaul the drinks trolley. It looked like a scene from a Bond film minus the MI6 agent, plus a suspicious amount of ouzo.

"Well," Caroline declared, sweeping toward them in a kaftan that defied geometry, "I hope you're ready to be adored. We've chilled the wine, inflated the cushions, and even persuaded James to play something on that ridiculously handsome clarinet of his."

"Caroline," Aimee said, laughing, "what are you wearing?"

"Darling, it's vintage Athens. The woman swore it belonged to Melina Mercouri's second cousin or possibly a lampshade."

Linda appeared beside her with a quieter smile. "We're glad you're back. The place is less itself without you."

The group gathered on the terrace as the sun slipped behind the pine ridge, and glasses clinked like small declarations of affection. Serge raised his flute of rosé.

"To love at sea and ashore. And to this extraordinary family of misfits."

"Misfits?" Caroline huffed. "Speak for yourself. I'm extremely well adjusted."

"To being extraordinarily well adjusted, then," Lawrence said, raising his glass.

As the first stars pressed their soft weight into the sky, the sound of James's clarinet curled through the air like silk unwinding in moonlight. The tune was slow, wistful, and Aimee realised it was a version of the melody she'd been humming that morning. He'd caught it and answered. Linda watched him with an expression that bordered on luminous.

Later, Aimee slipped away, barefoot on the cool stone steps leading to the small side garden. She passed the pomegranate tree where new fruit was already forming, and the half-built arch where Caroline had insisted on wind chimes "to keep the spirits interested."

She found Michalis standing there, watching the sea. He didn't turn when she reached him. He simply opened his arm to let her in.

"You know," he said softly, "I never thought I'd feel this again."

She rested her head on his shoulder. "What?"

"This belonging."

She kissed his neck. "We make our own place. Every day."

They stood a long while in silence as the villa murmured behind them and the night carried the sound of distant bouzouki strings from the town. A new chapter was beginning not just for them, but for Villa Petrouni. And the guesthouse, and new guests, old ghosts, fragile roots reaching for light.

The sea was their past. But this this life they were shaping, with lemon trees and faded shutters, these souls who kept showing up with stories to tell this was the present. And perhaps, if they were careful with it, the future too.

Part 2:
Turning Tides

The next morning broke with a shimmer that kind of golden light that sifted through lemon leaves and made the white walls of Villa Petrouni hum with warmth. Catherine padded into the kitchen barefoot, her hair still scented with rosemary from the garden. A pot of strong Greek coffee was already on the boil, thanks to Lawrence, who was at the small courtyard table with his laptop open and reading glasses slipping down his nose.

"Working?" she asked, kissing the top of his head.

"Skimming," he replied. "It's a property case, nothing urgent. Besides, it's hard to feel litigious when there's a cicada chorus in B-flat outside your door."

Catherine poured two cups. "We've created something here, haven't we?"

Lawrence looked up at her, setting his glasses aside. "You've created something. I'm merely a helpful sidekick with an eye for pruning schedules and pension transfers."

She grinned and passed him his cup. "You? You're the patron saint of steady hands and clever exit clauses."

He shrugged, pleased nonetheless. "Speaking of which, what's the plan today?"

"We're walking through the new studio space with Aimee. The windows arrived yesterday. Pippi wants to talk about a storytelling circle in the evenings you know, tales, folk songs, bits of old island magic. And Caroline insists she's found a ceramicist who works by moonlight."

Lawrence raised an eyebrow. "By moonlight?"

"That's what she says. He's either a potter or a werewolf. Either way, he's on the list."

By mid-morning, the villa pulsed with gentle industry. Serge and Marco were in the garden, fussing with olive crates and fairy lights for some future soirée. Michalis was at the old hotel next door, talking logistics with Kosmas and marking possible wall removals with neon chalk. Aimee had her sketchbook out, sitting cross-legged in the sunlit studio room that now had one wide window overlooking the sea and another catching the shadow of the old fig tree.

Linda appeared with a clipboard and a practical smile. "Paint samples. Pale green, sun-drenched terracotta, or the one that looks like a peach was left too long in the sun?"

Aimee pointed to the latter. "It's soft, romantic, and a little bruised like most good things."

Linda chuckled and scribbled it down. "You've got the soul of a poet."

"I think it's just the view," Aimee replied. "And possibly the leftover ouzo from last night."

Caroline swept into the room, a riot of colour as usual. She wore linen trousers the colour of hibiscus and a shirt knotted at the waist in a shade that could only be described as 'sunset-meets-orange-sherbet.'

"Ladies, brace yourselves. A yacht has just moored at the far end of the quay and there's a man aboard with shoulders like a Greek statue and a beard that would make Poseidon weep. I nearly dropped my watermelon."

Linda raised an eyebrow. "Was he alone?"

"Tragically, no. He appears to be travelling with crates of lemons, a shaggy dog, and an older woman with a straight back and stern gaze, The intrigue!"

"Caroline," Aimee said carefully, "have you actually spoken to them?"

"Not yet. I waved. The dog barked. The man winked. The woman sneezed. Honestly, it felt like theatre."

Linda chuckled. "Let's not rush to invite the entire cast of *The Odyssey* to dinner."

But the villa thrived on such arrivals. That afternoon, the stranger appeared at the gate, following a grinning Kosmas who seemed entirely unfazed by the man's peculiar ensemble. The dog a long-legged island mutt with a pink tongue and wagging tail sniffed the rosemary and lay down under the olive tree as if born to it.

"May I introduce Hugo," Kosmas said. "From France. And his companion, Madame Adeline Lys.

They've sailed from Paros and are looking for... well, something new."

Hugo bowed slightly, his eyes crinkling at the edges with mirth and perhaps a bit of sunstroke. Madame Lys nodded curtly, her silver braid coiled around her head like a crown of command.

Caroline stepped forward and extended her hand. "Welcome. "We're either your salvation or your downfall depending on how much wine you can drink, and how good you are with a mop."

Madame Lys smiled. "I have mopped many floors and drunk even more wine. I believe I am qualified. I would like to settle here for a time."

Later, as dusk rose and the cicadas handed their chorus to the owls, the table was extended under the pergola. Hugo turned out to be an excellent guitarist, and when Caroline discovered this, she immediately insisted on a duet.

"What are you playing?" Linda asked.

Caroline glanced around dramatically. "A ballad of unrequited love and very expensive divorce settlements."

"Sounds catchy," said Lawrence.

The song, part torch song, part comic lament, had the whole table howling by the second verse. Adeline poured the wine with regal precision, occasionally whispering corrections in Greek to Michalis, who nodded with exaggerated humility. James watched the scene unfold, a smile playing on his lips. He caught Linda's eye and for a moment, everything fell away: the clinking of glasses, the chatter, the candlelight. Just her. Just him.

When the music ended, Aimee rose and raised her glass.

"To those who return, to those who arrive and to the beautiful mess we make of life when we're brave enough to really live it."

The glasses met in a chorus of hope.

Part 3:
Seeds and Signs

The next morning, Michalis and Hugo walked the edge of the slope between the villa and the old hotel, inspecting the olive trees and talking about soil types, wind currents, and what it meant to be tethered to a place. Hugo, it turned out, had once studied viticulture, only to abandon the vineyard for a decade at sea.

"It's strange," he said, stooping to examine a wild fennel plant ", how the sea calls you until one day it doesn't. And suddenly it's the earth calling instead."

Michalis nodded. "Yes. And some people spend a lifetime pretending they can't hear either voice."

Inside the villa, Catherine and Pippi were seated at the large pine table, surrounded by notebooks, coloured pencils, a weathered Greek-English dictionary, and a teetering pile of local folklore books. The new retreat programming was beginning to take shape art mornings, cooking sessions with Michalis, storytelling circles beneath the fig tree, and afternoon walks with Lawrence through history-rich ruins.

"I want it to feel like a gathering of spirits," Pippi said, sketching a rough calendar with loops and stars. The living and the lived-in. As if the land itself is part of the story we're telling."

"It already is," Catherine murmured, flipping through a yellowed volume of island folktales. "Listen to this: 'To walk the hill path after dusk is to walk among those who have walked it a thousand years before. The cypress remembers."

Pippi smiled. "Let's include that quote in the welcome pack."

Just outside, Eleni was standing in the garden, a small trowel in one hand, a basket of cuttings in the other. Aimee joined her, hands still stained with pastel chalks. For a moment, they just stood side by side in silence, admiring the unruly beauty of the climbing jasmine.

"My mother would have loved this place," Eleni said at last.

"I wish I could have met her," Aimee replied softly.

Eleni nodded. *"She wasn't soft. But she understood softness. There's a difference."*

They shared a look not quite familial, not yet, but easy, open.

"I've been meaning to ask," Aimee said. "Did she... choose the bracelet?"

Eleni nodded slowly. "She wore it the day she met my father. The day she said yes. She left it for Michalis, saying it should be for whoever gave him peace."

Aimee swallowed. "Then I'll try to live up to that."

"You already are."

Eleni walked away with her trowel and cuttings, and Aimee stood a little straighter in the shade of the fig.

By late afternoon, the air shimmered with heat. Caroline, in a straw sunhat the size of a fishing boat, was leading Madame Adeline Lys and Linda on a mission to find more outdoor seating for the upper terrace.

"I want something that says 'careless chic,' but also 'sturdy enough to survive a Greek winter, or at the very least be stackable'," Caroline explained, sweeping through the lane toward a dusty old shop that smelled of pine resin and leather.

The shopkeeper, a man of indeterminate age with a moustache that curled like the ends of an old violin scroll, offered coffee, ouzo, and exactly the kind of carved cedar bench Caroline had imagined. "It's a little cracked," he admitted, "but my grandfather made it during the war. It's survived shells, goats, and three ungrateful sons-in-law." "Perfect," Caroline declared. "We'll take it."

Back at the villa, James was sitting under the harbour with his sketchpad. He watched the shadows fall across the tiles, drawing the way the sun hit the folds of Linda's shirt as she carried a cushion inside. He didn't even realise what he was doing until he'd filled two pages with sketches of her soft angles, quiet strength, the way her eyes always seemed to be listening.

Lawrence, watering the beds nearby, glanced over and saw. He said nothing, but later, as they shared a beer on the lower terrace, he asked simply, "Have you told her?"

James looked down at his hands. "No. It's too soon."

Lawrence took a sip. "Sometimes, too soon becomes too late."

James said nothing. But the next morning, Linda would find the sketchbook on the kitchen table. Open to the page with the drawing of her laughing, her head thrown back, one hand shading her eyes from the sun. She felt the joy of the drawing settle in her and knew that things could never be the same again. With or without James, she was whole.

Dinner that night was on the lower terrace, near the herb garden. The food was simple lemon chicken with roasted potatoes, a tomato salad bursting with oregano and thick green oil, and slices of feta that had never seen plastic wrap. Serge had baked bread in the outdoor oven, and Marco had draped fresh-cut myrtle over the plates "because we must seduce the gods before we feed the mortals."

Hugo told stories of narrow harbours in the Cyclades where dolphins followed them like shadows. Pippi recited a line of Sappho, and Catherine translated it aloud. Madame Lys sang something in Breton that sounded like wind wrapped in wool. Aimee leaned into Michalis, and Caroline toasted them all.

"To the absurdity of time and the absolute necessity of courage."

The moon rose over the strait, full and pale gold. No one moved for a long time. Aimee looked around the table, the faces, the music of languages and laughter and felt something begin to settle inside her.

Home wasn't a place. It was a collection of hearts beating beside yours in the dark, still singing long after the candles went out.

Part 4:
The Wind Changes

The morning after the terrace dinner was hushed as if the house itself had exhaled into sleep and wasn't ready to wake. Aimee woke to birdsong and the quiet creak of shutters shifting in the breeze. She stepped out onto the balcony with a shawl over her shoulders, the sea glowing with a pearl-like stillness. Below, Catherine and Lawrence were seated side by side with coffee, not speaking, just sharing the silence.

She padded down to join them. Catherine reached over and squeezed her hand.

"Good day?" Aimee asked, her voice low.

"The best kind," Catherine murmured. "No demands. Just sun, a second coffee, and maybe a walk before the heat takes over."

Michalis emerged a few minutes later, hair damp, shirt half-buttoned, carrying warm bread wrapped in a clean linen cloth. "Bread," he said solemnly, setting it on the table, "and an idea."

Lawrence raised an eyebrow. "Dangerous combination."

Michalis ignored him, turning to Aimee The baker is retiring," he said. "Eleni told me this morning. If no one steps in, the shop may close. It's been in the same family for three generations."

Aimee blinked. "What does that mean?"

"It means I'm thinking. A café-bakery, with a book corner, simple dishes, island produce, and wine in the evenings. A place for music. And laughter."

Aimee leaned forward. "And you'd run it?"

"With someone, perhaps I've got enough big commitments as it is," he said. "It is going to be perfect for the right person.

Catherine smiled. "Let's keep it in mind."

He nodded. "If the retreat is the heart, maybe the café could be its hands, how it reaches into the village. A bridge."

Lawrence sipped his coffee. "Let's talk to Kosmas. And to the baker."

Just then, Pippi arrived with a notebook filled with scrawled ideas and half a poem. Her smile was slow and easy. Her sketches were fluid and beautiful.

"You look like conspirators," she said.

"We are," said Aimee. "We're plotting joy. And Pippi, you're very good at retail."

That afternoon, Caroline insisted they all go down to the shore towels, umbrellas, a portable speaker, and a bottle of retsina in a cool bag that may once have carried fish. The little beach was nearly deserted, save for an elderly couple who nodded at them and resumed playing backgammon under a faded umbrella.

Hugo and Michalis swam out to the rock where boys had once dared each other to dive. Aimee floated with her face to the sky. Linda and James sat hip to hip on a striped blanket, occasionally brushing hands as if by accident. Caroline read aloud to Madame Adeline, from an old copy of *Durrell's Prospero's Cell*, but mostly to herself.

Then Thanassis arrived.

He came down the track carrying a potted lemon verbena and a wide smile. "You forgot your herbs," he told Caroline. "And I had to see if your terrible impression of a plant expert had improved."

"It hasn't," she replied, not missing a beat. "But I've added sound effects."

They laughed that kind of laughter that folds something invisible between two people. He sat beside her and began naming wild plants she pointed at with exaggerated seriousness and dry wit.

"Is this love?" Caroline asked, holding up a sprig.

"Possibly," Thanassis said. "Though it might be thyme. Easy to mix them up."

That evening, after the sun had burned down to embers and the sky turned lavender over the hills, Aimee walked alone to the little chapel above the villa. It was small, whitewashed, with faded icons and candles melted into stubs. She lit one, then sat on the old bench under the cypress.

She thought of her life before Poros. Before Michalis. Before Caroline's ridiculously OTT outfits and Pippi's gentle grounding presence, before Linda's quiet strength, before Marco and Serge turned a sailboat into a second home, before Catherine's instinct had pulled her from the ruins of herself.

She let it all arrive. Let it sit beside her, the ache of it, the gift of it.

From the hill, she could see the flickering lights of the villa, hear the faint sound of someone playing the guitar, and see a faint path glowing with lanterns down to the micro-xenodocheio. Life was taking root. It had edges now. It had weight. It had shape.

She stood, walked slowly back down the path. A breeze lifted her hair, carrying jasmine, rosemary, woodsmoke, and sea salt everything that had become her world

At the gate, Michalis was waiting. He didn't speak. He simply held out his hand.

She took it.

And together, they stepped inside.

Chapter 13:
Aboard Samantha (Setting Out)

The lines were cast with a splash and a cheer. *Samantha*, her hull gleaming and canvas folded like a sleeping bird, eased away from the quay under the watchful gaze of Poros' old clock tower. The morning had begun with the clink of mugs and the rustle of canvas bags Catherine checking last-minute supplies while Lawrence stood back, half amused, half daunted by the flurry of preparations.

"Is it always this theatrical?" he asked, sipping his coffee as Serge barked an unintelligible command involving a winch and a fender.

"Oh, darling," Catherine said, brushing her curls back with a grin, "you've seen nothing yet."

Aimee and Michalis stood on deck, arms lightly brushing. Michalis, long accustomed to the sea's briny call, carried the calm steadiness of a man who had made peace with tides. Aimee, notebook already tucked into her woven bag, carried the hum of expectation beneath her skin.

Serge and Marco moved as a single mind Serge with sharp French precision, Marco with the languid ease of someone who understood boats the way some men understood wine or women. Marco adjusted the bow line and looked up at Catherine.

"Still remember how to tie a rolling hitch?" he teased.

"I remember how to make you think I've forgotten, so you'll do it for me," she replied, settling into the cockpit like a queen reclaiming her throne.

"*Allora!*" Marco called and *Samantha* turned her prow toward the open strait, the harbor shrinking behind them. A small cluster of locals waved from the quayside café. Even the cats, blinking from the hot walls, seemed to say: *Bon voyage, mad ones.*

It didn't take long for the rhythm of the sail to take over the snap of wind in the rigging, the creak of rope and wood, salt on lips, and the low thrum of the engine that was eventually silenced in favor of wind.

Catherine stood at the helm, with Serge coaching her gently. Lawrence squinted at the GPS plotter as if it might suddenly reveal their future in Morse code.

Aimee had slipped off her sandals and padded barefoot along the teak decking. She leaned against the rail, sketchbook in hand, watching Michalis adjust a halyard with Marco.

"You look like you belong here," she said.

Michalis glanced over, smiling. "The sea and I understand each other. We both have moods. And we both hate being taken for granted."

She sketched the lines of his face as he turned back to the ropes the salt caught in his beard, the tension in his forearms. He was solid, sun-warmed,

187

impossibly real. The boat gave a gentle heave and she felt it the shift from land to sea, the subtle letting go of everything that had once felt fixed.

Below deck, Catherine was reorganizing the galley with the satisfaction of someone who believed deeply in proper order pepper to the left of salt, plates nested by size, wine bottles padded with towels in the cool bin.

Lawrence appeared at the foot of the steps.

"Do I dare ask where you've hidden the coffee?"

"In the locker beside the spice rack. Next to the emergency baklava."

"There's emergency baklava?"

"I don't go anywhere without it."

He laughed and stepped forward to kiss her. "You are a marvel."

"Tell me again when we're becalmed near Ermioni and you're cranky without espresso."

On deck, the wind picked up and *Samantha* heeled slightly, her sails full. Island coastlines slid by like painted panels in an ancient theatre. Pine-covered hills dipped to secluded coves, and the sea scattered silver flecks across the bow.

Catherine joined Aimee at the rail, both women leaning out slightly, hair tangled in the breeze.

"You know," Catherine murmured, "there were years I thought we'd never do this again. Just the sea, and laughter, and nothing urgent."

Aimee nodded, eyes still on the horizon. "It's different now."

"It is. But better, somehow. We've all been through the fire a little. Even Lawrence for all his calm, he's softer around the edges here."

"And Michalis?"

Aimee smiled. "He doesn't fill space. He makes room. That's rare."

Catherine took her hand and squeezed it. "I'm proud of you, you know. You came back to yourself."

"I didn't think I could."

"That's the thing about the sea, Aim. It always brings something back if you let it."

Behind them, the men were debating whether to anchor near Ermioni's western cove or swing out toward the inlet past the pine spit. Serge argued for depth. Marco argued for light. Michalis, ever the mediator, suggested they toss a coin. Lawrence, who had eased into his role aboard with surprising grace, offered to row ashore once they moored.

"Anything to justify the hat Catherine insisted I bring," he said, pulling out a wide-brimmed straw number from below deck.

Everyone groaned.

That evening, *Samantha* moored in the quiet of a near-forgotten cove. The sky burned down from rose to violet, and the water stilled into a mirror of some other world. Dinner was simple grilled fish, lemons squeezed by hand, a tomato salad bursting with salt and oil. They ate on deck, legs stretched out, wine glasses catching the moonlight.

Marco raised his glass. "To old sails, new companions, and the improbable magic of six people afloat."

Aimee looked around at Catherine glowing in the candlelight, Lawrence teasing Serge about wine preferences, Marco leaning easily against Michalis, who rested a hand on Aimee's knee.

It was, she thought, the kind of moment that asked for nothing.

It just *was*.

Like the sea.

Like love when it's real

Part 1:
The Glass Sea

By mid-morning of their second sailing day, *Samantha* was gliding toward Paralia Astros a quiet crescent of the Peloponnesian coast where low hills met the sea with barely a whisper. The sails hung slack, their canvas breathing in and out like the lungs of a resting giant. Then, the wind gave out altogether.

It was as though someone had pressed pause on the world.

The sea moments ago ruffled with playful gusts lay suddenly still, a flawless sheet of blue glass. Sunlight scattered rainbow iridescence across the surface, shimmering and silent, broken only by the occasional lazy slap of rope against mast. Serge checked the wind vane, tilted his head, and gave a low whistle.

"Completely becalmed."

Marco emerged from below deck holding a tray of olives and almonds. He blinked at the stillness, then grinned. "Well, if Aeolus won't lend us a breath, perhaps it's time for a swim."

Aimee looked up from her sketchbook. "Are we allowed to just… stop?"

Michalis was already untying the painter from the inflatable dinghy. "This is the best kind of stopping."

They dropped anchor in twenty metres of water so clear you could see the pebbles on the seabed. A breeze more imagined than real stirred the hairs on their arms but didn't so much as wrinkle the water's skin.

Catherine stood at the stern platform, toes curled, eyes wide. "It's like a dream."

Then she jumped.

A perfect dive clean, sure disappearing into the blue with barely a splash. Seconds later, she surfaced, laughter ringing out across the bay like a bell.

"It's like silk!" she cried. "Come in! It's like the water isn't even wet!"

Lawrence followed with a theatrical flourish, clutching his nose like a child and splashing in with far less grace. Aimee stripped down to her swimsuit, casting a look at Michalis, who was already shirtless and smiling.

"Race you," he said and dove like a knife into water.

Aimee stood for a moment longer sun above, silence all around then jumped.

The water wrapped her like a second skin. Cool. Perfect. Endless. Beneath her, the sea shimmered in sapphire and silver, light refracting into fractals. She surfaced and floated, arms wide, watching the sky merge with the sea in a seamless dome. All around, the others bobbed like sea nymphs and poets in exile. Even Serge had surrendered to the stillness, floating on his back with a beatific smile and closed eyes.

No one spoke.

There was no need.

It was the kind of silence that healed things

Later, they lay scattered across the deck towels, limbs, hair drying in the sun. Marco had made iced coffees. Lawrence read aloud from a battered paperback, skipping the bits everyone found pretentious.

Aimee sat beside Michalis, feet dangling into the blue.

"Why does this feel like a memory already?" she whispered.

"Because it's the kind of moment you never forget," he said. "It imprints."

Catherine, still damp and wrapped in a towel, sipped her coffee and spoke without looking up. "They say when the sea is like this glassy, luminous it's because the gods are watching."

"Watching what?" asked Serge, towel-drying his beard.

"To see who remembers to be grateful."

Aimee looked up. The sun dazzled overhead, tracing a slow arc through their journey.

"I think they'll be pleased," she said.

By late afternoon, a whisper of wind returned. The sails were raised again with quiet reverence, and *Samantha* moved onward toward Paralia Astros. The coastline inched closer white buildings clinging to the hills, fig trees casting shadows on ancient stone.

As they neared the harbour, Catherine looped an arm around Aimee's waist from behind.

"What are you thinking?"

"That nothing can ever top today."

Catherine smiled. "Ah, but that's the thing, Aim. Greece always finds a way."

They docked just as the sun spilled low and orange across the water. A man on a moped waved them into the mooring with the sleepy generosity of someone who'd done it a thousand times. He handed them a long, rusty key.

"Toilets and showers. They're clean enough. Don't flush the paper."

They laughed and thanked him, then wandered up the quay to find a taverna, or maybe not. Maybe just a bottle of wine and some leftover bread beneath the stars.

Behind them, the sea lay like a memory.

But the feeling that wide, still joy travelled with them ashore.

Part 2:
Under the Cypress Moon

The quay at Paralia Astros was quiet the kind of quiet that settles like fine dust after a long summer's day. A lone fisherman mended his net beneath a faded blue awning. A dog barked lazily, reconsidered, then stretched into sleep. The group wandered up from the mooring barefoot or in sandals, sun-glazed and gently giddy.

They found a taverna just past the square more a scattering of tables beneath cypress and fig trees than a formal restaurant, but the scent of grilled sardines and slow-cooked lamb was magnetic.

"Should we ask for a menu?" Lawrence murmured.

Michalis laughed softly. "This is the kind of place where you ask what's good today, and the answer is: everything my wife cooked."

And so it was.

The owner's wife a woman with arms like bread dough and a gaze that softened only when she smiled ushered them to a long table beneath a fig tree and listed the offerings like a prayer. No menu. Just trust.

Plates arrived like chapters in a family story: roasted aubergine with garlic and yoghurt, zucchini fritters crisped with mint, chickpeas slow-baked with lemon and thyme, lamb that fell apart with a sigh. Bread, still warm from a wood-fired oven. Wine in a tin jug cold, local, just sweet enough to surprise the tongue.

The sun slipped into the sea. Streetlamps clicked on with a gentle hum. Cicadas sang. Somewhere, faintly, a transistor radio played a rembetiko ballad.

Catherine leaned toward Serge and Marco. "Remember that night in Nafplio? When you both insisted we could dance the hasapiko after a carafe and a half of ouzo?"

Marco placed a hand on his chest. "I remember performing it flawlessly."

"You kicked a waiter's chair over," said Serge, not looking up.

"It was part of the choreography."

Lawrence chuckled, one arm draped over the back of Catherine's chair. "This all feels... not quite real."

"That's how you know it is," said Aimee, watching the candlelight flicker across Michalis's face. "The best things do."

They lingered long after the last spoonful of yoghurt and walnuts had been scraped clean. The owner brought a complimentary bottle of tsipouro, pouring it with ceremonial gravity. The conversation softened, unravelling into quieter threads fragments of memory, old poetry, laughter that started low and tumbled into surprise.

In a quiet corner, Aimee sketched. Her pencil captured the curve of Catherine's hand around her wineglass, the flick of Serge's hair in the wind, the glint of candlelight in Marco's glasses. But again and again, her lines were pulled toward Michalis the tilt of his head, the shadow beneath his cheekbone, the way his smile looked when he didn't know he was smiling.

Catherine had chosen a slightly removed seat, under an olive tree with a better view of the harbour. She was reading an old French novel she insisted she hated, pausing only to look up when Marco's laugh rose or when the waiter, a handsome young man with shoulders shaped like possibility, passed with more cutlery.

"Catherine, come back to the table!" Aimee called. "You're missing the toast."

"What's the toast?"

"To what comes next," Aimee said, raising her glass.

Catherine closed the book and stood. "Then count me in."

Later, they returned to the boat by torchlight feet dusty, hearts unreasonably light. The moon hung above the water like a pearl strung on invisible thread. Michalis and Lawrence adjusted the mooring lines while Serge and Marco murmured over weather forecasts, debating possible winds near Hydra.

Catherine climbed to the bow with a cushion and a shawl. Aimee followed, settling beside her with a sigh.

"We're changing, aren't we?" Aimee asked.

Catherine looked at her. "Yes. All of us. Not away from who we are but into who we're becoming."

"It's strange. I thought it would feel like a loss."

"It doesn't?"

"No," Aimee whispered. "It feels like more."

They sat in silence for a while, until Lawrence joined them with two mugs of tea and a biscuit wrapped in a napkin.

"To ward off tsipouro-induced poetry," he said, handing one to Catherine.

"Too late," she replied. "I've already written a haiku about feta."

He groaned. "Please tell me it doesn't rhyme."

"Don't challenge me."

Aimee smiled, watching them. The yacht rocked gently in its berth, the sea lapping against the hull like a lullaby. Below deck: the clink of cups, Marco humming, Serge's footsteps. Above deck: stars, so thick and close they felt like velvet draped across the sky.

In that moment, surrounded by old friendships shifting into new rhythms, love growing quietly, the sea stretched out into the night. Aimee felt time dissolve.

Not lost. Just... irrelevant.

Everything that mattered was here:

On this boat. In this breath. Under this cypress moon.

Part 3:
Homeward Light

They left Hydra in the morning hush, sails full but tempered as though the boat, too, sensed the voyage drawing gently to a close. The sea was placid, glittering with long ribbons of silver, and the air carried the faint scent of thyme from the island cliffs.

Marco stood at the helm, sunhat slightly askew, while Serge scrawled notes in the logbook. Catherine lounged aft with a novel she wasn't reading. Lawrence watched the horizon with the look of someone mentally sketching each curve of the land. Aimee leaned against the boom beside Michalis, one leg curled up, sketchpad in her lap, though all she'd drawn so far was the outline of a cloud that looked suspiciously like a cat.

"We'll make Frog Island by midday," Serge announced, tapping the chart.

"Frog Island?" Lawrence asked, bemused.

Marco pointed ahead. "Tiny, uninhabited. Looks exactly like a frog from the south side. We always stop there."

"Don't argue with tradition," Catherine added.

By the time they reached it, Frog Island did indeed reveal itself as a lazy green hump in the sea, with two smaller islets near its head, giving it the uncanny silhouette of a lounging amphibian. They anchored just offshore in shallow, impossibly blue water and declared it lunchtime.

But supplies were dwindling. What remained: a tin of vine leaves, a block of feta, the dregs of an oregano jar, half a loaf of bread, three beers, two peaches, and a slightly damp packet of crisps.

Marco surveyed the meagre bounty, clapped his hands together, and said, "Aha! We shall dine à la cordon bleu. Observe."

With flair worthy of a Parisian bistro, he assembled feta-and-crisp sandwiches, layering chips between slices of bread smeared with soft cheese and dusted with oregano. Catherine found a lemon and squeezed it over the top. Serge produced a picnic knife and carved everything into tidy triangles.

They ate sprawled on deck, feet up on the rails, salt still clinging to their skin.

"This," said Lawrence, biting into his sandwich, "is culinary genius."

"It's crunchy," said Michalis, "and tragic."

"I'd put this on a tasting menu," Aimee added, licking lemon from her fingers.

Catherine lifted her can of beer. "To the humble crisp. May it always rise to the occasion."

They toasted. They laughed. They finished every last crumb.

An hour later, *Samantha* raised her anchor and made her slow, deliberate way toward Poros. The sea had flattened to a perfect plane again, and the boat glided as if drawn by unseen hands.

That's when Marco, peering over the stern, spotted a shape in the distance, a long, elegant craft approaching on a complementary heading.

"Is that?" he began.

"It is," Serge confirmed. "*Angelika.*"

The sleek vessel came alongside with practised ease. Standing at her helm, grinning from behind a pair of outrageous sunglasses, was Anton, an old sailing friend with skin the colour of walnut wood and a laugh that could unmoor clouds.

"Thought I'd catch you before you made port!" he called. "You've got that smug, 'we've had a magical trip and we're too tanned for sympathy' look about you!"

They shouted greetings over the water, exchanged outrageous compliments, and Anton held up a bottle of chilled retsina.

"For when you dock. Consider it a bribe for stories."

With a wave and a wink, he turned his vessel slightly and fell into a gentle parallel course. The two boats sailed together like siblings in step, the final leg into Poros Strait.

The town unfurled before them in its usual splendour: terracotta rooftops catching the golden hour, whitewashed houses tumbling toward the harbour, the old clock tower watching it all with impassive grace.

And there, on the jetty, as though arranged by fate or a very deliberate phone call, stood Linda, James, and Caroline. The latter had clearly dressed for dramatic effect in flowing linen, enormous sunglasses, and a posture of casual regality. Beside her, carrying a crate of herbs and looking slightly dazed but undeniably smitten, was Thanassis.

"There they are!" Caroline shouted. "About bloody time!"

Linda waved with both arms. James offered a quiet, contented smile that somehow said everything.

As Samantha glided into her berth in reverse, stern-first, ropes thrown and caught with ease, Aimee felt something shift deep in her chest. A breath she hadn't realised she'd been holding.

The end of the journey, yes.

But not an ending.

Michalis stepped off first and was immediately tackled in a hug by Caroline, who then promptly offered him a glass of something suspiciously strong and herbal.

James helped Aimee ashore with understated grace. "Good trip?"

Better than good," she said. "Restorative."

Linda embraced Catherine, whispering something that made them both laugh and blush. Serge leapt to the dock and clapped Thanassis on the shoulder.

"You survived the Caroline hurricane, I see."

Thanassis merely nodded. "She talks. A lot."

"And you're still here?"

"She smells like roses," he said. "And talks to plants. I like that."

The last of the gear was passed ashore. The sun slid behind the hills. And the two boats, Samantha and Angelika, moored side by side like old friends. Anton bid everyone farewell. He'd been at sea nearly four weeks and insisted he needed to find his land legs again, but promised to visit the evolving hotel soon.

Marco looked at the group, now mingling and laughing, already planning dinner or drinks or some half-made dream. Stories of the becalming near Astros were already percolating.

He nudged Serge. "New sails. New crew."

"And a very fine home port," Serge said.

As twilight deepened, they all began walking up the hill together back to Villa Petrouni, back to a waiting table, back to the next chapter.

Because some journeys don't end.

They just arrive exactly where they're meant to.

Chapter: 14:
Return to Xenodocheio
(What Is Still to Be Built)

Mikro xenodocheio breathed differently now. The scent of sawdust and basil drifted from open shutters. Sunlight poured into spaces once closed tight. Voices, laughter, instruction, and the occasional curse in three languages echoed through every floor.

Six rooms remained unfinished. But in the hands of this accidental collective of lovers, dreamers, exiles, and hopefuls, the project had taken on a life of its own.

On their first morning back, Caroline found Thanassis in the herb garden behind the lower terrace. He was unloading a basket of rooted lemon balm and pink, rain-fed verbena, soil clinging to his hands as if it belonged there.

Still barefoot and robe-clad, she intercepted him before he reached the planters.

"You're early."

"I never left," he said simply, handing her a sprig of verbena.

She rolled it in her palms, breathing in its scent.

They sat beneath the fig tree, dirt beneath their nails, and something softer rising between their words. When she joked about her chaotic ways, he

205

didn't laugh; he simply looked. And when she faltered, he only said,

"I saw it early. The shyness under the sparkle. The echo behind the laugh. You don't have to pretend with me."

It unsettled her and steadied her.

He left to tie back the bougainvillea, and she followed him with a watering can she had no intention of using just to be near him. Just to feel seen without performance.

Inside, each room had begun to suggest who it might one day shelter.

Catherine had quietly claimed what she called *The Sanctuary Room,* north-facing, cool in the afternoons, with walls the colour of buttermilk and the scent of lavender creeping through a cracked shutter. She envisioned it as a space for writers, thinkers, and anyone seeking silence that felt like balm.

Lawrence, clipboard in hand, liaised between contractors and tradespeople with unassuming charm. His Greek was awkward but endearing; his patience, infinite. He made friends with the stone mason, negotiated discounts with the tile supplier, and kept the work moving through three island holidays and two power outages.

Linda gravitated toward the orchard-view suite. It had been neglected for decades, with cracked tiles and dust-thick windows, but beneath the grime, she discovered a mosaic border of pomegranate and acanthus, still vibrant. She oversaw every inch of its restoration. Fabrics were chosen from a quiet shop in Athens. Clay lamps came from Maria, the potter. The palette was pale green, shell pink, and soft sand.

"It's a room for someone rebuilding," she said one morning. "Like I was."

James helped her without speaking of it. He lifted boxes, brewed coffee, and held sketches for comparison. And sometimes, when she wasn't looking, he sketched her brushing her hair back as she chose tile, resting a hand on her hip while she eyed up light fittings.

Aimee and Marco were elbow-deep in the Bay Room, whose half-moon view of the strait made it a favourite. They sanded shutters, painted the walls a soft sea-glass blue, and added brushed brass fittings. Aimee painted a mural of a trailing vine that crept from floor to ceiling, gold-veined leaves unfurling between the light and shadow.

"This is a place people come to begin," she said.

"And remember," Marco added.

Pippi, newly returned from London where she'd been disentangling a chaotic consultancy contract and a brief, ill-advised romance with a sound designer who owned more headphones than convictions, arrived at Villa Petrouni lighter somehow. The very act of coming back had shorn her of unnecessary weight.

She took up the top-floor studio, a space few others had managed to make work. The ceiling sloped dramatically. The beams were low enough to bump one's head if one is not careful. But the morning light poured in with theatrical insistence. To Pippi, it was a perfect crow's nest, she called it, high above the comings and goings, close enough to the sea to feel it in her bones.

She wasted no time making it unmistakably hers. Faded red and ochre kilims softened the tiled floor. The walls were pinned with ephemera: black-and-white photos of Greek widows laughing on plastic chairs, a torn receipt from a taverna in Sifnos, a line from Sappho inked in gold on brown parcel paper. Sculptures made of driftwood and rope sat beside thumbed poetry anthologies. A bowl of sea glass gathered over the years from beaches across the Cyclades rested on the sill. No one dared move it. The glass was her oracle, she said. When unsure, she'd reach in blindly, letting shape or colour guide her mood.

"Absurd," she admitted. "But absurdity is underrated."

Cream linen curtains swayed gently in the breeze, edged with a Greek key motif she had hand-stitched on a ferry from Rhodes. The studio smelled of beeswax, rosemary, and the particular salt of cotton sheets dried in the sun.

Visitors often paused at the doorframe, unsure whether to enter. It had the hush of a chapel. Or perhaps a sanctuary.

"It's for someone who needs to create something," she told Catherine one morning, barefoot, hair still damp from the sea, "but doesn't know what yet."

She wasn't entirely referring to herself, but she wasn't exempt either.

Pippi had always been that sort of woman, a revealer of truths through indirection. A weaver of space and feeling rather than declarations. She didn't force outcomes. She let them steep.

People gravitated toward her not because she was effusive, but because she was deeply present. She listened in a way that made others feel smart, seen, and somehow amusing. She had a knack for unearthing the one thing someone had forgotten they loved, a childhood hobby, a half-finished song, a recipe written in their grandmother's hand.

It was why Catherine had wanted her there from the beginning, why Aimee trusted her instincts completely. Why, even the most taciturn guests found themselves laughing or crying within an hour.

At night, Pippi sat by the studio's open shutters with a glass of retsina and a notebook on her knee, watching the stars embroider themselves into the sky. She said she was writing a play "only five characters, but each one thinks they're the protagonist." Whether she ever finished it didn't seem to matter.

The act of sitting with it, of opening the possibility, was enough.

The studio became more than a room. It became a kind of threshold, a place between what was and what could be. And without ever saying so, Pippi made it clear: the door would always be open, for whoever next found themselves in need of such a space.

Caroline's domain, predictably, was the wildest. The room had uneven walls, smoke-scented plaster, and a rusted metal bedframe that she insisted had *narrative potential.* She sourced fabric from retired theatrical costumers, convinced the island's last tinsmith to fix the window latches and make two wall sconces, and used an olive root lamp built by Thanassis as her centrepiece.

It became a haven not tidy, but fiercely alive.

One evening, she looked up from sanding a stool and found Thanassis watching her.

"I thought I had to dazzle to be loved," she said.

"You already shine," he replied. "But what you've started doing that's something rarer. You let people stay."

She blinked hard, then reached for the wine. *This man,* she thought, and took a long sip.

THE WORK BEFORE THE WELCOME

The days ran long but sweet. They rose with the sun and collapsed into dusk with tired hands and wine-stained laughter. Some days were all dust and delay. Others saw entire rooms bloom into beauty. Mikro xenodocheio, once just a promise of potential, now felt like a gathering of intentions, each person adding a piece of themselves.

Catherine managed bookings and outreach, her laptop propped on crates as she replied to enquiries from writers, yoga instructors, and a group of Danish retirees requesting *"cooking and mythological instruction, please."*

Lawrence dealt with a surprise boiler explosion at 3 a.m. one morning, and a water pressure mystery that had everyone showering in shifts. He handled both with dry wit and a head torch, dubbing himself the *"Patron Saint of Plumbing Emergencies."* A new head tank was duly ordered along with an emergency backup.

Linda's room was nearly done. She stood in the doorway one evening, arms folded, watching the soft light catch on her pale curtains.

"It feels like a woman lives here already," she said.

"She does," James replied, without hesitation.

They didn't speak of it again. But she held his hand under the table that night at dinner.

211

Thanassis brought Caroline a small lemon tree in a pot.

"It's still young," he said. "But it will fruit if you stay long enough."

She looked at him. "I'm tired of leaving."

"Then plant something."

She placed the tree by the stone step of her room.

And for the first time in years, she unpacked every one of her bags.

Part 1:
What Was Hidden

The west side of the property had always been a bit of a mystery, dense with growth, half-swallowed by a plumbago thicket that flowered like madness and defied every attempt to tame it. The blooms, brilliant in electric blue, tumbled in waves over stone and cracked masonry, cascading over a rusted wire gate so lost in foliage it looked like a relic from another world.

Lawrence and James took it on without ceremony one hot Tuesday morning, already sweat-slicked before the first vine was cut.

"This thing's like a siege engine," Lawrence muttered, yanking at a root thicker than his wrist.

"It's also oddly beautiful," James admitted, watching how the light played through the petals.

They hacked and cut and dragged and burned, pausing only to sip water and exchange the kind of brief, satisfied nods that only men doing brutal, simple work can truly appreciate. Every metre gained revealed more mystery, the outline of an old stone wall, a series of terracotta shards, what looked like a rough baking table long consumed by vines.

And then they found the door.

It was small, half-submerged in soil, its top beam bowed and cracked, but unmistakably a lintel.

213

Lawrence knelt, brushing away leaves and spider webs to reveal what might once have been a carved date eroded, barely legible, but still: 1891.

"Can we open it?" James asked.

"Not yet. Let's not take the door off before we know what's holding it."

It took two days of patient clearing and help from Michalis, who arrived with pry bars, a crowbar, and two plates of hot spanakopita from the village bakery. When the door finally gave, it did so with a sigh and a scatter of dry earth that felt like it had been waiting a century to exhale.

Inside: cool shadow, the scent of ash and history. The room was deeper than expected, partially carved into the slope. Beams arched across the ceiling, not standard beams, but old ship timbers, curved and dark, some still bearing faint tool marks and sea-salt notches.

Brushwood had been woven between them not for strength, but for insulation and breathability, an old trick in island *fournos.* The oven itself stood like a stone altar at the back of the room, wide-mouthed, blackened with ancient fire, and half-filled with the remains of charred fig wood and brittle olive branches.

"Well," Lawrence said, brushing dust from his arm. "This just became my favourite room in the house."

James, brushing cobwebs from a niche in the wall, said nothing. He simply stood, turning in slow circles, taking it all in the smoke trails on the stone,

214

the silence that wasn't empty, but full of stories waiting to be heard.

They lit a candle. It burned cleanly. No draught, no must.

Aimee and Catherine arrived not long after, drawn by the noise and the silence that followed.

"Good god," Catherine said, stepping inside. "It's like a shipwreck made a love child with a monastery."

"It's the old fourno," Michalis confirmed, running a hand along the hearthstones. "This would've fed twenty people, maybe more. Probably the communal oven when the house belonged to the farmstead."

Aimee was quiet. She walked to the back wall, touching the stones, then looked up at the brushwood ceiling, light filtering through the old curves of wood.

"We have to preserve it," she said.

"No doubt," Lawrence agreed. "But we should use it too. It deserves flame again."

The following week, they cleared a narrow footpath leading to the room, lit lanterns along its edge, and repointed some of the outer wall by hand. Serge suggested turning it into a space for slow-cooking kleftiko, bread, and even fire-roasted quince when the season turned. Marco wanted to hold poetry readings by candlelight. Pippi proposed teaching guests to make storytelling bread, where each fold held a memory.

Thanassis and Michalis passed a gorse bush brush down the chimney on ropes, emerging covered in soot from many years.

Linda, who had stood in the doorway watching it all unfold, said simply: "I think it might be the heart of the whole place."

That night, they gathered just outside the newly revealed room. The old hearth was scrubbed and ready. Lawrence had baked flatbreads with rosemary. Michalis roasted feta in fig leaves. They opened the wine and passed the plates hand to hand. The fire crackled behind them, not roaring, but breathing again.

Caroline lit a candle in a niche by the oven mouth and whispered something no one quite caught. Thanassis, beside her, smiled.

"You're putting roots down," he said.

"I'm trying."

"They're holding."

No one made speeches. No one needed to.

But they all felt it that the house, the land, the stones themselves had given something back.

Not just a room.

But a memory of time rediscovered.

And the promise of warmth to come.

Part 2:
Goat-Sized Setbacks and Lemon-Scented Certainties

The weather turned without warning, as it always does on Greek islands, like a character flaw in an otherwise perfect guest. One moment, the sky was chalky blue; the next, a quilt of thunderheads rolled in from the south, scattering light like theatre spots before a dramatic act.

The storm hit at dusk.

The garden lanterns flickered. The shutters rattled. Aimee stood in the doorway of the newly opened fourno room, wind twisting her hair around her face, the scent of woodsmoke clinging to her sleeves.

"Quick!" she called. "Marco's rugs!"

Upstairs, Linda was calmly unplugging the router, drying laundry and saving three documents at once. At the same time, Lawrence attempted to reason with the plumbing system, which had begun to groan in sympathy with the thunder. Serge was already outside, chasing tarps and muttering in three languages.

Michalis ran along the southern path, grabbing a bundle of tools and shouting into the wind. When he reached the lower gate, he found Caroline and Thanassis huddled in the open storage alcove, trying to protect the lemon tree in its cracked terracotta pot.

"It's too young for this," Caroline said, crouched low, shielding it with her body.

Thanassis draped his jacket around the pot. "So were we once."

The storm passed in less than an hour, but it left behind a trail of damp towels, upturned chairs, and a scent of ozone sharp enough to taste.

It also flushed out some of the island's most elusive residents.

The goats arrived at dawn.

It was Linda who spotted them first, eleven of them, including one mottled leader with a bell and an unreasonable swagger. They had found a gap in the boundary wall behind the hotel and entered like tourists checking in for breakfast...

By the time the group assembled in alarm, the goats had already sampled the rosemary, knocked over a sack of lime plaster, and chewed one of Caroline's espadrilles.

"Oh, for god's sake," she moaned. "I loved those shoes."

"They were entirely impractical," Catherine muttered.

"Exactly why I loved them."

It took two hours, a bag of barley, and some firm negotiating from Michalis to coax them back out. James, having documented the entire operation in sketches, declared it "deeply educational and strangely inspiring."

Later that afternoon, with the goats gone and order restored, Kosmas arrived at the gate, wiping sweat from his brow and waving a battered manila folder above his head.

"It's done!" he shouted. "Signed, sealed, certified by Athens!"

He strode triumphantly onto the terrace, greeted by applause, mock cheers, and Caroline throwing a tea towel in the air like a victory flag.

Inside the folder: final confirmation that ownership of the small hotel had officially passed to Linda and Michalis, equal partners under a shared agreement, with titles split, but tied in a deed of cooperation that ensured mutual input, shared profit and risk, and independent living space for each of them.

Michalis read it through, lips barely moving. Linda stood beside him, not touching, but shoulder to shoulder. When he nodded and held out his hand, she took it. It had already been legalised at the notary before works started, but it was lovely to see the final documents crisp with a myriad of stamps and official-looking seals.

"Shall we make something beautiful?" he asked.

She smiled. "Only if it's complicated."

"Oh, it will be."

By sunset, they were all gathered again, this time on the upper balcony of the hotel, where the roof had finally been repaired and a long reclaimed table set under festoon lights that swayed in the post-storm air. Aimee had cooked grilled peaches, soft goat's cheese (from a source more willing), rosemary flatbreads, and a salad that Catherine swore tasted like the last day of summer.

Wine flowed. Thanassis brought jars of preserved lemons. Caroline forgave the goats and toasted her surviving shoe. Marco performed a goat impression so accurate that Serge wept into his wine glass. The ringleader goat had munched well on a young laurel bay, so he was christened Lorenzo of the Bay. Marco acted out the scene.

And Linda?

She stood quietly at the railing, watching the horizon blush into indigo. James stepped beside her and said nothing, just placed one hand over hers, and let the moment root itself without the need for flowers.

Later, after the table had been cleared and the last bottle opened, Kosmas raised his glass.

"To good madness. To useful chaos. And to turning broken things into homes."

They drank. And for once, no one tried to follow it with a joke.

221

Because the truth was, here on this weather-worn slope above Poros with its stubborn olive trees and goat-prone footpaths, they were making something worth staying for.

Something honest.

Something whole.

Chapter 15:
The Edge of Staying (Lemon Trees and Unasked Questions)

The lemon tree outside Caroline's room was flowering again. It hadn't been expected to fruit until next spring, but there it was a scattering of pale blooms opening along its young branches like a whisper of promise.

Thanassis noticed first. He said nothing. Just fetched a small length of olivewood stake and tied the slender trunk with fresh jute, anchoring it gently against the wind.

Caroline watched him from the doorway, arms folded, oversized shirt falling off one shoulder like casual rebellion.

"You treat everything like it might break," she said.

"I treat things like they deserve to last."

She stepped down barefoot, the morning warm on the stone. "And people?"

He looked at her. "Even more so."

They were quiet after that, surrounded by birdsong and the soft sound of shutters opening across the terrace. Somewhere down by the fourth room, Serge was singing to himself something vaguely operatic. Marco responded with a theatrical groan.

Caroline smiled, then turned away before it could grow into something more vulnerable.

Thanassis followed her gaze. "You still want to run."

She didn't answer. Not yet. She plucked a flower from the lemon tree and rolled it between her fingers.

"It's easier to charm someone than to let them love you," she said.

"I know."

"Do you?"

"Yes."

"Then why haven't you run?"

He stepped closer, gently taking the crushed blossom from her hand.

"Because you don't frighten me. I see you, Caroline."

Later that morning, she found Linda in the garden, her sleeves rolled, a notebook in her lap filled with lists, fabric swatches, and receipts carefully paper clipped with colour-coded tabs.

"God, you're organised," Caroline said, flopping beside her on the bench. "It's terrifying."

"It's survival," Linda replied. "Without order, I fall apart."

Caroline laughed, then didn't. She stared at the orange tree beyond the trellis for a while, then said quietly, "I think I might be in trouble."

Linda looked up. "With Thanassis?"

"He's…" Caroline trailed off, searching. "He's the sort who'd build a house for you stone by stone, even if you only asked for a garden bench."

"And that's a bad thing?"

"That's the terrifying part," she replied. "He waits. He listens. He sees through every deflection. And the worst part is, I like it."

Linda didn't answer. She waited, calmly, like Thanassis might have.

"I've never really done this," Caroline said. "Not properly. I flirt, I fly, I disappear. I've left before it got real. Or I stayed just long enough to mess it up before they could."

"And now?"

"I think he's… real. And I'm terrified I'll crack him."

Linda reached over and took her hand.

"Caroline. We're not as dangerous as we think we are."

Caroline's throat tightened. "You always make it sound so simple."

"It's not. But it's worth staying for. You don't have to run from someone who sees you. You just have to let them keep looking."

You're such a loyal friend. Remember when you took me into your London flat after the divorce? I didn't have a brass sou but you were there. Just... be there now. But for yourself."

They sat in silence for a while. The breeze shifted. Somewhere, Catherine was shouting instructions about missing curtain hooks. Michalis was arguing cheerfully with a delivery man about the weight of terracotta basins.

Caroline looked up at the sky. "Do you think people like us get to settle?"

Linda squeezed her hand. "I think we're already doing it."

Caroline smiled then. A real one. Quiet, unguarded.

And for once, she didn't make a joke to follow it.

PART 1: THINGS THAT GROW

The light was thickening by late afternoon, that golden, honey-warm hour when even the stones seemed to exhale. Caroline had taken to sitting in the garden between tasks, half-heartedly replanting herbs while watching Thanassis work on the slope near the rear wall.

He was barefoot, as usual, sleeves rolled, a pencil tucked behind his ear. He moved like someone who trusted the earth and, more strangely, like someone who trusted himself. That unsettled her more than she cared to admit.

"Do you always work like you're tending something sacred?" she asked, standing now in the shade of the fig tree.

Thanassis didn't turn. "Isn't everything given the chance?"

"That's not a normal answer."

"I'm not a normal man."

She laughed, coming to lean against the low stone wall, brushing the dust from her dress. "I gathered that the first time you corrected my plant names and still complimented my perfume."

He set down the trowel and finally turned. "I have something to show you."

Caroline blinked. "Is this the part where you lead me into the trees and reveal your secret fig orchard or some other metaphor?"

"No," he said. "But close."

He led her across the terrace, past the pomegranate tree and the pots she had rearranged four times in a single week. Down a small, partly hidden path just beyond the tool shed, one she hadn't quite noticed before. It was lined with rosemary and old roof tiles, and ended at a small, crooked gate that creaked open onto a clearing that looked like something out of a forgotten painting.

There, amidst wild oregano and creeping ivy, stood a single almond tree not young, but not ancient either. Its bark was silvered and split, and at its base was a low, curved bench made of stone and salvaged wood.

"I planted this when I was twenty-one," Thanassis said. "The year after my father died. We lived just up there on the ridge."

Caroline's breath caught. "You've never shown anyone this?"

He shook his head. "Not even my mother. It was my place for years. I came here when I couldn't speak for myself, when I was trying not to disappear. I was shy and so sad."

She stood still, her hands resting lightly on the bench's edge. "Why now?"

Thanassis looked at her, then not hard, not questioning. Just... seeing.

"Because you're still deciding if you'll let yourself be known. And I wanted to go first."

Caroline sat, folding her hands in her lap. The breeze shifted, carrying with it the faint scent of wild thyme. The almond tree above them rustled quietly, as if nodding approval.

"I'm afraid of needing someone," she said, not looking at him. "Of liking someone too much. Of them, seeing everything and choosing to walk away."

"I won't," he said.

She turned to him. "You can't promise that."

"I can promise I'm here now. And that I've seen enough already to know I want to keep looking."

Her throat tightened. "I'm a bit of a handful."

"I noticed! And I'm not looking for someone tidy."

There was a silence then, not awkward, not staged. Just filled with meaning. And then Caroline did something she hadn't done in years.

She leaned forward.

And kissed him.

Fully herself.

A release.

It wasn't dramatic. It wasn't a performance. It was soft, almost unsure, but it was hers fully and freely given.

Thanassis didn't move to take more than she offered. He simply kissed her back with the same steadiness he used to tend trees. With care. With patience. As if she were something growing and precious.

When they broke apart, she didn't look away. She rested her forehead against his and whispered, "Now I'm in real trouble."

He smiled. "Not trouble. Just rooted."

And for the first time in a long, long time, Caroline let herself be still.

230

Part 1:
First Impressions and Quiet Triumphs

The first guest was due on Friday.

This time, there were no last-minute delivery crises, no broken pipes, no goat incursions, only a palpable buzz moving through the villa like an electrical current. Aimee arranged bowls of figs and late-summer grapes in each room. Linda ironed napkins. Catherine read over her welcome letter aloud while Lawrence re-checked the guest Wi-Fi and muttered about routers and miracles.

The local electrical store had sent a man to look at Wi-Fi extenders. He let out an involuntary gasp and said, "Near impossible. I am calling Father Panayiotis." Lawrence was surprised it was so bad that it needed divine intervention.

Later that afternoon, a priest arrived. His pressed black robes were neat and tidy. On his vestments: a badge reading *Cosmote Greece*. He worked for the phone company and for God.

"Yes, yes," smiled Father Panayiotis. "I have a direct line, so your internet will be solved."

With that, he set to work, scurrying around the rooms, fixing a better modem and boosters where needed. He explained over Greek coffee that he had his day job and his calling, and that both worked well together. He blessed the house on departure.

Caroline, to everyone's astonishment, was early.

She swept into the salon in cream trousers, a loose indigo shirt, and a scarf she claimed once belonged to an Italian heiress. In her arms: fresh-cut verbena, two lemon muffins, and a pomegranate she'd polished to a shine.

"Darling, where do you want the glamour?" she asked, already fluffing a pillow.

Marco peeked over the balcony and applauded. "She's early! Serge owes me five euros!"

Serge appeared from the kitchen, hands floury, holding a bowl of what might have been frittata or possibly an experimental quiche.

"She's possessed," he said. "Call a priest get Father Panayiotis back!"

Caroline smirked. "Possessed by Thanassis, more likely."

There was a beat of mock shock, then laughter. But the truth hung gently in the air: she was different. More grounded, somehow not dulled, but anchored. She moved through the space like someone who had chosen to stay. To give herself space and time. Her London apartment was now let, freeing both time and funds to make things happen.

The guest arrived just past noon: A Londoner named Steve, early fifties, solo traveller, former architect turned memoirist. Tall, with silvered hair and an expression that toggled between curious and tired. He stepped out of the taxi with a well-worn duffel and looked up at the villa with a mixture of wariness and hope.

Caroline, naturally, was the first to greet him.

"Welcome to your unravelling," she said. "In the best possible way."

Steve blinked, then smiled. "That's... oddly perfect."

Catherine offered chilled water and showed him to the Sanctuary Room. Linda had left a handwritten card on the desk with a small quote: *To be alone is not to be lost.*

He read it twice. Touched it once.

Later, Aimee caught a glimpse of him through the hallway window, standing in the garden, hand outstretched as a butterfly landed briefly on his wrist. He didn't move.

The first guest had arrived.

And the house, quietly, had begun to breathe differently.

That evening, after the dishes were cleared and the lanterns lit, Caroline made her way to the old stone bench on the east terrace, where Serge and Marco were already sharing a bottle of wine and laughing about wallpaper decisions.

"I still think the coral print in Room Four is too loud," Serge was saying.

Marco rolled his eyes. "It's not loud. It's bold. This place needs bold."

"You've been saying that since Mykonos in 2010."

"That's because I was right."

Caroline slipped into the space between them like a missing puzzle piece.

"Well, look who's domesticated," Serge teased, pouring her a glass.

"I'm not," she said. "I'm... selectively settled."

Marco lifted his glass. "To selective roots, then."

They clinked gently, the warm breeze tugging at the hem of her shirt.

"I always thought I was too much," she admitted. "Too loud. Too much story. Too much appetite. You know what you always say, I may have a lot of luggage, but at least it's Louis Vuitton. Thanassis... he doesn't flinch."

Serge looked at her with a softness few had ever earned. "Darling, you were never too much. The world was just a bit too small."

Caroline blinked hard. "How do you do that?"

"I've had years of practice."

They sat in companionable silence for a time. The moon rose. Somewhere, Steve, the new guest, played a single tentative note on the villa's old mandolin, the sound drifting like a question over the lemon trees.

"You think this will last?" Caroline asked.

Marco nodded. "It already has. You're here."

And she was.

For once, entirely.

Part 2:
A Light in the Fourno Room

Steve had begun to soften.

On his second morning, he joined James in the garden with a mug of coffee and asked softly about the best beach for swimming unobserved. By afternoon, he had discovered the almond tree behind the tool shed and returned with a sketch of its branches curling like script against the sky.

Caroline found him there as the light dipped, holding a pencil, sight narrowed like a spyglass.

"You sketch?" she asked.

"I used to design buildings," he said, "before I realised I was always drawing places for other people to live in. I never really imagined my own."

She sat beside him on the bench. "That's changing now?"

"Perhaps. This place makes you think about shape not just of walls, but of time."

Caroline offered him a slice of plum cake wrapped in a paper napkin. He accepted it, and they watched the light fall through the fig leaves without needing to speak again.

That night, Thanassis found Caroline beneath the olive tree with her feet bare and her hair plaited loosely, reading a book with no cover.

He held up a lantern. "Come with me."

"No questions?"

"No questions."

She followed him down the garden path, their shadows stretching long and intertwined. In the fourno room, the stone doorway flickered with candlelight. Inside, Serge and Marco had swept the floor, spread rugs, and placed cushions in a circle. A table held olives, bread, wine, and a gramophone that looked suspiciously like it had been pilfered from Catherine's reading nook.

Catherine was already seated, wearing a scarf tied as a headband and sipping ouzo. James leaned against the wall, sketchbook in lap. Aimee and Michalis stood arm-in-arm, humming quietly to themselves.

Caroline looked around. "This was supposed to be a storeroom."

Serge grinned. "Then we stored something, joy."

Marco clapped his hands twice. "Tonight, we dance. No cameras. No plans. Just music and bread and people who chose each other."

Thanassis stepped behind Caroline, hand brushing her back. "Do you dance?"

"Not well," she said. "And not unless I've had three glasses of wine."

He handed her a glass. "Then we wait."

The gramophone crackled, and a tsifteteli filled the space sinuous and aching and beautiful. Aimee began to sway. Michalis joined her, his hands slow and sure at her hips. Catherine stood and pulled Lawrence into the light, laughing as she tried to teach him the steps.

Caroline leaned into Thanassis and whispered, "This is dangerous."

"It's delicious," he replied, and spun her gently into the centre.

They moved with the song, not choreographed, but somehow in time. She danced without armour. He held her without need. Around them, their strange, beloved tribe began to whirl and laugh and clap.

Then Serge took Marco's hand and began to waltz, exaggerated and theatrical at first, then tender, elegant, and real. The group cheered. Someone started singing. Linda threw her head back and joined in, her voice steadier than anyone expected.

Candles burned low. Wine disappeared. The walls echoed not with age, but with the sound of something beginning.

Aimee turned to Catherine and said, "This is what I hoped we'd build."

Catherine smiled, her arm around Lawrence. "We didn't build it. We became it."

Outside, the stars gathered in conspiratorial silence.

And in the old stone oven room, once cold with disuse and time, the fire had returned truly.

Chapter 16:
Guests and Guardians (Doors Opening)

The October sun had shifted slightly, no less warm, but somehow more golden, more reflective. The mornings were cooler, crisper, carrying a hint of autumn that left dew on the pomegranate leaves and the first fig husks soft underfoot.

Mikro xenodocheio had found its rhythm. There were guests now, not just one or two, but a small stream of arrivals, each bringing their strange music to the harmony. Some stayed quietly, as if trying not to disturb the peace of the place. Others arrived like storms in linen trousers, loud with ideas and longing.

It was Catherine who spotted Hugo again in the same spot by the olive tree, notebook in lap, mug of something dark in hand. His elderly travelling companion, Miss Adeline Lys, arrived beside him in a hat large enough to shade a donkey and a shawl large enough to double as a picnic blanket.

"They're back. Something medical, Adeline had to go to Athens," Catherine whispered to Lawrence as she passed the breakfast veranda.

He looked up. "Hugo and... the Duchess?"

"She's not a duchess."

"She certainly could be."

Adeline Lys had the aura of someone who might have once declined an invitation to Buckingham Palace because the weather was unfavourable. She walked with two ivory-handled canes and always carried a satchel that no one had ever seen her open.

Hugo, young and wire-thin, kept pace with her attentively but never intrusively. It wasn't clear if he was her grandson, nephew, career, or latest protogé. Caroline was sure someone had said aunt. What was clear was that they travelled together, moved like a unit, and had returned with the same unspoken grace.

"I remembered the olives," Adeline said to Aimee as she passed, pressing a sealed jar into her hands.

"You didn't need to bring anything."

"Of course I did," she replied. "Places like this should be paid in more than currency. I am so happy to be back."

The new guests arrived just after midday.

First came Peter and Anne, an art curator and a retired theatre set designer from Paisley. She wore long scarves in warm weather and spoke with her hands. He had white hair in a ponytail and carried a fold-up bicycle he never used.

Next: Satin and Mehdi, a married couple from Marseille, travelling with sketchbooks, a tripod, and a profound commitment to olive oil. She was studying Byzantine icons; he was photographing wild herbs for a book he hadn't yet titled.

They were all greeted with warmth and wine, and within an hour were seated under the pergola comparing sea-swim temperatures and debating the difference between serenity and mere boredom.

It was Hugo who drew the sketch. Quietly, without fanfare. A charcoal rendering of the garden corner, Satin reaching for a lemon, Mehdi squinting at the sun, Adeline asleep in her chair with one hand still gripping her cane like a sceptre.

Catherine looked over his shoulder. "You see everything."

"I only draw what's already there," he said.

That evening, after the new arrivals had found their corners of comfort rooms that already seemed to know what each person needed, Caroline wandered down to the side garden where Thanassis had been planting the late-flowering jasmine.

He was crouched low, one knee pressed to the earth, tying back stems with fine cotton twine. A lamp flickered beside him. The shadows danced across his forearms and neck.

She sat near him on a stone bench, legs folded beneath her, arms bare to the night.

"Do you believe," she said slowly, "that people can start over, no matter what came before?"

Thanassis tied the knot carefully, tested its hold, then looked at her. "Not only do I believe it. I see it every day."

"In plants?"

"In people. But yes, plants too."

She leaned forward, elbows on knees. "Even the wild ones? Even the ones that grew in the wrong place for too long?"

He smiled. "Those are the ones that survive anything. They just need a little help remembering they belong."

There was a pause, then not heavy, but full.

Caroline tilted her head. "Do you ever get scared?"

"Every day."

"But you don't show it."

He shrugged. "I don't need to. Fear doesn't stop me from planting."

And then, without an agenda, without tension, he reached across and rested his hand gently over hers.

It was not possessive. Not dramatic. Just certain.

And for the first time in years, she didn't pull away.

PART 1: SMALL ACTS OF
KNOWING

The rhythm of the house shifted again not disrupted by the new guests, but deepened by them. It was as if the place had inhaled and found a wider lungful of breath.

Each person seemed to fall into their own tempo. Anne spent hours in the wild garden, sketching pomegranate shadows with a stick of vine charcoal. Peter curated imaginary exhibitions on the breakfast terrace, narrating each imagined piece to a rotating, bemused audience.

Satin was seen most often cross-legged on a cushion in the herb corner, painting a single olive leaf over and over. Mehdi, her husband, had claimed the old garden wall as his station, photographing thyme, ants, and the morning light on limestone like a poet disguised as a botanist.

It was a kind of dance, a slow one, but everyone moved in time.

Adeline had taken to afternoon chess matches with Lawrence, using a small set of ceramic pieces that seemed to have once belonged in a museum. Their games were long and involved more stories than moves.

"I once beat the Deputy Foreign Minister of Portugal in under seven minutes," she said over a particularly intense board.

Lawrence, brow furrowed, moved his bishop two squares and paused. "Were you playing with or against him?"

"That," she said, sipping mint tea, "is classified."

Theo, meanwhile, began to surface like a man from a long dive. He took walks with Linda through the lemon orchard, sat quietly with Hugo in the evenings, and slowly began to share fragments of a book he hadn't told anyone he was writing.

"You ever write for yourself?" he asked Aimee one morning as they both looked out toward the sea.

"All the time," she said. "It just takes longer to admit it."

Caroline watched all this with a sense of disoriented wonder.

It had been a long time since she'd stayed still long enough to see people in this light when they began to glow, just softly, from the inside out. She saw it in Linda when James walked by and brushed her shoulder. She saw it in Catherine when Lawrence adjusted a shutter without her asking.

And, she realised with a start, she saw it in herself.

She'd stopped performing.

Even stranger no one seemed to miss it. A strange truth about being the jester: the one who says what others only think.

Thanassis had begun building a low bench in the orchard, using offcuts of driftwood and stones from the creek bed. When Caroline asked why, he simply said, "Because someone will need it. Maybe not yet."

That evening, she did something uncharacteristic.

She went to the small bookshop in town, the one with creaking floors and a poetry-cat that refused to move, and asked the woman behind the desk if they had any books about Cretan and Peloponnese plants.

The woman blinked. "For reading or impressing someone?"

Caroline grinned. "Bit of both."

She returned with a slim paperback and three postcards pressed between its pages. On her way back, she stopped to buy bread, a jar of quince paste, and a tiny bottle of tsikoudia with a hand-painted label.

By the time she returned, dusk was settling in.

Thanassis was at the far edge of the garden, kneeling beside a struggling laurel bush. She didn't call out. She just walked up, placed the book and the jar beside him, and said, "For your library. And your sweet tooth."

He looked up, surprised. Not by the gesture, but by the expression on her face something shy and direct at once.

"You didn't have to," he said softly.

"I know," she replied. "That's the point."

He took the book in his hands like it was a gift far more precious than its modest cover implied.

And for the second time that week, Caroline surprised herself.

She stayed.

Later that night, the lights of the micro xenodoheio glowed like small lanterns against the hillside. The guests dined together on the expansive terrace. Theo brought a bottle of red wine he'd once hidden in a hiking sock "just in case," and Anne passed around figs she'd poached in cinnamon.

Adeline raised a toast. "To those who return. To those who stay. And to those still deciding. Thank you, everyone, you know I truly love it here."

Glasses clinked. Bread was broken. Stars came out like a secret remembered.

Caroline looked across the table at Thanassis.

He didn't raise his glass. He just nodded one of those deep, quiet nods that held everything.

And she, for once, didn't look away.

247

Part 1:
Keys and Candles

The house settled into twilight with the grace of a place that had learned not to chase silence but to invite it. Lamps flickered behind old shutters. The stone walls held the day's warmth. Somewhere in the orchard, cicadas tuned their final chorus of the season.

In the garden, Adeline and Hugo sat on a bench near the rosemary beds, the light behind them soft as parchment. She wore her shawl pulled tightly around her, and Hugo held a small notebook open on his knees.

"They think I'm your companion," Hugo said, half-smiling.

"You are," Adeline replied. "Only not perhaps in the way or the reason they assume."

He didn't look at her. "Do you think we've fooled them?"

"We haven't tried," she said. "That's why it works."

He turned the notebook toward her. A sketch: her hand, veined and strong, holding the edge of a book. Nothing else. Just that gesture. Just her presence.

"You've drawn me like a character from an epic," she murmured.

"You are one," he said. **"You just haven't told them the ending yet."**

Adeline gazed at him, something tremulous in the corners of her mouth. "Promise me, when the time comes... you'll let them remember me this way."

He nodded, quiet and sure. "Of course. But only if you promise to stay as long as you can."

She reached for his hand, held it in both of hers, warm, weathered, steady.

"I intend to. This feels right."

Elsewhere in the house, Serge was in his element.

He had commandeered the fourno room like a theatrical set designer preparing for a clandestine gala. Rugs layered the stone floor. Candles glowed at various heights, some tucked into alcoves, others floating in shallow ceramic dishes. Wild herbs and cut olive branches were woven around the old hearth. A table was set for two, lit by a hanging lamp with a soft amber shade. Marco and Serge had sent the invite.

Marco leaned in the doorway, watching. "You've outdone yourself."

Serge adjusted a napkin and smirked. "If this doesn't bring James and Linda together, then I give up."

Linda arrived, drawn by the scent of rosemary and woodsmoke. She wore a soft linen dress and a bracelet of sea-glass beads Aimee had gifted her weeks ago. When she stepped inside, her breath caught.

The room glowed. The air felt sacred.

James was waiting, dressed simply, nervously adjusting his cuffs until he saw her.

"You planned this?" she asked.

"Not entirely. Serge insisted. But I wanted the time. With you."

She smiled. "Then let's not waste it."

They ate slowly roasted vegetables, warm bread, a bottle of Peloponnesian red Marco had stashed for "emergencies of the heart." They talked about gardens. About books. About the loneliness of living at half-volume for years.

At one point, Linda reached across and touched James' wrist.

"I'm not entirely whole," she said.

"You're not meant to be," he replied gently. "You're meant to be real."

She looked at him for a long time, then nodded.

And when he stood and offered his hand, she took it.

No music.

No performance.

Just two people learning the rhythm of something honest.

They danced without music, holding to each other, and to life to come.

On the edge of the orchard, Thanassis waited under the almond tree.

Caroline arrived ten minutes late and unapologetic, wearing a faded denim jacket and carrying a paper bag of pistachios.

"You said I should plant roots," she said, handing him the bag. "So I came bearing snacks."

He smiled and offered her a minor brass key.

She blinked. "What's this?"

"My front door."

Caroline hesitated, then took it. It was warm from his hand.

"You want me to visit?"

"I want you to know where I live. In case you ever want to come without asking."

She turned the key over in her palm.

"You're serious about this."

"Yes."

"And what if I'm not ready?"

"I'll wait."

She looked at him, the silence between them wrapped in starlight.

"Maybe I'll come," she said.

"I am waiting."

Later that night, she placed the key on her bedside table.

Next to it: the book on Cretan flora, a small jar of honey, and a pressed almond leaf.

She didn't have to decide tonight.

But she certainly knew the direction she was facing.

Part 2:
The Key Turns

The courtyard lanterns had been strung that morning, soft golden bulbs suspended from olive trees and old beams, Marco and Michalis balanced on ladders, arguing about symmetry. Catherine declared the whole scene "a little Tuscan, a little Elysian," and Serge threatened to print it on brochures.

By sundown, the micro xenodoheio glowed like the stage of an open-air amphitheatre. Long cushions were arranged beneath the jasmine trellis. Bread and olives were passed, wine uncorked. Plates of grilled figs, soft cheese, and tiny spinach pies appeared like offerings to the muses.

It was Aimee's idea for a night for everyone to bring something of themselves: a drawing, a story, a piece of music, a memory.

"There's no pressure," she'd said. "Just presence."

Peter began the evening with a theatrical reading from a fake catalogue of imaginary art. Anne followed with a haunting sea-themed sketch, holding it to the candlelight so the shadows danced in the ink. Mehdi sang a soft French lullaby. Satin read a few lines from a notebook she insisted was private, and everyone applauded just the same.

When it was Hugo's turn, he hesitated.

Adeline touched his arm. "It's time."

He stood slowly and walked to the centre, notebook in hand.

"I wasn't sure I would," he said, voice quiet. "But this place... It's a sort of confessional, isn't it? Only there's no priest, just people with good bread and better listening."

A chuckle rippled through the group.

"This isn't poetry," he continued. "But it's mine."

He read not from a script, but a letter. Addressed, it seemed, to no one. Or to all of them.

"I thought I was here to care for someone. To protect, to assist. But the truth is, I was running from my own life. And this formidable woman beside me didn't let me. She gave me a routine. And in it, I found myself. So here, in this small corner of the world, I stopped hiding."

He closed the book. Adeline reached for his hand and spoke.

"I may not have so long. But the best is yet to come. None of it would be possible without Hugo."

No one applauded. Not yet. They just sat with it, the bravery, the precision of it. Then Caroline stood and offered him a glass of wine, and the circle breathed again.

As the evening faded into music and stories half-finished, Caroline slipped away.

254

She passed beneath the arbour, up the thyme-lined path, past her room and toward the olive grove's edge.

She held Thanassis' key in her hand.

The walk was short, but her thoughts were not.

She paused by the fig tree, again beneath the almond branches. Then continued.

His house was simple, built low into the hillside of stone, timber, and a soft light behind one curtain. She stepped to the door, her heart loud in her ears.

The key turned easily. Silently.

She opened the door and stepped inside.

Thanassis was there, seated at a small table with a single lamp and a plate of olives. He looked up without surprise—only warmth.

"I was just thinking," he said, rising, "that it might be a good night for soup."

Caroline shut the door behind her.

"I don't know how to do this," she said softly.

"You're already doing it."

She exhaled. "Then make me soup."

He smiled. "You'll stay?"

She nodded.

Not just for a night.

But for something that might finally last.

Chapter 17:
The Measure of Days (When the Light Changes)

The days had begun to soften. Not shortened, exactly the sun still lingered, but the light had changed in quality. It filtered more slowly through the pines, glowed more gently off the tiles. Mornings came with a cool edge that hinted at departures.

Adeline moved a little slower, too.

She still walked the garden in the early light, shawl draped over her shoulders, canes tapping against the stones like a second heartbeat. She still asked questions, pointed, precise ones about the pomegranate harvest, or whether the rosemary by the oven room was overwatered.

But she sat more often now. Drifted into silence mid-sentence, as if listening for something only she could hear. Looked out at the horizon as though reading a familiar story written on the sea.

It was Hugo who answered for her, sometimes. Not presumptively, just gently. As if they'd rehearsed these silences together.

It was Catherine who noticed first.

She said nothing, but she folded a thicker blanket over Adeline's chair one morning and added extra honey to her tea. It was Serge who later placed a stool beneath her feet when she sat by the west wall, watching the sun.

No one asked. Not yet. But something had shifted, and they all felt it keenly.

But it was Linda who felt it most sharply.

She hadn't meant to cry. But it caught her by surprise, a slow, rising tide of emotion that spilt over as she stood by the kitchen window and watched Hugo tie Adeline's hat beneath her chin.

The tenderness undid her.

She stepped outside, past the lemon trees, down the back path toward the potting bench. There, among the tools and half-planted lavender cuttings, she folded into herself and let the tears fall.

Aimee found her there.

She said nothing. Just sat beside her and waited.

Linda wiped her eyes with the back of her hand. "It's silly. I am just getting to know her."

Aimee shook her head. "It's not silly."

"She reminds me of my mother," Linda said quietly. "The way she still insists. The way he helps without smothering. It's so... dignified."

She sniffed. "I can't bear to watch it again. And yet I can't look away."

Aimee placed her hand over Linda's. "Maybe that's what love does. It stays with you. Even when it hurts."

Linda nodded, slow and raw. "It's still close. Four years. You'd think I'd be steadier.

To tell the truth, Aimee… it was the final nail in the coffin for my marriage. He just gave no support, not when I needed it most."

Aimee didn't reply. She didn't need to.

Some griefs are like root systems invisible but vast, rising to the surface with a look, a scent, or a memory.

That afternoon, Adeline asked Hugo to take her to the upper olive terrace. It was a longer walk, but she wanted the view. He helped her gently, without fuss, and when they reached the stone bench, she settled beside him with a sigh that carried both effort and peace.

"I think it's time," she said.

Hugo looked at her, unreadable. "Are you sure?"

She nodded. "If I wait much longer, I'll be the story they tell after I'm gone. I'd rather tell it myself."

They sat there a long while, saying nothing.

Just watching the hills in the distance, the sea, and the haze of light over everything they still had.

That evening, Adeline asked Catherine if she might speak at dinner.

"Nothing dramatic," she said, touching Catherine's wrist. "Just honest."

Catherine only nodded her eyes, already shining.

Part 1:
The Telling

Dinner that evening was simple: white bean stew with rosemary, grilled bread, and a salad of torn basil and tomatoes still warm from the sun.

The wine was soft, slightly chilled, poured by Lawrence with steady hands.

The group gathered beneath the pergola, the candles flickering in terracotta bowls, shadows playing across the stone.

Adeline waited until plates had been cleared, until conversation had found a lull.

Then she rose.

No dramatic pause. No clink of glass. Just the quiet strength of someone who had held court in far more formidable places than this.

"I asked Catherine if I might say something tonight," she began, her voice even but low.

Hugo looked up to her left, his hands still loosely folded. His gaze never wavered.

"I want to thank you all," she continued. "Not just for your kindness, or the olives, or the sunshine, though they've all been restorative. But for the way you've allowed me to be part of this moment in your lives without demand or expectation."

She paused, eyes scanning the group.

259

Some, perhaps, already knew. Others, Caroline, Mehdi sat frozen, feeling the shape of something before it took form.

"I am, as some of you may have sensed, nearing the end of my time."

The words landed gently like rain on dry earth.

"I won't catalogue the diagnosis or the details. That isn't the point. The point is I chose to be here. I chose to spend these days in a place that feels alive. Among people who are not afraid of silence, or laughter, or truth."

She looked to Hugo, then back to the others.

"This young man," she said, placing a hand over his, "is my companion, my confidant and, though he would never say it, the guardian of my better self.

He has not asked for thanks, but I give it anyway. And I ask one thing of all of you: when I leave, I will not let him carry me alone. Share the weight. Share the memory."

No one moved.

Not out of shock, but reverence.

Then James raised his glass first. "To Adeline."

"To Adeline," echoed Linda, voice thick, wiping her eyes with a napkin.

"To the days that matter," Serge added.

And so the toasts came simple, unadorned. Real.

Adeline sat down. Her hand still rested lightly on Hugo's.

Later that night, Hugo stepped outside to catch his breath. The stars had spilt across the sky in a great, aching arc too beautiful to bear alone.

Linda found him there barefoot, silent.

"I'm sorry," she said, not for the first time that day.

"Don't be," he replied.

"She's extraordinary," Linda said.

"She always has been."

There was a pause. Then Linda asked, "How long have you known?"

"Two years. She told me one night in Vienna after a Chopin recital. Said if I was going to follow her across Europe, I might as well know the real itinerary."

Linda gave a soft, astonished laugh. "But you stayed."

"I didn't think of it as staying. It was just... where I was meant to be."

She nodded. "You're remarkable."

"No," Hugo said, shaking his head. "She is. I'm just lucky enough to witness it."

And for the first time in days, Linda didn't cry. She stood beside him and looked up at the stars, letting the silence say what words never could.

Part 2:
A Fire in the Hearth

The weather turned quietly.

One morning, the garden smelled of dry leaves and thyme, and Linda noticed the lemon tree had lost its gloss. The shadows stretched earlier, and the whitewashed walls of the micro xenodoheio held the gold of the sun a little longer before giving it back.

In the evenings, shawls reappeared. Tea replaced wine. And the old fourno room, once a summer refuge of cool stone and filtered light, became again what it had always been: a hearth.

Adeline liked to sit there after lunch. The sun reached just far enough to warm the flagstones, and Serge had added a woven rug beneath the table, a silent kindness that needed no mention. The room smelled faintly of fennel seeds and old wood.

On this particular afternoon, Linda arrived with a teapot and two delicate cups wrapped in a towel to keep them warm. She found Adeline already seated by the small arched window, a blanket over her knees, a letter in her lap. "You always bring the right thing," Adeline said, smiling.

"Years of making do," Linda replied. "And paying attention."

They sat in companionable silence, sipping. Outside, a breeze rattled the bay leaves.

Eventually, Adeline spoke.

"I've been thinking about endings," she said, glancing down at the letter.

"Not surprising," Linda said gently.

"No," Adeline agreed. "But it's not just the leaving I'm thinking of. It's what's left behind. Who it falls to."

Linda set down her cup. "Go on."

"I'm not without means," Adeline said plainly. "In fact, I have more money than Hugo suspects. He's never asked one of his many beautiful faults. He assumes I've always travelled on charm, a pension, and accumulated air miles."

Linda smiled but said nothing.

"I need someone," Adeline continued, "who isn't dazzled. Who knows what things cost, not just in money? Someone who will see to things properly when I'm gone." "You mean…"

"Yes. I'd like you to be one of my executors."

Linda blinked, caught off guard.

"I don't even know your surname," she said softly.

"De Lys. Adeline De Lys," Adeline said. "But what matters is that I know yours. I've seen you. You're sensible, you're kind, and you don't flinch. You'll keep Hugo safe not just from grief, but from the vultures I suspect may circle once the dust settles. I have the remnants of a disagreeable family hovering."

263

Linda felt her throat tighten. "That's a lot to ask."

"I know."

Linda took a breath. Looked around the room. The plaster flaked in places. A sprig of thyme lay on the sill. Autumn crept in at the edges, soft and slow.

"You've seen me, too," she said.

Adeline smiled. "Of course I have. You're not easy to miss, once someone knows how to look."

They sat together, the moment unfolding like a late fig, rich, ripe, just a little bitter.

After a while, Adeline handed her the letter.

"This outlines the terms," she said. "There's a trust, and a foundation, and yes, a house in Antibes no one's lived in since my brother died. I need you to make sure it goes where it should. Hugo will have anything he needs but not more than he can bear."

Linda took the envelope, weighing it in her hands like a living thing.

"I'll do it," she said.

"I never doubted you would. And thank you, I feel a weight has lifted."

That night, Linda walked out to the sea path, the letter tucked in her coat.

She paused by the water, eyes stinging, and whispered into the dark, "I hope I get this right, Mum."

The tide answered with a sigh.

Part 3:
Where the Roots Take Hold

Sunday morning dawned soft and golden, the kind of autumn day that arrived like a benediction. The sea below Villa Petrouni shimmered in pewter tones, and a hush seemed to rest over the citrus groves, as though even the trees knew something meaningful was unfolding.

Aimee had been up since first light, sleeves rolled, cheeks flushed with kitchen warmth. The scent of cinnamon, roasted tomatoes, and garlic drifted from the open windows. Michalis, ever the conductor of calm chaos, managed three pans at once while sending Caroline out for last-minute herbs and welcoming early guests with a kiss to each cheek.

The tables had been laid beneath the pergola in the courtyard between the villa and the micro xenodoheio. Long mismatched cloths, jugs of cut bay leaves and olive branches, old plates and tumblers of deep-red wine. Serge had found wild persimmons and arranged them in bowls with walnuts and fennel sprigs. Pippi, in a linen apron three sizes too big, floated around setting candles and stealing grapes from the platters.

By midday, the courtyard was full of laughter and voices, the music of many lives woven together, old guests, new friends, a child from the neighbouring

265

house chasing a chicken in great arcs around the fig tree.

Adeline was helped to her seat beneath the olive tree closest to the oven room, a place of honour where she could see everything and speak little, if she chose. She wore her navy cashmere shawl and a silver pin shaped like a quill. Hugo sat beside her, steady and smiling, his hand never far from hers.

"I feel like a very loved tree," she whispered. "One last glorious autumn."

"You're not done turning leaves yet," he murmured back.

After the third course, roast lamb with wild oregano and crushed lemon potatoes, Michalis stood and tapped a spoon against his glass.

"We began this season with dust on our shoes and just an idea," he said. "And now, somehow, we've filled rooms with strangers who became companions, meals with stories, and gardens with laughter."

He looked around at the gathered group: Serge, Marco, Catherine, Lawrence, Caroline, Thanassis, Linda, James, and the ever-gentle Hugo, with Adeline. "This little xenodoheio this guesthouse of souls gave us more than we ever gave it. So thank you. For planting something here. For tending it."

Aimee stepped forward and kissed his cheek. "And here's to next season and to finishing the roof tiles."

Laughter rose like birds startled from the orchard.

Later, as the sun dipped low, James and Lawrence carried out baskets of seedlings: sage, thyme, trailing rosemary, tiny cyclamen with deep pink blossoms like butterflies. Thanassis joined them with a small trowel in his belt and a paper bundle of crocus bulbs.

"We'll plant along the northern slope," he said, pointing to the edge of the path. "Winter rain will do the rest."

Lawrence nodded. "There's something comforting about it, isn't there? Planting now, not for ourselves, but for spring."

James pressed a clump of soil in his hand. "The hope it carries. That life cycles forward. That roots take even when we can't see them."

Michalis joined them, sleeves rolled and eyes bright. "It's what we do. Here in this country, in this life. We plant. We wait. We believe."

Adeline, watching from her chair, smiled. "And you do it without guarantees. That's what makes it beautiful."

As twilight deepened, torches were lit, music played low from Marco's Bluetooth speaker tucked in a wine crate, and the courtyard

shimmered with candlelight and the kind of fatigue that comes only from joy.

Caroline danced once with Thanassis, her arms around his neck, her forehead to his chest.

"You smell like pine needles and wine," she said.

"And you smell like home," he replied.

Catherine caught Aimee's hand at one point and whispered, "You've built something here. Something real."

"I think we all have," Aimee replied, watching Michalis pass a plate of olives to Adeline with the care of a man handling treasure.

And at last, as the sky turned velvet and stars began to appear one by one, Hugo helped Adeline to her feet.

"Just for a moment," she said.

She stood in the centre of the courtyard, and everyone gathered loosely around her like petals around a bloom.

"I want to say," she began, "that life is rarely what we plan. But if we are lucky, truly lucky, it becomes something even better. Because of others. Because of their love, their stubbornness, their willingness to invite us into their mess and their miracle."

She looked to Linda. "Thank you for seeing me clearly."

To Caroline. "Thank you for reminding me what fierce joy looks like."

To James. "For your gentleness."

To Catherine and Lawrence. "For opening your hearts and your home."

And finally, to Hugo. "For everything."

Then she said nothing more.

There was no need

That night, after the last dish was washed, the fire dimmed, and the guests drifted to their rooms, Adeline and Hugo sat once more beneath the olive tree.

In the silence, he took out his notebook.

"May I?" he asked.

She nodded.

And so he sketched.

Not as a portrait. Not a symbol.

But simply as she was luminous, fading, rooted, and reaching.

A woman who had planted so much and asked only that it be tended.

Further up the hill, a window in the old fourno room flickered gently with firelight.

Chapter 18:
The Autumn Garden (The Terrace)

They began at the top of the land, where olive trees gave way to rough terraces and bramble. The early October air was a softer kind of warm, heavy with sage and earth. Catherine was the first to see the shape: a natural amphitheatre with views down to the sea, the kind of place that called out for something fragrant, low to the ground, and humming with bees. The autumn wind carried a chill and the faint scent of wood smoke from village chimneys.

Thanassis, boots already dusted with ochre, walked the land like a man listening to old stories. He crouched at the edge of a stone wall, crumbling soil in his palm.

"Thyme and lavender will do well here," he said. "But we'll have to mind the drainage. This ground doesn't forget the rain."

He was right. The first layout, neat rows of young lavender interspersed with thyme and marjoram, was lovingly arranged over three long afternoons. Serge and Marco placed a turquoise amphora in the centre, found by Kosmas at a salvage yard in Pelion. Its glaze caught the morning sun and turned deep green by evening.

Beneath the amphora, a hidden pump fed water into a small stone-lined pool. Aimee had suggested it was something that reflected both sky and planting, a mirror in the earth. Caroline declared it "utterly Grecian," which everyone took as approval.

Thanassis oversaw the work with quiet attention. He did not speak often, but when he did, it mattered. He trimmed one of the thyme plants with his fingers, sniffed the stem, and nodded. "This one will thrive. That one move is half a metre. Too shaded."

James, helping rake out the mulch one morning, leaned over and asked, "How do you know?"

Thanassis looked at him and said, "Same way you know when someone's in love. You just... see it."

Then the rains came.

Not a gentle misting, but a night of furious wind driving in from the east, drenching everything, filling the dry riverbed below the villa and dragging half the mulch down with it. In the morning, the terrace was a mess: soil slumped, roots exposed, three of the young lavenders stripped bare.

Caroline stood at the edge, arms crossed, wind tugging at her scarf.

"Well," she said, "every beauty gets flattened now and then."

It was Thanassis who led the response, calm, unfussed, already laying out timber boards to reshape the beds. Kosmas came by that afternoon with new plans and a gentle reminder: they'd need a proper building licence if the walls were to be reinforced. Ever practical, he even had the forms in his bag.

"We'll do it properly this time," said Michalis, laying out a new curve for the stone edging. "Something that will last."

Stone from Pelion was ordered smooth, green-hued, quarried just above Volos and known for keeping calm even in high summer. When it arrived, Serge clapped his hands like a child at a festival. "It looks like sea glass."

They worked slowly this time. Two weeks passed. The walls took shape. The soil was layered back in this time, mixed with compost and pumice. The pool beneath the amphora was re-lined with tiles Aimee had found in a back street of Nafplio, each one patterned with stars, small galaxies underfoot.

Thanassis waited to replant until the moon waned. "The plants don't like too much pulling when the moon is full," he explained. No one argued.

It was Adeline who asked, one afternoon, if she might add something.

She stood at the edge of the terrace, Hugo at her side, and looked out at the low hum of bees already returning.

"There's a kind of tree," she said, "that grew in the garden of my childhood home in Antibes. Almond. Every spring, it would bloom in a flurry of pale petals like the first snow of warmth."

273

She turned to Catherine and Aimee. "Would you allow me to plant one at each corner? A kind of blessing."

No one hesitated.

Linda squeezed her hand. "They'll be beautiful here."

"I hope so," Adeline said. "I may not see them flower. But someone will."

Thanassis walked over and nodded solemnly. "We'll find good stock. Strong roots. They'll be happy on this slope. And you *will* smell the blossom, Adeline."

By the week's end, four almond trees had arrived, delicate yet tall, their leaves just beginning to yellow with the season. James and Lawrence dug the holes, and Thanassis placed each tree himself, stepping back after every one to adjust the angle, as if composing a piece of music only he could hear.

When the last was planted, Aimee lit four small lanterns, one at the base of each tree, and they stood together in the early dusk, watching as light and shadow settled between the leaves.

"It feels... right," Catherine said quietly.

"It feels like faith," Hugo added.

Adeline smiled, her eyes glinting in the lantern light. "It feels like home."

Part 1:
The Return of Pippi

The early morning ferry from Piraeus nosed into Poros harbour just as the mist was lifting off the strait. Among the first to disembark was a small, determined figure with a straw hat slung over one shoulder, two large tote bags bumping at her sides, and a grin that hadn't left her face since Hydra.

Pippi had returned.

She'd texted no one, wanting the arrival to be a surprise, but Caroline happened to be at the harbour with Thanassis collecting a box of olive tree stakes when she spotted her weaving through the crowd.

"For God's sake," Caroline called, dropping the clipboard she'd been holding. "She's back from the real world."

Pippi dropped her bags and launched into her arms. "Don't exaggerate. London barely qualifies."

Thanassis, watching the reunion with a bemused expression, picked up the clipboard and made a polite half-bow. "I see your reinforcements have arrived."

"Oh, he's still handsome," Pippi whispered to Caroline. "Hasn't run for the hills yet?"

"Not yet," Caroline muttered. "But don't jinx it."

Pippi's return sent a ripple through the household. She had been part of so many summers' sailing trips, winter dinners, long, half-drunken nights of Greek salad and soul-baring that it felt strange she'd ever left.

Aimee found her that afternoon on the new lavender terrace, kneeling beside one of the re-planted thyme clumps, fingers stained with soil.

"You're supposed to be a guest," Aimee teased, crouching beside her.

"I'm a guest with opinions," Pippi replied. "And honestly, these thyme roots look like they need more mulch. Has Thanassis checked them?"

"He checked everything. Twice."

The two women paused, leaning on their knees, heads almost touching.

"I've missed this," said Aimee.

"So have I," said Pippi. "London is exhausting. Everyone's on the verge of being brilliant or broken."

"And which are you?"

"Somewhere in the middle. But then I thought why wait? Why not be somewhere that's real?" She looked across the terrace, where Caroline was gesturing dramatically at something Thanassis had just said. "Where people know who you are not just what you do."

Later that morning, the garden buzzed with activity. Serge was attempting to train a rambling rose along the trellis with the solemnity of a fencing master. Lawrence and James unloaded another crate of Pelion stone, while Michalis returned from the village with three bags of compost and a loaf of sesame bread tucked under his arm.

Pippi found herself walking the perimeter with Thanassis, helping him space out a row of young marjoram plants.

"Place them like guests at a good dinner table," he advised. "Enough room to talk, not enough to gossip."

Pippi laughed. "Is that a Greek proverb?"

"No. That one's mine."

Near the almond tree Adeline had chosen for the eastern corner, Caroline knelt with a spade, frowning at a scrap of paper scrawled in Greek.

"Is this a planting schedule or a spell?" she muttered.

Thanassis wandered over, peered at it, and gave a small smile. "It says, 'Plant here when the wind comes from the west, and the cats lie low.'"

Caroline stared. "What does that mean?"

"It means," he said, crouching beside her, "some things only thrive when the world is quiet."

Pippi, passing with a tray of coffee mugs, laughed so hard she nearly dropped them. "I missed this. All of it."

By midday, the terrace smelled of sun-warmed stone and crushed thyme. The turquoise amphora gurgled softly. Adeline sat beneath her almond tree again, Hugo beside her, reading aloud from a battered volume of Neruda. Linda had placed a folding table beside them with figs, cheese, and almonds.

"Adeline's trees are doing well," said Catherine, standing with Aimee on the upper path.

"They feel like they've always belonged," Aimee replied. "Like she planted something in all of us."

Caroline and Thanassis, seated nearby with mugs of mountain tea, glanced over as a breeze caught Adeline's scarf and lifted it lightly off her shoulder. She looked utterly still, content, but not unmoved.

Thanassis rested his hand beside Caroline's.

"She planted with love," he said. "That's why they'll grow."

Caroline was quiet for a long moment. Then she nodded. "I know. It's just... I'm not sure I'm brave enough for all that."

"You are," he said. "You just think too loudly to hear it."

The afternoon ended with a small, impromptu gathering, cushions dragged onto the terrace, Serge playing a slow tune on a borrowed guitar, and James sketching while Linda leaned into his side. Catherine passed around slices of a fig and walnut cake that

Pippi had miraculously conjured from the pantry, and even Thanassis allowed himself a second piece.

As the sun dipped low and the first lights came on across the harbour, the garden glowed.

It wasn't finished. It probably never would be.

But it was loved.

And things planted in love have a way of lasting.

Part 2:
The Cost of Beauty

Linda sat at the long pine table in the kitchen with the ledger open and a pencil resting against her lips. The window behind her framed the first gold of evening, but she barely noticed. Her fingers tapped lightly on the wood as she ran the numbers again.

It was the third time.

The total was undeniable.

They'd gone over.

Stone from Pelion, specialist compost, that infernal pump for the amphora (which Serge had insisted needed a pressure adjuster to create "just the right ripple"), it had all added up and so had the wages for the local crew, the unplanned drainage channel after the storm, and the last-minute trip to Nafplio for those blasted tiles.

She closed the ledger, exhaled, and went to find Michalis.

He was in the side storeroom, folding old tablecloths with the care of a man born into a generation that knew the value of linens. He looked up and smiled.

"Need something?"

"We need to talk," she said, motioning for him to sit.

They settled onto the bench, the room cool and scented faintly of lavender and starch.

"I've been through the accounts," she said. "We're about eleven thousand euros over what we set."

Michalis didn't flinch. He listened, eyes focused, expression   still.
"That's a lot," he said finally.

"It is. And it's mostly the garden, the terrace, the amphora, the pool. The almond trees, of course, are not included. All good choices. But we've lost our buffer."

He nodded. "I don't regret a single one. But I see what you mean. We need to rein things in."

Linda leaned back slightly, arms folded.

"This next phase the final interior rooms, any external painting we need to cost first. And commit only after."

"I agree," he said. "You've done a brilliant job, Linda. Without you, this would've been chaos."

"You're kind," she said. "But kindness doesn't pay for tile grout."

They laughed a quiet release of unspoken tension.

Michalis stood and pulled a small envelope from his back pocket. "I've been meaning to show you this. I asked Kosmas to model a minimal guest season six months, Five rooms. His numbers say we can break even in two years. Maybe less."

Linda unfolded the papers. They were clean, careful, thorough. "Thank you," she said. "This helps. All of it helps."

She stood, brushing imaginary dust from her skirt. "And Michalis we're going to make this work. But no more Pelion stone. Not unless it comes with its own donkey."

He smiled, broad and grateful. "Deal."

Unbeknownst to either of them, two days earlier, Adeline had met quietly with Kosmas in the corner of the terrace garden.

Hugo had gone into town for bread. The others were knee-deep in planting. She wore her navy shawl and her silver pin and looked out over the project with a steady eye.

"I want you to add something to the garden fund," she told him. "Quietly. Anonymously, if possible."

Kosmas, always one for discretion, merely raised an eyebrow.
"How much?"

She named the figure just over the total Linda had tallied.

He nodded. "I'll arrange it."

Adeline smiled, satisfied. "Consider it insurance. For a spring I may not see. But which I want very much to arrive."

Back on the main terrace that evening, Pippi lit a string of copper-wire fairy lights across the almond trees. Caroline poured a round of chilled tsipouro,

282

and Catherine passed out the leftover cheese pies from lunch.

James and Lawrence returned from the storeroom with baskets of kindling, and Serge had found a crate of dried sage for the fire.

As the first flames took hold and the group gathered once more around the long table, Linda leaned close to Michalis.

"We'll be fine, you know," she whispered.

"I know," he replied, eyes warm.

And high on the shelf above them, in a weathered envelope marked only with the Greek letter phi, sat the quiet promise of a gift waiting to be discovered.

Part 3:
Hearth and Heart

The fire was lit in the main lounge with great ceremony.

Lawrence had fetched kindling. Michalis coaxed the flame. Caroline theatrically produced a basket of pinecones she'd been hoarding like a dragon. Serge and Marco rearranged the furniture into a loose crescent, each armchair draped in one of the soft wool throws Catherine had found at the Athens market.

Everyone gathered early, wine poured, snacks scattered, the last of the day's blue dimming through the shuttered windows.

"Feels like a house now," said Pippi, tucking her legs under herself on the sofa. "Not just a project."

Catherine nodded. "It's got soul."

Michalis added a log to the fire and frowned.

"Although, has anyone noticed it's warm near the chimney but absolutely freezing by the door?"

James, ever the architect's son, got up and waved his hand above the mantle.

"Ah," he said. "The design draws the heat straight up the flue. Very stylish. Very Greek."

"Translation," muttered Caroline, "it heats the roof tiles and the neighbour's cat, but not the humans inside."

They laughed. Thanassis offered a rare smile. "That is the purpose of blankets."

Pippi passed around mugs of cinnamon tea. Catherine added a tray of honeyed nuts and small savoury pastries. They toasted to the season to what had grown, what had weathered, and what might still bloom.

At some point, Kosmas approached Linda. He handed her an envelope and gestured toward the side table.

"I was instructed to give you this once the work was done."

Linda turned it over, brow furrowed.

"What is it?"

"You'll see."

She stepped into the hallway and opened it beneath the antique lamp.

Inside was a handwritten letter in Adeline's sloping script.

Dearest Linda,

I wanted this to be quiet, and perhaps a little unexpected like blossom in early spring.

I've asked Kosmas to place a contribution into the fund. It's more than what has been spent I know this because I asked him to be honest with me about the overages. He's very good at his job, even when I bribe him with some good French wine…

I do this not as a patron, but as a friend. You have given your strength, your care, your steadiness to this place and it shows. Let this gift take the strain from your shoulders, so that you might walk into the next season lighter.

I ask only one thing in return: let the garden have a name.

Yours, in friendship and gratitude. Adeline

Linda read it twice. Then again.

Her shoulders loosened. Her breath caught. And somewhere deep in her chest, something unfurled quiet, old, and dear.

Acceptance. Grace.

She folded the letter into her coat pocket, returned to the lounge, and said nothing not yet. She simply sat beside James, took his hand, and smiled into the firelight.

The next morning, after the fire's ash had cooled and the crumbs swept away, the group gathered again this time outside, beneath the soft rustle of almond leaves.

Linda had asked Serge to make a nameplate.

He'd fashioned a small plaque, its letters etched with quiet flourish. It had been Catherine's idea, but it was Thanassis who had chosen the words.

They unveiled it together.

"The Garden of the First Rain"

In honour of what begins again.

No speeches were made. None were needed.

Aimee brushed her hand over the lavender. Caroline looped an arm through Thanassis's. Hugo read the words twice and kissed Adeline's hand.

She simply said, "Now it belongs to all of you."

And just like that the season had turned.

Chapter 19:
Winter's Reckoning (Drains and Radiators)

The weather turned suddenly, as it often did on the island once the olive harvest ended. Winds blew in from the north, rattling shutters and lifting the scent of pine and woodsmoke into the air. Fires were lit earlier each day, and woollen blankets migrated from closets to every surface. In town, rugs stored since spring were unfurled, beaten, and taken into lounges and bedrooms. Winter curtains appeared where simple muslin had been.

The talk turned to olives and the harvest every *kafenio* had a different take. A good year. A bad year. The worst ever. The local cooperative, where olives were pressed and handled for the farmers, buzzed with industry. Maria, the manager, surveyed the scene like a general at war. She spotted those trying to jump the line and sent them to the back without a word. All went like clockwork under her command.

Thanassis collected many bags of waste skins and used them as mulch in the garden. "No good for some plants," he pointed out. "Too bitter to bear. But for others perfect protection."

Lawrence and James helped him for several long days, dragging and layering, wheelbarrow after wheelbarrow. Roses and trees needed their own special mix, which had a distinct smell of goat.

"*Copria*," said Thanassis the Greek word for manure. The gentlemen were banished to the outdoor shower before dinner.

At Villa Petrouni and the adjacent *micro xenodohio*, routines shifted subtly. Morning coffee was now drunk indoors, chairs angled toward warmth. The terrace lay quieter, the paths slick with fallen leaves and the occasional damp fig. Still, something glowed beneath it all a sense of gathered lives, of inward turning, of a nest prepared.

One evening, with rain sluicing against the windows, the group gathered in the main lounge again. Serge had found a half-bottle of brandy, and Marco was carefully slicing apples for a tarte Tatin that seemed overly ambitious for the small oven.

Catherine had brought in a basket of logs that turned out to be riddled with damp, and Michalis was laughing as he tried to coax a sulky flame into life. Eventually, the fire caught as they always did in this house and the talk turned slow and warm.

It was Pippi who said it first. "You know, someone once told me there are two kinds of people: drains and radiators."

A pause. Then a chuckle from Caroline. "Radiators?"

"Yes," said Pippi. "You know the ones who give off warmth, make everything easier, lighter. And drains they pull the joy from the room. You don't even realise it until you leave and feel lighter."

"God," said Linda, sinking deeper into her chair. "That describes half of my marriage."

The room went quiet. Not awkward just thoughtful.

Linda continued, more to the fire than anyone else.

"Graham was... well, on paper he was perfect. Generous, charming, the kind of man who made friends on trains. But it was always about him. If I was tired, he needed more. If I was sick, he was suddenly worse. If I was happy he'd find a way to turn it sideways."

She stopped, swallowed. "And I allowed it. For years. Until I didn't. When I nursed my mother, and she died, he showed zero compassion. Just seemed rather put out that the attention wasn't on him."

No one spoke. There was no need.

James, sitting across from her, looked up slowly "You know... I loved someone who radiated. My wife. She gave without asking, smiled before I even realised I was upset. And when she got sick, it was like her light dimmed... but she still gave it. Until the very last."

He blinked, eyes steadying. "Since then, I've been careful not to expect warmth. I suppose I assumed I'd had my share."

Caroline leaned forward, glass in hand. "I think I've been a radiator wrapped in tinfoil. All shine, no heat."

That got a laugh the kind that sounds like a sigh.

"I made everything look fun," she went on. "But I kept my coat on, metaphorically speaking. Every man I dated, I knew from the start they wouldn't last. I picked them for that. No risk of actual hurt."

Thanassis, seated beside her, didn't speak. He simply reached out and took her hand. She let him.

Across the room, Aimee spoke softly "Richard... my ex... was the coldest person I ever knew. Not obviously he was witty, loved in public. But when it was just us... I was a mirror for his moods. If he was low, I had to fix him. If I was low, I was weak."

She exhaled. "I didn't realise how cold I'd become, just trying to keep him warm."

Michalis shifted beside her, placing an arm around her   shoulder. "Not anymore."

"No," she agreed. "Not anymore. I have my own radiator, *Agapi mou*."

Outside, the wind howled briefly, then fell silent as if listening.

In the flicker of firelight, the group sat still. Thoughtful. Not broken. Not sad. But seen.

Catherine stood and placed another log on the fire carefully, deliberately.

"You know," she said, "radiators don't always look how we expect. And drains can wear silk ties and smile just right."

She turned to face them, her voice low but clear. "But when you find people who warm you without effort you hold on. That's how we survive the winters. That's how we grow gardens in spring."

A pause. "And this old fireplace needs a wood burner. It's hopeless."

Outside, the olive trees leaned into the wind. Inside, warmth gathered in the bones of the house.

Part 1:
The Real Radiator

By early December, the wind had taken on a damp, determined edge. The island quieted. Ferries came less often, the light shifted, and porches stayed shuttered until midday. But inside the walls of Villa Petrouni and the small guesthouse next door something entirely different was happening.

Christmas was coming not just as a date, but as a feeling.

Preparations began modestly. Catherine, ever the organiser, pulled down boxes from the attic marked with years and musty labels: *"Xmas 2012 – Sussex," "Greek String Lights – Broken?"* and *"Napkins (Stains?)."* Marco and Serge took charge of the kitchen calendar, already debating how many courses were *too* many for a Christmas Eve dinner.

Pippi, returning from a trip to the mainland, brought back bags of candied orange peel, pistachios, dried cherries, and a lopsided paper star she insisted had been blessed by a monk from Tinos.

"Or possibly a baker," she admitted. "He had flour on his shoes."

Linda unearthed a dusty tin of brass bells and found herself unexpectedly sentimental about it. James, without a word, cleaned each one and hung them from a beam with delicate string.

But the biggest surprise arrived on a Thursday morning with a truck from Athens and two grumpy delivery men who spoke rapid French and not a word of Greek.

"What on earth?" said Caroline, staring at the enormous wooden crate being wheeled up the hill.

Lawrence checked the paperwork, squinting. "It's addressed to the *xenodohio*... from Strasbourg."

"Strasbourg?" said Michalis. "That's not a Greek island."

Marco clapped his hands together. "It's the wood burner! I forgot I ordered it the first night we tried to have a hopeless fire. This is a Christmas present from Serge and me. May we always give you warmth."

A cheer went up followed by a brief but determined panic about how to get it through the doorway.

Three hours later, the wood burner stood proudly in the main room of the micro guesthouse installed with the help of a borrowed trolley, Tasos from the village with his building skills and much cursing, and Thanassis' impressive grip strength. It was flanked by two battered armchairs from the flea market, which Catherine and Aimee had covered with bright woollen throws.

It was a sleek, cast-iron beauty, all ornate flourishes and a small warming oven built into the top.

"Perfect for apple pie," asserted Serge.

294

It looked wildly out of place and yet, somehow, perfect.

Catherine ran her hand along the polished metal. "So... not only do we have real radiators in our lives, but we also now have an actual one."

Everyone laughed even Linda, who had been quietly calculating the fitting cost.

The first fire was lit with ceremony. Pippi opened the wine. Serge produced a tin of roasted chestnuts from nowhere. Caroline, caught in a rare moment of introspection, stood with Thanassis watching the flames catch and rise, her arm around him.

"It's funny," she murmured. "All that talk about drains and radiators... and then this turns up. A real one. An actual warm heart."

Thanassis looked at her, his eyes reflecting the firelight. "Maybe we needed to say it to see it."

"Maybe," she said. "Or maybe it just took the long road from France. Now... how can we bake some apples in this little oven bit?"

The season gathered momentum. Adeline, quieter now, spent her days near the fire, knitting long strips of scarlet yarn that she refused to explain. Hugo had found a vintage record player at a local market and brought it back with cracked old albums of Greek Christmas songs and French lullabies.

One evening, Serge and Marco decorated the tree, a crooked pine from the hillside above the house and insisted on hanging clove-studded oranges.

"For luck," Serge said, "and because it hides the smell of damp plaster."

Aimee and Michalis crafted wreaths from olive branches. James carved tiny angels from driftwood. Pippi, with help from Thanassis, hung a long garland of rosemary and bay over the guesthouse threshold.

Even Caroline helped painting signs for the guesthouse door.

"No Drains Welcome"

"Radiators Only, Please Knock."

Each evening, they gathered by the fire, surrounded by stories and sparks, the cold locked outside by thick stone walls and new insulation courtesy of Lawrence's obsession with winterising.

It wasn't just a holiday.

It was a season of turning inward and healing from old patterns. Of embracing the unlikely, imperfect family they had become.

And as the flames of the French wood burner flickered and danced, the laughter rising with the scent of cinnamon and pine, no one could deny:

They were radiating now.

Part 2:
A Froth of Pearls

The night before Christmas arrived quietly, under a sky of pale stars and rustling olive branches. The fire in the French wood burner flickered with a steady rhythm, casting long shadows across the walls of the lounge. A hush had settled over the house, not from absence, but from fullness.

They had dressed in their best, which, in this house, meant soft knits, scarves of varying flamboyance, and a general disregard for matching socks. Catherine wore her signature cashmere. Adeline, a velvet wraps the colour of red wine. Hugo, dashing in a moth-bitten cravat, brought his French manners to the table, greeting each guest as though they were arriving at a royal salon.

Dinner was served in the largest room of the guesthouse, the long table set with wild bay leaves, flickering votives, and plates in a joyful mismatch of patterns. Serge's tarte tatin, by some miracle, had survived a second attempt. Marco had made a cinnamon-stewed lamb that smelled like mountain Christmases and ancient kitchens.

As they raised their glasses, Pippi stood, holding a plate of almond biscuits.

"I propose a toast," she said. "To radiators the people, not the appliances, who keep us warm, even when we don't know we're cold."

Laughter and agreement rang out.

"And to the year ahead," added Catherine, "in whatever shape it arrives."

"Round," muttered James. "From this food, definitely round."

After dessert and more brandy than was strictly sensible, the group moved to the sitting room. The chairs had been rearranged in a semicircle, the lights dimmed, and a small stack of wrapped gifts had appeared beneath a rosemary bush pressed into service as an extra Christmas tree.

Aimee and Michalis exchanged a wrapped sketchbook and a small carved box of olive wood. Caroline gave Thanassis a leather-bound field guide to Mediterranean plants "for all the ones I pretend to know." He, in turn, gave her a hand-carved mortar and pestle and a tiny poem, translated from Cretan dialect. She didn't speak, but she folded the page and kissed his cheek.

Linda had found a delicate brooch in Poros, a silver almond blossom, which she gave to Adeline with a trembling hand. Adeline's gift to Hugo, characteristically unexpected, was a bound set of handwritten pages: the first half of her memoir.

"I thought," she said, "if I go first, you'll know how the story began."

He cried silently as he hugged her.

Then, with a quiet flourish, Lawrence stood and approached Catherine. In his hand: a slender black box.

"This," he said, "is a froth of pearls. A muddle. A tangle. A beautiful accident. Just like our life."

Inside was the necklace.

Thin gold wires curled like wind across water, layered and light. Scattered between the strands were creamy pearls of varying sizes and, nestled between them, small diamonds that caught the light like moonlit sea spray.

Everyone gasped.

"It's from Anthi the jeweller in the main square," Lawrence added. "She made it over three weeks. Called it 'utter madness,' and then wouldn't let it leave until she was sure it danced."

Catherine touched it, speechless.

"It does dance," she whispered. "And so do I."

He fastened it around her neck, his fingers steady, and kissed her shoulder.

"It's art. She's a true artist," said Marco.

"No," said Serge. "It's love."

Later, when the fire was low and tea had replaced the brandy, Adeline reached for the long bundle of scarlet yarn she had been knitting since the first frost.

Without a word, she began to drape it, looping it from one beam to another, forming a gentle arc above the table. As she moved, she spoke softly.

"In my family, we had a tradition. A red thread to tie the year together. To remind us of what holds."

Loop by loop, the yarn took shape, not perfect, not planned, but holding.

"Some years it was longer. Some years it broke. But we always tied it again."

When she had finished with Hugo's help, it stretched from wall to wall, a soft scarlet curve above their heads.

Aimee stood and touched it. "It's beautiful."

"It's ours," said Adeline. "And it will stay until spring."

Part 3:
Threads That Hold

The morning came slow and silver. Light spilt gently over the hills, brushing the tops of almond branches and dew-drenched rosemary. The air was still not empty, but reverent, like a church without walls.

In the kitchen, Michalis was already brewing coffee, the old copper pot hissing like a contented sigh. He crept, letting the others rest the warmth of the previous night still hanging in the air like a shawl around the house.

Adeline sat by the window of the old fourno room, wrapped in her deep-red velvet. Her breath misted the pane as she stared at the corner where the almond trees had been planted. Tiny buds already promised spring.

Linda entered quietly, carrying two cups.

"You're up early," she said, handing one to Adeline.

"I always am," Adeline replied. "Each morning is a gift I wasn't promised."

They sat in silence for a moment, letting the weight of it settle.

Then Adeline turned, her gaze soft but intent. "I wanted to speak with you. Something personal."

"Of course," said Linda, instantly sensing the gravity.

"I've updated my will," Adeline began. "It's all quite simple. Hugo will have everything he needs. I've made sure of it. He's never asked. Never pried. That's why I must make sure he's protected."

Linda nodded, her throat tight.

"But French law..." Adeline continued, "I require that I leave something to my blood relatives. However distant. They've never cared for me, not as a child, and certainly not as an adult. When I was ill the first time, they didn't even call. But still... the law insists."

"What will you do?" Linda asked gently.

"I've left them one thousand euros each," Adeline said. "Just enough to fulfil the law. No more. It ensures they cannot challenge anything."

"That's wise," Linda said. "And important. Not just legally... emotionally."

Adeline's eyes glistened. "I needed someone to know why. And I trust you."

Linda reached for her hand. "I do know. And I'll make sure it's honoured. And Adeline, I can't thank you enough for your donation to the garden, but we will fall out if you do that again."

Adeline smiled quietly. "It is nothing, compared to the peace and dignity you've allowed me."

Outside, the light shifted golden now, catching the shimmer of dew on almond bark.

Elsewhere in the house, Aimee and Catherine had taken their coffee to the upper terrace. Wrapped in blankets, they leaned against the warm stone and watched the horizon brighten with delicate confidence.

"You know," Catherine said, "I never imagined this would be our life."

"Me neither," Aimee replied, eyes on the water. "But I don't think I imagined any life at all for a while. Just one long holding pattern."

They were silent.

Then Aimee smiled. "And now? There's colour. Warmth. Even noise."

"Especially noise," Catherine laughed. "I heard Marco singing in the pantry this morning."

They sipped their coffee in sync.

"I think I'm finally happy," Aimee said softly. "Not just in love. Not just busy. But... peaceful."

Catherine nodded. "You deserve that."

"So do you."

The wind picked up briefly, ruffling the remnants of last summer's pink bougainvillea clinging to the villa's sun-worn façade. Aimee turned her face into it.

"I wonder what Mum would've thought," she murmured.

"She'd have loved Michalis," Catherine said immediately. "And hated Richard."

Aimee chuckled. "She did hate Richard."

Catherine smiled. "And she'd have loved this house. Especially the ridiculous stairs."

They both laughed, now tears at the corners of their eyes, though neither named them.

Down below, Hugo appeared in the garden, chasing a rogue napkin, while Pippi emerged sleepily from the guesthouse wearing one of Serge's jumpers and singing something vaguely familiar.

Caroline and Thanassis strolled up from the path arm in arm, her hair in wild disarray, his coat wrapped tightly around her shoulders.

And in the window of the fourno room, Adeline stood, watching the almond trees, her eyes full, but unblinking.

Inside the guesthouse lounge, the scarlet thread still hung across the ceiling. No one had touched it. It had become something more a symbol of the year just lived, of the ties that had held. Linda flicked a duster over it from time to time, but it had to stay.

And beneath it, in quiet smiles and exchanged glances, lived the knowledge that something rare had been made here.

Not just warmth.
But home.

Chapter 20:
The Halcyon Days (Fava and Forecasts)

The sun had returned with theatrical intent. January's brittle gloom gave way to that rare and celebrated spell of Greek midwinter, the Halcyon Days. A fortnight of blue skies, windless days, and a quality of light so clean and golden it made the lemon leaves shine like lacquer. Locals whispered it was the best in years.

And, true to form, Marco had taken it as a sign from the gods.

"Today," he declared, standing in the doorway of the Poros townhouse, "we resolve the fava question."

Fava: A Greek staple, simmered with love and split yellow dried peas.

Inside, Serge turned off the kettle and raised an eyebrow. "Is there a question?"

"There is a rivalry," replied Michalis, appearing with a bundle of split peas, garlic, and something he refused to name. "And I'm about to settle it."

Within the hour, the kitchen was a tangle of aromas and one-upmanship, Marco's onions caramelising with thyme, Michalis' mix of peas and garlic bubbling over a low, flickering flame. Serge, ever the master of hospitality, set the table with mismatched ceramics and linen napkins, a loaf of bread still warm from the bakery resting at its centre.

Catherine arrived bearing lemons from Villa Petrouni. Aimee followed with a bottle of early-pressed olive oil from a farmer in Methana. Caroline and Linda trailed in, laughing one with paint swatches, the other clutching a bulging notebook of renovation plans.

"Blind tasting," Serge announced. "Strict rules. No peeking."

The two bowls were marked only A and B. Everyone sat, tore pieces of bread, and dipped them in near reverence.

No one spoke during the tasting, not from decorum, but out of culinary concentration.

When it was done and the votes were counted, Marco won by a clean margin. He roared with delight and danced a little victory jig on the tiled floor. Michalis sank into his chair with theatrical despair.

"I am disgraced," he cried. "This is a Greek national humiliation."

"You used too much garlic," Caroline muttered.

"That's called *flavour*," Michalis retorted.

Peace or something close to it was restored with the timely arrival of Eleni, who swept in with a bottle of *rakamelo* wrapped in brown paper—much more fun than the fava.

"Raki, honey, cinnamon," she said. "And one secret ingredient."

She wouldn't say what it was, only that her great-aunt in Sitia swore by it. It was poured into small glasses, warmed, and sipped slowly, the heat blooming in everyone's chest.

As the sun began to drift lower over the Saronic Gulf, Serge cleared his throat and stood by the window, squinting at the sky.

"There's something we've been thinking about," he said. "Marco and I. If this weather holds and it looks like it will, we're considering taking *Samantha* down to Crete."

"Crete?" said James. "In January?"

"Not for a holiday," Marco explained. "There's a boatyard down there. One we trust. Good facilities, excellent carpentry, and honest rates. It's time she had her winter work haul-out, antifoul, and fittings inspected. We'd leave her there until spring."

Lawrence, who had been buttering bread, looked up. "And how long a sail is that?"

"Four to six days," said Serge. "If we go inside Kythira, hugging the Peloponnese at first. Could be magical."

James nodded slowly. "I'll make sandwiches."

The room buzzed with the idea of wind, sun, sea, the hush of a winter passage under the rare halcyon sky.

Linda placed her napkin on the table. "I'd love to come, but we've got fresh funds thanks to Adeline.

Plasterers are back next week. Room Four's finally getting sorted."

Caroline grinned. "And I've been seconded. My destiny is paintwork."

Aimee added, "And someone has to manage Hugo and Thanassis."

Michalis, ever dramatic, clutched his heart. "Abandoned by my own fiancée!"

Eleni snorted. "You're all mad."

"It's just a proposal," Serge said. "Nothing decided. But if the forecast holds..."

And for a while, they sat with the idea. That perfect kind of plan: ambitious, romantic, possibly ill-advised, and exactly the sort that takes root over shared food and winter sun.

Part 1:
Knots and Threads

They gathered at the quay just after sunrise, mist curling along the still waters of the Poros strait. *Samantha* bobbed gently at her mooring, already stocked with fuel, bread, and optimism. Marco stood barefoot on deck, tying and retying a bowline with theatrical precision, while Serge secured the last of the galley stores. Michalis appeared with two crates, one of oranges, the other of Eleni's still-warm koulouri and muttered something about not trusting shipboard breakfasts without sesame.

Lawrence and James hoisted a final bag aboard, grinning in that particular way men do when half-drunk on the excitement of leaving, even for something entirely practical. The others stood on the dock: Catherine in a scarf she'd borrowed from Aimee, who in turn had borrowed it from Caroline. Linda wore an apron smudged with paint, and Hugo had one of his flat caps pulled low over his eyebrows. Adeline, leaning gently on a carved cane no one had ever seen before, stood just back from the edge, smiling in a way that made them all blink against the light.

"Will you be warm enough?" Aimee asked her quietly.

"I have layers," Adeline said, patting her coat. "And a full pot of mischief."

The goodbyes were filled with ribbing and affection. Marco hugged Caroline like a brother, murmuring something about checking the olive trees at the boatyard. Serge kissed Catherine's forehead and made her promise not to do any actual plastering. Michalis lingered with Aimee, their embrace longer, slower, no drama, just warmth and the unspoken wish to fast-forward the following week.

And then they were gone, lines loosened, fenders drawn up, sails catching the whisper of wind that slid in with the tide. *Samantha* moved like a memory into the channel, her white hull catching the morning sun.

They watched until the boat was no longer visible, just a suggestion of canvas and wake, heading toward the open Saronic and then south, toward Cape Maleas, Kythera, Crete, and whatever came after.

Back at the small guesthouse, the fire had already been lit. The day was crisp but clear. Adeline settled into one of the large armchairs, a shawl tucked around her shoulders and an absurdly bright ball of wool rolling about her lap like a citrus comet.

"What on earth are you making?" asked Caroline, sinking onto the couch beside her.

"Something lime green and entirely impractical," Adeline replied. "Which, incidentally, could describe most of my wardrobe choices from the 1970s."

Linda appeared from the kitchen with a teapot and three mismatched mugs. "It's meant to be a scarf, I think," she said. "But it may end up as a table runner. Or a protest banner."

They laughed the easy kind of laughter that comes only when women know they are safe and understood.

As the fire crackled, Adeline began to speak slowly at first, then more fluidly. She told them about her younger days: her work as a museum curator in Aix-en-Provence, years spent dusting Roman glass and translating Byzantine inscriptions by candlelight during power outages. Of how she'd fallen in love with a Spanish archaeologist who wore silk scarves and vanished into the Moroccan desert without goodbye. Of her family, brittle and cold, and the aunt who left her a lot of money and a lot of doubt.

"I built a life out of fragments," she said, gazing into the flames. "But it was beautiful, in its way."

She looked at Linda, then Caroline.

"I've asked Linda to be my executor," she said plainly.

Caroline blinked, then reached for her hand without hesitation. "I can think of no better person."

Adeline smiled. "I see bits of myself in you both. The practical and the flamboyant. The part that hoards emotions like porcelain, and the part that spills them like red wine on a white blouse."

Linda, usually so composed, felt tears sting unexpectedly at the corners of her eyes.

"You're family," Adeline continued. "Not by blood. But that's never mattered to me. You've both given me something that feels like home."

There was a pause. Not silence but the kind of quiet that matters.

"And Hugo?" Caroline asked gently.

Adeline sighed. "He won't talk about the future. Says it's morbid. But I want him looked after. He's never asked about my finances, not once. Which is why I must ensure he never has to worry."

Just then, the door opened, and a gust of cold air brought with it a flurry of energy in the shape of Pippi's cheeks pink from the chill, a knitted beret slightly askew, and a bottle of *rakamelo* wrapped in a tea towel.

"I found a new one!" she declared. "Locally made. It's got a hint of clove and possibly a trace of mischief."

The mood lifted instantly. Mugs were swapped for tiny glasses. Cushions were rearranged. Pippi lit two more candles and flung herself down between Linda and Caroline with a theatrical sigh.

"I leave for London and come back to an emotional confessional and lime-green knitting," she said. "Remind me never to leave again."

And they laughed long and loud until the wind outside died down and the flames inside danced higher. That evening, as they passed around stories and secrets and steaming glasses of sweetened fire, the room felt entirely outside of time, stitched together by memory, love, and women who understood that life was too short not to wrap it in colour and drink it down.

Part 2:
Kythera's Welcome

By the fourth day of sailing, *Samantha* had settled into a rhythm the kind known only to seasoned crews and old friends. The sea south of Hydra had offered them glittering calm, then a steady Aegean breath as they rounded Cape Maleas. Each man had taken turns at the helm, and the wheel passed like a talisman. There were hours, whole golden hours, where they spoke only in glances and half-grins, the sea doing all the talking.

It was Lawrence who spotted the island first.

A blur at first, low, blue-grey, indistinct on the horizon. Then, as they drew nearer, Kythera emerged in full: rugged and romantic, ancient and elemental—Rock, scrub, olive, sky. There was something unspoiled about it, something that reached backwards—the true birthplace of Aphrodite.

The port of Agia Pelagia appeared like a hidden smile on the island's northeast coast a modest marina ringed by pale buildings, their shutters closed for winter. The town seemed asleep. Not lifeless just paused.

A young policeman stood alone at the quay, hands deep in his jacket pockets, wind tugging at his collar. He stepped forward just as *Samantha* turned into her

314

berth and, with practised ease, caught the lines Lawrence tossed from the bow.

He was, by all accounts, unreasonably handsome.

"Welcome," he said in perfect English, flashing a smile that caused a visible shift in Marco's balance. "Kythera is honoured you chose us."

"I thought this island was asleep," James whispered. "Turns out she's dreaming in Technicolour."

The officer helped secure the lines, nodded toward the only open café, and vanished with the polite efficiency of someone raised on both *xenia* and discretion. His name, they later learned, was Andreas. And it would take several rakis before Marco stopped mentioning him.

They found two rooms at a modest *xenodocheio* overlooking the harbour, run by an old woman who seemed surprised but delighted by their presence. The sheets were heavy cotton. The windows rattled in their frames. The heating was largely theoretical. But it felt like an adventure wrapped in wool blankets and sea salt.

At dusk, the wind dropped entirely, and Agia Pelagia glowed in silence. They wandered the harbour until they found the taverna shutters closed, chairs stacked, a faded blue sign swinging in the breeze: *Η Παραλία του Τάκης*.

"Closed until Easter," read a chalkboard in Greek.

Just as they turned to go, a voice called out from the shadows.

"You'll eat here," said the man. "I'm Takis. The food's better when no one's watching."

He disappeared inside and returned five minutes later with four chairs and a bottle of wine already open. "Sit. I'll see what's left in the kitchen. Sardines. Beans. Bread."

It turned out there was more than that. Much more.

Out came a steaming tray of *gigantes* with tomato and dill, crusty bread blistered from a wood-fired oven, *kalitsounia* sweet cheese pastries, still warm and a slow-cooked rabbit stew with hints of mountain thyme and something none of them could name.

They toasted him with wine that tasted of iron and fig leaves.

"You should not be open," Serge said.

Takis waved a hand. "I am closed. You are not strangers. You are sailors. And sailors do not eat alone on Kythera."

His wife appeared from the kitchen and introduced herself as Cathy, she'd come on holiday from England and never left. She produced a tray of brownies she'd baked for the Sunday market. One bite, and Marco closed his eyes.

"What is that extra taste? I've never had anything so magnificent."

Cathy and Takis beamed. "It's the Kythera sea salt," Cathy said with a smile. "A little Greek addition."

They lingered late into the evening, the tiny dining room lit by a flickering heater and the soft amber of old bulbs. There was no music, only the clatter of cutlery and the murmur of sea air through cracked shutters.

"This is *filoxenia*," Michalis said softly. "The old way. Kindness to a stranger. Food for the road."

James nodded, wiping a tear from his eye from laughter or wine or simply the absurd perfection of it all.

Later, as they walked back to *Samantha*, stars scattered like spilt sugar overhead, and they spoke little.

No one wanted to disturb the spell Kythera had cast. It was somewhere they would all return one day, without question.

Part 3:
Saltwater Bonds

The next morning, wrapped in scarves and bravado, the crew of *Samantha* set out early for a chilly dip at Agia Patrika, a narrow cove just east of Agia Pelagia, reachable only by water and flanked by honey-coloured cliffs. The sun was up but pale, offering light without warmth. The water was shockingly cold, crystalline, cobalt, and utterly inviting in the way only winter seas can be.

"Madness," James declared, stripping to his trunks. "Glorious madness."

One by one, they plunged in, gasping, howling, laughing as their limbs adjusted. It was Lawrence who first spotted the slow, steady movement below. Sea turtles three of them gliding beneath like shadows made of patience and ancient grace.

They all fell quiet in the water.

The turtles passed without alarm, weaving through the shallows as if blessing the moment.

Later, as they dried themselves on the deck with towels that did little to help, Michalis murmured, "We'll come back. We have to. The girls will love this too."

They all nodded. No vote was needed.

Kythera was a talisman.

The wind was with them as they made their way southeast. The sea, ever changeable, offered a soft rise and fall a lullaby in motion.

But mid-afternoon, as they cleared the edge of the Peloponnese, the engine gave a protesting cough and stuttered to silence.

Marco was below before anyone could say a word.

Half an hour later, he emerged, sleeves rolled and hands dark with oil.

"Loose fuel line. Nothing dramatic," he said. "But if I hadn't checked..." He shrugged.

"Hero," Serge said, handing him a tin cup of strong coffee and a kiss.

"Oh, not done yet," Marco replied. "There's a leak under the galley sink. I can hear it."

He'd barely said the words before Serge was crouched inside the cupboard, wrench in hand, flashlight between his teeth.

"You two," said Lawrence, watching. "You're basically an Anglo-Greek-Italian rescue unit."

James chuckled. "I hope you don't mind me saying, but... this isn't what most people picture when they think of a gay married couple."

Serge glanced up, wiping his hands. "What do they picture?"

"Soft furnishings and scented candles?" Michalis offered, cheeky.

Marco grinned. "We like those too. But someone's got to keep the boat afloat."

There was laughter easy, unguarded, then a silence that carried weight.

"I'll tell you what I see," Lawrence said finally.

"I see two men who love each other deeply, fix what's broken, laugh more than they complain, and get on with things."

"Exactly," James added. "More capable than most and with better taste in food and fashion."

"Time's long past for preconceptions," said Michalis.

Marco and Serge exchanged a look that needed no translation; it was pride, humility, and gratitude wrapped in the glance of those who've weathered both storms and stereotypes.

Later, as the sun dipped low and Crete came into view as a soft silhouette against the sky, the men sat in quiet communion, the bond between them strengthened by salt, sweat, and small acts of grace.

When they arrived at the boatyard the next day sunburnt, wind-kissed, and travel-worn *Samantha* slid into her cradle like a bird returning to roost. Marco oversaw the haul-out. Serge handled the paperwork. The others stood back, watching the vessel they all loved rise into the air.

"She's earned her rest," Marco said.

"So have we," added Lawrence.

But even as they packed bags and checked flights, each knew something had shifted.

They had sailed together as friends.

They returned as brothers.

Chapter 21:
Winter Returns Softly (The Final Rooms)

The morning light slanted through Villa Petrouni with a kind of expectant hush, the sort of stillness that only follows a night of wild wind and rain. The shutters were dappled with dew, and below, the garden wore the night's weather like a cloak flung off in haste.

In the kitchen, Caroline hummed off-key to an old Ella Fitzgerald track on the Bluetooth speaker as she handed a steaming mug of mountain tea to Linda.

"Message just came through," Linda said, reading from her phone. "They're safe in Crete. Marco says *Samantha* was hauled out this morning, with no issues. They'll be on a plane to Athens tonight, and back in Poros tomorrow."

Caroline raised her cup like a toast. "And not a single call for help."

"Well," Linda smiled, "you know Serge and Marco would only radio in if the mast were on fire."

Out the window, Thanassis stood by the almond trees Adeline had donated, adjusting the last of the winter stakes. The lavender and thyme terrace now shimmered with small green shoots just visible if you knew where to look, and behind him, Hugo was attempting a quiet serenade on the mandolin, stopping every few chords to consult his handwritten notes. The gentle domesticity of it all felt like a warm scarf wrapped around the shoulders of the cold season.

Inside the guesthouse, the scent of plaster and fresh paint mingled with the faintest echo of the sea. The final two rooms, the last part of the season's significant push, were both well underway.

Room Five was the more classical of the two. Aimee had returned from Athens weeks earlier with a sketchbook full of sea lilies and faded frieze patterns from the National Archaeological Museum. There had been something about the worn elegance of those terracotta and pale pink motifs, the memory of things that had survived storms, wars, centuries. With Catherine's help, she'd begun to translate them onto the walls in a series of quiet, mural-like details: stylised florals and curling lines, the brushwork delicate and timeless.

In the adjoining bathroom, handmade ceramic tiles in shades of dusty rose met brass fittings salvaged from an antique market near Monastiraki and buffed to within an inch of their lives. Everything whispered of heritage, a room built like an homage to the past, but grounded in the future.

Next door, Room Six was a different creature entirely. Where the previous room reached back in time, this one leaned into the now. Linda had suggested a cleaner palette, something soothing. Pale grey silk had been sourced from a boutique on Ermou

Street, soft as breath and embroidered with a minimalist Greek key motif in fine silver thread. The bedspread shimmered under light from the new polished pewter reading lamps, which Serge had personally adjusted to perfection. The artwork was Aimee's diptych in cool blues and graphite, inspired by the straits of Poros and the way the wind carved pathways through the sea.

Catherine stood in the doorway with Pippi, who had arrived back from London just the day before, cheeks still pink from the flight and arms full of wrapped surprises.

"You've made poetry," Pippi said quietly, touching the silk. "Rooms that breathe."

"They're the last," Catherine murmured. "And in a way, they're the first. We're starting something permanent."

As if on cue, the phone rang, Eleni from the port, announcing that the ferry had arrived. Five familiar names were on the passenger list.

Pippi grinned. "Shall we go and meet our sailors?"

Part 1:
Return of the Sailors

The port of Poros held a particular kind of light that afternoon, golden and slanting, as if trying to reassure the island that the worst of winter had passed. The ferry from Piraeus pulled in with a low murmur, gulls scattering, fishermen nodding at its slow approach like old friends reunited after a season apart.

On the jetty stood Catherine, Aimee, Caroline, Pippi, and Linda, with Thanassis and Hugo in tow, a motley welcoming committee of scarves, coats, and bright eyes. Hugo held a cardboard sign that read **"SS Poseidon Survivors"** in large, childish script, which made Caroline laugh aloud.

"They'll love that," she said, nudging his arm.

The first off the gangway was Marco, wind-flushed and grinning, rolling a battered case behind him. Serge followed, elegantly unruffled, with a tote bag that looked suspiciously like it had been used for ferrying herbs and engine parts. Behind them came Michalis, looking fitter than ever and smelling of salt and sun. Then James, who had grown a beard so stylish that Pippi immediately declared him "dashing." Lawrence brought up the rear, clutching a paper bag of pastries he'd picked up from Athens airport.

"For the ladies," he said, bowing.

325

There were embraces, real ones, warm and long, the kind that made up for the time apart. No one seemed to mind the slight drizzle that had started. They walked back up the slope together, a moving caravan of chatter and sea tales, everyone talking over everyone else.

At Villa Petrouni, the fire had already been lit by Thanassis, who had a gift for coaxing reluctant logs into flame. Marco and Serge's townhouse contributed platters of preserved olives, cheese, and slices of marinated artichoke hearts. Linda produced a warm spanakopita from the oven, the perfect blend of olive oil pastry, spinach, and salty feta. Caroline poured tumblers of red wine with no sense of reason or rationing.

The evening unfolded like an impromptu festival, stories spilt out like uncorked bottles. They laughed about the turtles of Agia Patrika, the surprise of Takis and Cathy opening their winter-closed taverna, the leak under the sink, the engine glitch mid-crossing, and how Marco and Serge had solved both without so much as a grumble. Serge, slightly tipsy, mimed his own heroics with a wrench and a tea towel, and everyone clapped.

Caroline leaned into Thanassis and whispered, "This. This is what I always wanted without knowing it."

He didn't answer in words, but he rested his hand lightly over hers on the bench, warm, weathered, steady, loving.

Later, as Hugo strummed the mandolin and Pippi sang a haunting verse from a *rebetiko* song she barely remembered learning, Aimee and Catherine stood at the edge of the terrace. The stars were out, and from this height, they could see the lights of fishing boats like fireflies on the sea.

"We've made something, haven't we?" Aimee said quietly.

Catherine nodded. "Something lasting. Not just for us, but for all of them."

They looked toward the *micro xenodocheio,* its silhouette against the dark hillside softened by the glow from within. Two rooms remained, nearly ready. And now, everyone was home.

Part 2:
Morning's Stillness

The next morning broke quietly, with only the subtle shift in the light giving away the hour. A low mist clung to the hills above Poros, the kind that vanished the moment it was touched by sun. Down in the kitchens of both Villa Petrouni and the guesthouse, kettles began to whisper before they sang.

Aimee padded softly across the tiles barefoot, drawn to the smell of coffee and the promise of a new rhythm settling in.

In the standard room of the *micro xenodocheio*, James was already seated with a sketchpad and a mug, watching the way the steam coiled like a phantom from his cup. He didn't draw yet, but simply observed. Linda entered next, in her thick cardigan and slipper socks, her hair slightly askew. She sat beside him and placed a hand lightly on his knee.

"It's a good stillness," she said.

"It is," James replied. "Like the world inhaled and held it."

The pair sat in companionable silence. From the terrace, they could hear Pippi laughing in the garden with Caroline, who was already trying to coax some life into the new beds with her usual blend of enthusiasm and total lack of horticultural knowledge. Thanassis was somewhere up the slope, no doubt already inspecting root growth and soil depth like a man decoding scripture.

Inside, Catherine and Lawrence emerged with the last of the pastries from Athens and declared breakfast open. The long table in the lounge was soon filled with people, light chatter, and the smell of warm bread, hard cheese, and preserved figs, Greek yoghurt with honey and walnuts, of course, never far away.

Aimee brought out her sketches from Athens. As everyone looked on, she explained her vision for the ancient frieze-inspired room: the sea lilies, the palettes of faded pinks and sandy terracotta, the sense of old stones whispering stories.

Marco leaned over the paper with an approving grunt. "It's not just a room," he said. "It's a memory with walls."

"Then we better get the rest right," Catherine added, smiling. "It's nearly ready, this place. Ready to be exactly what we dreamed."

There was a hush as that truth settled around them. After so many months of paint and plumbing, stone and setbacks, laughter and heartbreak, it was happening. Slowly, with love and intention, they had built something not just functional, but meaningful.

As the breakfast plates were cleared and Serge began drafting a list for the final curtain fittings, Michalis read aloud a message from Irini, the previous owner. She'd be coming next week, bringing *tsoureki* and her usual sharp eye for everything.

Everyone groaned in mock dread and real affection.

From the far side of the garden, Hugo struck up a slow tune on the mandolin, and the wind carried it uphill like a blessing.

Linda reached for her notebook. "Shall we make today the day we finally price out the room packages?" she said, practical as ever.

James smiled. "Only if you let me write the welcome note."

Part 3:
Beneath the Almond Tree

Later that afternoon, when the sun had warmed the flagstones and the wind lay quiet in the lemon trees, James found Adeline seated on a low bench just beyond the almond trees she'd donated. The terrace above glowed faintly with lavenders and thymes now beginning to root. A pale shawl was draped around her shoulders, her cheeks coloured by the cool air and something more elusive, a kind of serenity that seemed to sit lightly on her.

James approached with two mugs of tea. "Thanassis says these are doing well," he said, nodding toward the saplings.

"They remind me of Antibes," Adeline replied. "My mother used to say the blossom fell like confetti. It felt like the trees were blessing the earth."

She sipped her tea, then turned slightly to study James.

"Do you know what I see when I look at you?"

He shook his head gently, a little wary.

"I see a man who loved well. Who didn't let grief turn him to stone. That takes more strength than most people ever find. You are remarkable, James."

James didn't speak for a while. When he did, his voice was quiet. "I thought I'd lost that part of myself. The part that could be given again."

Adeline smiled. "But you haven't. I see it in the way you look at Linda. It's quiet, and careful, and very real. There's nothing louder than real love, James, even when it whispers."

They sat for a moment, the only sound a soft rustle from the olive leaves.

"You've been a gift to us," he said eventually. "To this whole strange, wonderful group."

She laughed lightly, then coughed, and recovered. "I don't have many seasons left," she said, not sadly but as a simple truth. "But I have enough. Enough to make sure Hugo is cared for. Enough to dance once or twice more. And enough, I think, to make certain this place remembers joy."

She turned to face him more fully.

"You'll help them remember, won't you?"

James nodded. "I promise."

From down in the garden, laughter rang out Caroline calling out in mock protest as Thanassis showed her how to water "without drowning the poor things," and Pippi chiding them both like a summer camp counsellor.

Adeline closed her eyes for a moment, listening. "Yes," she said softly. "This place is alive."

Above them, a breeze stirred the almond branches already studded with the tight promise of spring blossom.

Chapter 22:
The Lantern-Hung Courtyard

The scent of orange blossom drifted up from the lower garden, carried by a soft breeze that stirred the last threads of early spring. Lanterns were strung between the lemon trees and across the courtyard, their warm golden globes beginning to glow as dusk approached. Catherine stood at the edge of the courtyard, arms folded across her chest, watching as the final touches were added, white linens smoothed, glassware twinkling, soft music warming the stones underfoot. She wore a long cashmere wrap over her shoulders, knowing the night air would turn sharp, but for now, the moment brimmed with promise.

Lawrence came up behind her, kissed her shoulder gently, and handed her a glass of wine.

"It's all come together," he said.

"It really has," she replied, blinking as if the truth of it needed adjusting to.

Guests began to arrive slowly at first, the kind-faced carpenter who had reshaped the old window frames with such care, the plumber who had once wept laughing when the ancient boiler exploded, Thanassis, already teasing Caroline about her choice of shoes. Linda and James appeared arm-in-arm, her dress the softest green, his linen jacket creased with character. Pippi followed, bursting through the gate with her usual energy, a potted herb in one hand and a bottle of wine in the other.

Adeline was helped down the path by Hugo. She wore a dress in deep lilac and pearls that shimmered faintly under the lights, her white hair coiled at the nape of her neck. Everyone stopped for a moment to greet her, each one grateful that she could be there.

As the courtyard filled with laughter bubbling, plates clinking, the mayor of Poros arrived with his wife, a quietly elegant woman with keen eyes and a fondness for kalamata olives. He gave a short, warm speech beneath the olive tree, praising the spirit of community, the resilience of the project, and the beauty of what had been created. He raised a glass to Villa Petrouni and the *micro xenodocheio*, to *filoxenia* reborn, and to the people who had made it so.

Music followed strings and bouzouki at first, later joined by Thanassis with his wild, rhythmic drumming on an old ceramic pot. Serge and Marco danced first, exuberantly, pulling Michalis and Aimee in. Catherine and Lawrence followed. Then Caroline arms flung wide caught in the joy of the evening.

Eleni arrived just as the first dance ended. She stood at the edge, watching for a moment, her eyes catching Aimee's across the crowd. She gave a small nod and stepped forward, kissing Aimee warmly on both cheeks.

"You've made him very happy," she whispered.

"And you," Aimee replied, "have helped make this home."

They stood a moment longer, quiet but full. Arms linked and strong.

As the music surged again, Catherine and Aimee twirled each other into the centre of the courtyard, laughing, flushed, utterly content in a way they hadn't been in years. Sisters in every sense tethered by memory, by loss, and now by this beautiful, improbable chapter that had somehow unfolded before them.

And above it all, the almond trees rustled faintly, their blossoms just beginning to loosen.

Part 1:
Her Dance

As the music settled into something slower a gently swaying *zeibekiko*, with threads of longing stitched into its rhythm the courtyard lights softened, and the hum of conversation gave way to the rustle of silk skirts and murmured laughter. Hugo, standing a little apart with a glass in hand, glanced across the lantern-lit space to where Adeline sat beneath the climbing jasmine. She was watching the dancers with a wistful smile, her hands folded in her lap, her eyes shining with something that ran deeper than the evening.

Without a word, he crossed the courtyard.

"Would you do me the honour, Addie?"

She looked up, surprised, then nodded, and with quiet dignity, took his hand.

There was a hush as they stepped onto the stones together. Someone turned the music down just slightly. The crowd parted without instruction, instinctively aware that something was unfolding.

Adeline moved slowly, her spine still straight, her head held high. Hugo supported her carefully, not guiding so much as offering steadiness. Around them, the almond petals loosened by the breeze began to fall. A few caught in her hair, others on his shoulders. They danced with a grace that was neither youthful nor frail, but something entirely their own, built on memory, on companionship, on the kind of love that had never needed to declare itself loudly.

It was James who felt it first, the tightness in the chest, the way the heart seemed to stretch and ache at once. Linda touched his arm lightly. She, too, was crying.

Caroline blinked rapidly, and even Thanassis seemed to swallow hard, his usual broad stance folded into a kind of reverence. Catherine leaned her head against Lawrence's shoulder, her hand slipping into his.

Aimee, watching from the side, understood in that moment:
Some dances are not for joy alone.

Some are for goodbye.

When the music ended, no one applauded. Instead, there was a kind of breath held across the whole courtyard. Hugo led Adeline back to her seat beneath the almond trees and placed a shawl over her shoulders. He knelt beside her, kissed her hand, and said something none of them could hear.

But they didn't need to.

The petals spoke louder than words, pale, soft, infinite in their descent.

Part 2:
The Quiet Unravelling

The courtyard never fully resumed its earlier rapture. After Adeline's dance, the evening folded inward like petals closing at dusk. The music softened to a background hush, more undertone than presence. People moved more slowly now, their laughter tinged with warmth, their conversations quieter, more intimate.

Catherine made her way between tables, offering thanks to each person, the mayor and his wife for their kind words, to the local carpenter for the beautiful archway over the entrance, to Anthi the jeweller, who had crafted each room's delicate door plaques by hand. Every gesture, every piece, every contribution had been part of this shared resurrection. She felt the weight and wonder of it with every hug and nod of gratitude.

Lawrence stood with Kosmas and Michalis near the old olive press, glasses in hand, watching the last of the night unfold. Kosmas spoke about permits, of course, a new idea for a shaded pergola, perhaps even a kitchen garden. But beneath the bureaucracy was affection, pride in what had been created. He was a remarkable young man of quiet strength and firm resolve. Michalis smiled at them both and said simply, "It feels like home now."

338

Linda, still a little teary from the dance, had found her way to the old bench beneath the pomegranate tree. James sat beside her, offering her a handkerchief and his quiet presence.

"That was..." he began, then stopped.

"I know," she said softly. Then, after a breath, "I love you, Lawrence."

He blinked, then laughed a sound that cracked through the quiet like sunlight. "I love you too, my darling Linda."

No more was needed. They kissed again, under the pomegranate tree.

Caroline and Thanassis lingered near the kitchen doors, sharing the last of a sweet dessert wine and a quiet conversation about fig trees. Their voices were low, their laughter soft. She brushed a petal from his hair and murmured, "It's all rather perfect, isn't it?"

"Not perfect," he said, "but right."

Adeline remained beneath the almond trees, now wrapped in a wool blanket Hugo had brought down from her room. Her eyes were half-closed, her expression one of soft, steady joy. Pippi crouched beside her with a small plate of something sticky and sweet.

"Darling," Pippi whispered, "I hope you know this place is forever yours."

Adeline smiled without opening her eyes. "It already was."

As the night deepened, guests began to slip away in pairs and threes, their goodbyes whispered, their footsteps light. Hugs lingered. Eyes shone with wine and gratitude. The mayor shook hands once more with Lawrence, promising future visits. Anthi kissed Catherine's cheeks and pressed a tiny velvet pouch into her hand.

"For luck," she whispered.

One by one, the lanterns were dimmed. Aimee and Michalis, arms around each other's waists, stood on the veranda steps watching the last shadows pass. Somewhere in town, a dog barked once, and then silence returned.

In the morning, the blossoms would have fallen more thickly across the paving stones.

But tonight, under their soft snowfall, everything was still.

Part 3:
The Falling of Petals

It happened just before dawn.

The courtyard was empty now, save for Hugo, who had insisted on staying with Adeline beneath the almond trees. She had insisted on staying to see the petals fall. The blanket was still tucked around her shoulders, her hands resting gently in her lap. For some time, Hugo had spoken to her softly of stories of childhood and travel, of paintings she had loved, of the way she always entered a room without claiming it, yet never went unnoticed.

He had thought she was asleep.

But the breath between her last two sentences had been too long.

And now, there were no more.

He didn't cry. Not at first. He didn't move. The blanket still wrapped her like a benediction, the petals drifting down in a slow, pale fall. One landed on her cheek and stayed there.

Hugo sat utterly still, his hand still holding hers. The world tilted slightly, a hush settling over the courtyard as if it, too, recognised what had passed.

It was Linda who found them first, slipping outside before the light had risen correctly, drawn by a feeling she couldn't name. She paused when she saw them, one hand resting on the old wooden post, her heart breaking with the softness of it.

Then Caroline appeared behind her, barefoot, her shawl trailing on the ground. Together, they moved into the courtyard with the grace of dancers in mourning. No words were exchanged. Caroline went to Hugo's side and placed a hand on his shoulder. Linda knelt before Adeline and took her other hand.

"She's gone," Hugo whispered, as if saying it aloud made it real.

"Yes," Linda said gently, brushing the petal from Adeline's cheek. "But only just. She waited for the quiet. For the blossoms."

For a while, they stayed like that, the three of them in the early light. Caroline stroked Hugo's back, murmuring soft nothings. Linda kept vigil, her heart too full for words. They had all known it was coming. Adeline had known it. But the beauty of her leaving, the timing, the stillness, the petals was more than any of them had expected. Or wanted.

Later, the others would wake to the news

To Catherine weeping into Lawrence's shoulder.

To Aimee and Michalis holding each other in stunned stillness.

To Thanassis lighting a small candle in the fourno and laying an olive branch beside it.

To Pippi taking charge of the calls.

To the mayor sending flowers.

To Anthi, arriving with a silver bracelet she had once promised Adeline and never delivered, leaving it on her pillow with a handwritten note.

But for now, in the hush of morning, they simply sat.

The sun crept slowly up behind the hills.

The almond trees shivered once in the breeze.

And then we were still.

Chapter 23:
Under the Almond Trees

The courtyard had never looked more peaceful.

It was early afternoon, the kind of soft golden day that seemed stitched with memory. The breeze was low and warm, rustling the almond branches just enough to dislodge the occasional blossom. These floated down like notes in a silent score, each one a tender reminder.

Aimee and Catherine had arranged the chairs in a semi-circle facing the centre, where an old wooden table had been brought out from the dining room. Upon it lay a simple white cloth and a photograph of Adeline in her younger years, standing in front of a marble sculpture, eyes bright, one hand mid-gesture, as though explaining something essential and beautiful. A tiny bronze amphora sat beside it, filled with wild thyme and lavender.

There were no black clothes.

Adeline had said once during one of her fiercely honest dinners, *"I've worn enough black for a lifetime. When I go, let there be colour, and laughter, and people with sun on their backs."* And so there was. Everyone came dressed in soft tones, the colours of sea glass, olive leaves, and island clay.

Hugo had chosen a linen shirt in the shade of faded cornflower. He sat quietly, composed but distant, as though watching a scene from very far away. Linda,

344

always practical, had gently arranged tissues beside his chair, a bottle of water within reach. Caroline sat next to him, her fingers entwined with his, whenever required or not.

Kosmas stood just behind the group, not quite part of the family circle, but present all the same. Even Takis and Cathy, the taverna owners from Kythera, had sent a note and a bottle of island tsipouro, which stood unopened beside the photograph.

Lawrence opened the small ceremony with quiet words.

"We are not here to say goodbye," he began, "but rather to give thanks for love, for beauty, for courage in the face of life's untidiness. And for Adeline, who showed us all how to live with taste and boldness, and above all, grace."

Each person had been asked, if they wished, to speak.

Pippi was the first. She stepped up to the table and placed a smooth white stone on its surface.

"I found this the day she and I walked to the point, past the goats and the fennel," she said. "She picked one up, too; hers was streaked with pink. She told me, *'Everything of value begins plain, and is shaped by pressure.'*" Her voice caught. "I still have it. The lesson she gave me. I'll always have it."

Michalis followed, recounting the night Adeline first ate in his taverna, how she insisted on sitting by the kitchen to watch him plate the food, then demanded to know who had prepared the fig compote.

"She told me, *'You'll never be ordinary, unless you start thinking you are.'* And then she asked for the recipe."

Catherine read a short passage from a letter Adeline had once written her, a fragment full of wry humour, clear-eyed wisdom, and that particular way she had of seeing people fully, even when they couldn't see themselves.

"It's astonishing," Catherine said softly, "how someone can live in your heart before you know it. And then never leave."

When Thanassis stepped forward, even Caroline looked surprised. He cleared his throat and held a small slip of paper in one hand.

"Adeline used to ask about the garden every day," he said. "She'd touch the leaves, smell the soil, tell me what she liked and didn't. She told me once she didn't know much about plants, but she knew about survival. I think that's why she loved the almond trees. Because they bloom even in the cold."

He nodded toward Hugo, then sat down.

No one hurried.

No one rushed to fill the silences.

Instead, they let them linger soft pauses between memories, like breath between lines of poetry.

Part 1:
Light and Memory

As the last words faded into the hush of the courtyard, Catherine stepped forward once more, this time holding a slight taper. She paused beside the wooden table and looked at Hugo, who gave a faint nod. With quiet care, she lit the single candle in the bronze amphora.

The flame was gentle, barely flickering in the late afternoon breeze.

Others followed.

Each person who had loved Adeline deeply, quietly, or even from afar took a moment to step forward and light a candle of their own. Linda moved with steady hands, placing hers close beside Hugo's. Caroline's hand trembled just slightly, but her jaw was set with fierce resolve. James lit two, one for himself, and one, he said softly, for the love he had lost before he ever met Adeline, whose absence had long shaped his own journey through grief.

The pool of light grew steadily.

Serge and Marco arrived late; they'd been setting up the lounge for the quiet gathering to follow and placed a small votive together, side by side, without speaking.

Pippi brought a sprig of rosemary from the kitchen garden and laid it beside the photograph.

Then came Hugo.

He stood slowly, not out of weakness but with reverence. The courtyard was utterly still as he moved to the centre, the petals continuing to fall, the sun casting long, golden shadows behind him.

"I don't know how to do this," he said simply, his voice carrying clearly. "She would have told me not to try. *'Just be,'* she said. *'Just be.'*"

He looked around at the people gathered, the friends, the unlikely family that had grown around him like a wild and unexpected garden.

"You all gave her something she hadn't had in a very long time: a reason to get out of bed in the morning, to care about linen colours and lemon cake again, to argue about what the blue in the hallway should really be called. She loved this place. She loved all of you. And she... she loved me."

His voice cracked then. But he didn't turn away.

"She told me once," he continued, "that some people arrive late in your life but manage to take up the most room. She was my late arrival. And now... she is everything."

Silence followed completely, and beautifully.

Then Caroline, of all people, stepped into the space beside him and raised a small glass of tsipouro.

"To Adeline," she said, her voice fierce. "For teaching us that joy is a decision. That good olive oil is non-negotiable. And that we are never too old to fall in love, to change, or to begin again."

"To Adeline," they echoed, glass after glass lifted in her honour.

Aimee and Michalis brought out dishes, simple but full of love. Roast tomatoes filled with herbs and rice. Pomegranate salad with mint. Slivers of local manouri cheese on fig leaves. Wine flowed, but not too freely.

This was not a wake, nor a farewell with tears at the seams.

It was what Adeline had asked for: a pause. A toast. A few good stories, and some very good bread.

As dusk fell, Thanassis and James lit the lanterns strung across the courtyard. Their soft glow cast golden patterns on the stone. Laughter began to return tentatively at first, then fuller, with warmth.

And when it was truly dark, someone played music, a soft violin from Serge's playlist and Hugo, without a word, stepped once more beneath the almond trees.

This time, he danced.

Not a grand gesture, but a gentle sway.

Eyes closed.

One hand clasped, as if she were still there.

And in every way that mattered, she was.

Part 2:
The Plaque and the Promise

Two mornings after the memorial, the courtyard returned to its usual rhythm, filtered sunlight through the pergola, the clatter of plates from the kitchen, the humming of bees in the rosemary. But the almond trees swayed differently now, their slender branches marked by meaning, no longer simply ornamental.

It was Linda who took the small brass plaque from its cloth wrapping. She'd had it made quickly, but beautifully. The local jeweller, Anthi, had inscribed it in delicate, serifed Greek and English:

Adeline de Lys

Curator of beauty, keeper of wit, heart of this home

"Continue dancing."

She showed it to Hugo that morning.

He looked at it, then away. His hands were tightly curled around a chipped mug of black coffee.

"I don't know what to do," he said, his voice almost inaudible. "Every hour I expect her to walk in and tell me I've put the books in the wrong place again, or that the colour of the basil is off."

Linda sat beside him, not crowding, not offering platitudes.

"She left instructions," she said gently.

"No." He shook his head. "I don't want to hear them."

"Hugo," she said, turning to face him fully. "She trusted you. And she trusted me to help when it got too much. This isn't about sorting out a bank account. It's about making sure she's heard. That her last wishes were respected."

"I can't," he said again. "It makes it all too real."

"It's already real," Linda replied softly. "But it doesn't have to be unbearable."

She paused, watching his profile, the new lines grief had drawn, the gentle crumple that hadn't yet settled into shape.

"She's made sure everything is handled. A house in Antibes. The funds she never spoke of—a gift to the xenodohio. And most of all, she wanted you to be taken care of, not out of pity, but because she knew how much you gave her. Because she loved you."

That last word sat heavily between them.

After a long while, Hugo nodded. "She said... once... that legacy isn't money or fame. It's what you leave behind in the eyes of people who knew you best."

Linda touched his hand. "Then she'll be with us forever."

Later that afternoon, they walked slowly to the almond grove. Thanassis had already prepared the site where the plaque would go a low stone column made from local rock, shaped without flair but with

351

unmistakable grace. He gave them space and wandered off toward the thyme beds, pretending to adjust something.

Hugo took the plaque in both hands and fastened it to the stone.

There were no speeches this time. No songs. Only the sound of the wind in the trees, and the click of brass screws tightening against stone.

A single blossom drifted down and caught on the edge of the plaque.

Then fell away.

Part 3:
The Wish

That evening, Linda brought over a folded envelope from the desk drawer in the study. The handwriting on the front was instantly recognisable as Adeline's curling, elegant script, half-French, half-scholarly. It read simply:

To Hugo, when you're ready.

"I found it among her notebooks," Linda said, placing it gently in front of him. "She left another copy with me. I wasn't sure whether to give it now or later."

Hugo looked at the envelope. "I'm not ready."

"Then let's just sit," she said, settling into the armchair beside him. The lamps cast a soft gold light over the stone walls, and the fire crackled in the grate not because it was cold, but because it felt like something Adeline would have wanted lit.

They sat in silence for a long while, listening to the fire shift and sigh.

At last, Hugo picked up the envelope and opened it.

There was no great speech, no final philosophical essay, just a few pages, handwritten on thick paper, faintly scented with something floral and old.

He read aloud, slowly:

My darling Hugo,

If you're reading this, I'm gone. Not gone from you, I hope not entirely. I like to think we leave fingerprints on the hearts of those we love, and I hope mine linger, even if they smudge with time.

I want to say thank you. Not for anything you did, though you did plenty, but for who you were to me. You made me laugh again. You saw me when I thought I was invisible. You made me dance in a kitchen full of flour, and curse at the radio when it played that dreadful modern pop.

Don't close up now. Don't fold in like an envelope never meant to be opened again. I've left you some means, yes, but more than that, I want you to go on loving life. Find the unexpected joy. Accept the invitation. Sit in the sun, even when it's too bright.

And forgive me for going. I wanted to stay longer. But this was a good place to end with you, among friends, in the bloom of something new.

Yours, in every yesterday,

A.

When he finished, Hugo didn't speak. He didn't move. He simply closed his eyes and held the pages to his chest like a sail catching a breeze.

Linda reached for his hand and held it, letting the moment breathe.

"She really meant it," he said at last.

"Yes," Linda replied. "She always did."

He let out a long breath. "I don't know if I can ever feel that way again."

"You don't have to," she said. "But if you do let it come. Let it surprise you. That would be her greatest wish."

He looked over at her. "How do you know so much?"

She smiled faintly. "Because I've been where you are. Because I still feel it sometimes. And because she told me."

In the quiet that followed, the fire crackled again. Outside, the wind had calmed. The petals had all fallen.

But somewhere in the almond grove, there was still the faintest scent of spring.

Chapter: 24
Resurrection Light

The sun returned to the land like an old friend, not brash and demanding, but sure-footed and golden, touching the shutters of Villa Petrouni with quiet insistence. It coaxed the wild thyme into bloom, warmed the flagstones in the courtyard, and shimmered on the newly polished windows of the micro xenodohio, where Easter ribbons of red and gold fluttered on the door handles.

Greek Easter had arrived.

It was the season of renewal. Spring had painted the hillsides with cyclamen and poppies, and the faint echo of a distant goat bell was all that stirred the olive groves at dawn. In the kitchen, Catherine and Michalis had begun preparations early lamb marinated in garlic and lemon, rosemary gathered by Thanassis the day before, trays of koulourakia waiting for their sesame crowns. Aimee, barefoot on the terrace, was dyeing the eggs red with Eleni, the two women laughing over the failed first batch that turned out an odd purplish brown. The second, however, gleamed like jewels proper crimson, hard-shelled, and shining with the vinegar polish of tradition.

Linda had taken it upon herself to manage the guest list and bookings, which were, she noted with some surprise and satisfaction, almost entirely full through July.

"We're going to need more towels," she muttered, poring over the linen orders with a red pencil. Her former world all contracts and misaligned spreadsheets had never smelled of lavender and lemon oil. She found she preferred this one.

Caroline had cleared out a small outdoor area behind the kitchen and claimed it as her own spring salon. She'd added cushions, a blue iron mirror, and three pots of basil she named George, Lorraine, and Dean.

"For guests, obviously," she said to no one in particular and was later found sipping prosecco and humming along to old Ella Fitzgerald records as if she'd always been there.

But it was Hugo's quiet presence that stirred something deeper. He had asked, gently but firmly, if he might stay on not as a guest, but as part of the place. He now took coffee early on the upstairs balcony and wandered the garden in the late hours, lingering under the almond trees.

Linda, true to her word, had helped him begin arranging for him to meet Takis, the local counsellor who had once helped James find his feet after losing his wife.

Their first session was held in the garden near the amphora. Takis, unhurried and calm, offered Hugo not advice but space and that, Hugo realised, was the greatest kindness of all. He left that afternoon with a folded note in his pocket that read:

"It is not wrong to feel lost. Only to refuse the map."

That evening, the courtyard was alive with movement and colour. Serge and Marco had strung lanterns from the olive trees and hung bells from the bougainvillea that caught the breeze with a faint chime. A long table was laid under the stars, and in the centre, a bowl of red-dyed eggs shimmered like rubies. The spit had begun its slow turn, filling the air with the scent of rosemary smoke and crisping lamb.

James watched the preparations with a quiet smile, sketchbook in hand. Linda passed him a glass of chilled white wine and whispered, "Tonight we celebrate. But tomorrow the bookings continue."

He raised the glass in mock toast.

"To resurrection."

"To full laundry baskets and too many guests," she added, and they laughed like old loves who had known each other far longer than they had.

As the evening deepened, the church bells began to ring not in cacophony, but with steady joy, calling the faithful to midnight service. Candles were passed, wicks kissed with flame. The procession began down the lane, villagers and guests alike holding their candles high, whispering **Christos Anesti** into the starlit night.

Behind them, the villa glowed in the soft dark, a place of light, of laughter, and now, of something even more profound: belonging.

Part 1:
Greek Easter

By the time the congregation returned from the midnight procession, the villa's courtyard was aglow. Catherine had left a lantern trail of beeswax candles in mason jars, which now lit the path to the long Easter table. Pippi, who had only arrived that afternoon from London, stood smiling beside the others, her auburn hair catching the firelight, arms open wide for every embrace. She had brought a bottle of aged Scotch and a box of marzipan fruits from Fortnum's.

"For the inevitable sweet crisis after midnight," she announced, winking at Caroline.

"You're just in time," said Lawrence, handing her a glass of tsipouro and pulling her into the fold. The courtyard pulsed with an odd but perfect rhythm, a fusion of Greek hymns still hanging in the air and Billie Holiday from the kitchen speaker.

There was, of course, too much food. It spilled from platters and hands and hearts. Dishes of mayiritsa soup, lemony and rich, followed the lamb, now crisped at the edges and juicy at its core. Salads with dill and capers from the hillside, beetroot roasted in honey, Eleni's own tiropita still hot from the oven and in the centre of the table, those red eggs, waiting to be cracked in mock battles of luck.

The group had grown used to sharing everything, now meals, days, and even the unexpected currents of emotion that came with true closeness. There was an ease to it, a rhythm, as if each knew when to speak and when to be still.

Pippi sat beside Aimee, both women watching the scene before them with quiet joy.

"You seem lighter," Pippi said.

"I am," Aimee replied. "It took the weight of another life to realise how free this one could be."

"And Michalis?"

Aimee's smile deepened. "He sees me. Even the parts I'd hidden."

On the far side of the table, Michalis and Thanassis were laughing over something Caroline had said, a story involving an overambitious Easter bread, three bottles of wine, and a smoke alarm. Thanassis had taken to Caroline like a tree finding the sun slowly, deeply, without hesitation. And she, once wary of roots, had begun to grow into the possibility of being loved for exactly who she was.

Linda sat with James, passing him slices of bread and murmuring little thoughts about the morning's linen order, her hand brushing his just a second longer each time. Their bond had moved past the quiet stages of recognition into something lived-in and warming. He no longer sketched her so furtively. She no longer looked surprised when he did.

The night stretched on.

Hugo remained by the almond trees for a while, candlelight flickering beside him, Adeline's presence still strong in the roots, the soil, the very scent of the spring air. Later, he joined the others, eyes bright, smile true, helping clear plates, topping up wine glasses.

"You're staying then?" Pippi asked gently, catching him by the arm.

"If they'll have me," Hugo said.

"Oh, they'll have you," she replied. "They'll likely fight over who gets your help in the kitchen."

"I'm learning to dice onions the Greek way," he said proudly. "Eleni showed me. It's… precise. And I need you, Pippi, to show me the intricacies of bread making."

She laughed. "Then you're practically family."

And as the stars above Poros wheeled slowly in their springtime arc, the little courtyard of the micro xenodohio, the guesthouse that had become a haven, held its own kind of resurrection.

People who had thought they were finished with change, with love, with surprise, were finding that life had one more trick, one more sweetness, one more song to sing for them.

If they just let it in.

Easter Monday dawned with a clarity that seemed almost choreographed, the air crisp, the skies unmarred, and the bells from the monastery ringing faintly across the strait.

Catherine was the first up. She padded out in slippers and a wrapped shawl, mug in hand, to the terrace outside the villa. The almond trees were still dusted with pale blossoms, and beneath them lay the garden of memory, where Adeline's plaque nestled in soft shadow. She took a long sip of coffee and whispered her thanks.

Inside the micro xenodohio, Linda was already arranging breakfast with Eleni's help, baskets of warm koulouria, fig jam, thick yoghurt with wild thyme honey, and leftover red eggs, polished and cracked again just for fun.

Caroline appeared next, eyes bleary but delighted.

"Last night we were saints. This morning, we're sinners for sloth."

"I beg to differ," said Lawrence, walking in with a tray of fresh orange juice and slices of watermelon. "If we're up before nine, we're practically monks."

They sat wherever the sun warmed the benches best. Aimee arrived with a notebook under one arm, sketching the outline of the courtyard as people settled into its rhythm. Across the table, Pippi traced the rim of her coffee cup with one finger.

"I've been thinking…" she began.

"That usually means something excellent or dangerous," said Caroline.

"Why not both?" Pippi grinned. "What if we host a midsummer night's retreat? Something dreamy and slow. Sketching by moonlight. Writing beneath the jasmine. Wine that only comes out after ten."

"I love it," said Catherine. "That could be our theme for July."

"I can write the workshop plan," Aimee said. "And I know a poet she's based in Hydra now who might love to teach."

Michalis joined just then, balancing a plate of koulouria and a small jug of tsikoudia.

"Are we starting a new venture before I've had breakfast?"

"Always," said James, laughing.

The morning rolled into itself lazily. Hugo set to watering the garden, stopping now and then to stare at the view, as if checking it hadn't changed. The sea sparkled and shimmered as a mirror that offered no answers, only reassurance.

Later, Linda walked down the olive path with a bag of washing for the new machine. She and Caroline had commandeered the laundry room as their unofficial office. The renovations were complete, now all six rooms open and functioning, but there was still bedding to sort, invoices to double-check, and a line of receipts to translate.

"I found a marble soap dish in the shape of a fig," Caroline said, appearing behind her. "I think it needs to live in the sea-lily room."

Linda didn't even blink. "Then let it live there."

In the shade of the pomegranate tree, Thanassis was explaining grafting to Lawrence and James, using a split stick and an olive branch. "This one will bear the fruit of another tree," he said, binding the wound gently. "It takes trust. And patience. And good luck."

James looked down at the branch. "A bit like people."

Thanassis nodded. "Exactly like people."

That afternoon, a visitor arrived, a woman in her sixties with a straw hat pinned at an angle and a tote bag filled with what looked like manuscripts. Kosmas had sent her, apparently, and she was seeking a quiet place to revise a book.

"I need a few weeks of peace," she explained, as Catherine welcomed her to the courtyard. "Somewhere the world is kind and the sea is near."

"Then you've found the right place," Catherine said. "Come sit."

Her name was Livia, and she had once been an editor in Thessaloniki. Now semi-retired, she translated poetry and hosted a radio show about forgotten voices. By dinner, she had charmed nearly everyone with her dry humour and her ability to recite Greek poets from memory.

That night, under lanterns strung from lemon trees, the group ate spaghetti with slow-cooked tomato sauce, thick with cinnamon and basil. Livia told tales of the Thessaloniki art scene in the eighties, and Caroline added flourishes to every anecdote.

"Why is it," Livia asked at one point, "that all of you are here, together, in this place? It feels like a play I've arrived halfway through."

There was a long pause. Then Pippi answered.

"Because we each needed something healing, purpose, rest, love, and somehow this place offered all four."

Livia nodded. "Then may it keep offering."

And with that toast, they raised their glasses again, under stars newly returned from their winter sleep.

Part 2:
Greek Easter

The last of the Easter red egg shells had been swept from the steps, and the garden no longer echoed with firecrackers and midnight cheers. But a quieter joy remained, like the scent of lemon blossoms clinging to the air.

Hugo, for the first time in weeks, had slept until after sunrise. Linda found him on the courtyard bench, coffee in hand, looking less like a man adrift and more like someone beginning to imagine anchorage.

They had arranged to meet Adeline's lawyer in town for a brief meeting, she'd assured him. Just formalities.

But it had been more than that. The lawyer, a gentle woman with a steely sense of clarity, handed Hugo a slim folder and said simply,

She loved you. She wanted no questions left unanswered."

Inside, Hugo found letters two in Adeline's elegant, looping hand. One addressed to him, and one for Linda, tucked inside a crimson envelope. He could not bring himself to read it just yet, but he knew what it meant: she had not left him behind. She had thought forward, past her own death, and made sure he was included in whatever came next.

On the walk back up the hill, he asked Linda,

"Did you know she'd done all this?"

"She mentioned some things," Linda said. "But that was Adeline. She planned and protected always quietly, always with grace."

He nodded, and they paused at the top of the olive grove. The sea shimmered ahead, a mirror to the soft skies.

"I don't know what to do with it all yet," he admitted.

"You don't need to," Linda replied. "Just let it be for a while."

Back at the guesthouse, Caroline had transformed the lounge with armfuls of wildflowers and the scent of baked oranges. She twirled in with a basket of warm koulourakia.

"Today we celebrate! The first guests of May have checked in, and I didn't once call the booking system a 'satanic maze.'"

"Progress," Lawrence muttered, folding towels nearby.

"Also," Caroline added, raising an eyebrow, "Thanassis has agreed to build me a pergola. With jasmine and wisteria. A proper one. Not a wobbly contraption from a DIY nightmare."

"Did you ask him," Pippi teased, "or did you bat your lashes and threaten manual labour?"

"I may have offered to paint it naked," Caroline said with mock pride. "But only the undercoat."

The room dissolved into laughter, and Hugo, standing at the doorway, allowed himself to laugh too. The sound startled him. It felt honest.

Later, he returned to the almond tree garden. The plaque gleamed softly in the sun. He sat beside it for a long time, hands in his lap. No tears this time. Just quiet. Eventually, he began to speak aloud, as though to her.

"You were always more than I deserved," he said. "And I'm still here. That's the part I don't quite know what to do with. But I will."

The next day, a new guest arrived, a lecturer from Thessaly seeking silence. She was shown to the sea-lily room, and on the pillow lay a welcome card in Aimee's hand:

May you find what you didn't know you needed.

In the weeks ahead, the garden would be mapped for new shade beds, Caroline's pergola would slowly climb skyward, and Thanassis would sketch out a plan for a secret nook, a bench beneath the olive trees, dedicated to stillness.

And Hugo, for his part, would keep walking.

One morning at a time.

Chapter: 25
Collecting Samantha the return

The sea between Crete and the mainland stretched wide and glittering, a canvas of motion and memory. *Samantha* moved steadily across it, her sails full of promise. Serge stood at the helm, eyes scanning the horizon. At the same time, Marco, barefoot as always, double-checked their plotted course: a gentle arc northward, with one deliberate detour to Kapsali, then Agia Pelagia on beloved Kythera.

They had decided it without much discussion. Just a glance between Marco and Michalis when they lifted anchor from Agios Nikolaos, and a quiet nod from Serge. It was during their winter voyage that they'd first encountered Kythera's quiet warmth, the improbable kindness of strangers, the tranquil magic of its coastline. Now, in the rising light of spring, it felt right to return.

As *Samantha* swept past the jagged rocks of Cape Malea, the winds shifted, and Kapsali appeared like a pearl at the base of Kythera's southern cliffs. The horseshoe bay was calm, the twin lighthouses blinking like lazy guardians. Above them, the whitewashed houses of Chora clung to the hilltop like gulls.

A handsome young policeman, possibly the same one who had welcomed them in winter, waved them in and took their ropes with ease. He remembered them.

"Takis told me to keep a bottle ready. I'll call him," he said with a wink. "He says you owe him a rematch at *tavli*."

The small port of Kapsali is a tangle of pots outside the café, the slow scent of jasmine drifting on the breeze. A row of boats bobbed gently against the quay. Children darted barefoot through the alleyways. It was mid-afternoon, the light soft and long.

Serge exhaled. "This place feels like a held breath."

They loaded a few supplies and cast off for Agia Pelagia, on the northeast of the island.

Takis did indeed open his taverna for them once again, the chairs scrubbed, the wine simple but oh-so-generous, the food a cascade of local warmth: capers, olives, slow-cooked lamb, potatoes soaked in lemon. They ate under tiny lights strung across olive trees, sharing plates and toasts and stories that had never found their moment before.

Later, as stars settled over the dark ridge of Pelagia, Michalis walked the edge of the quay with James. They spoke of gardens and quiet grief, of Linda and the way she hummed when she worked. James mentioned the latest update from the villa: the last two rooms are nearly done, Linda is pacing herself, and Hugo is doing better.

They spent two days in Kapsali. Mornings began with coffee and sea swims, and ended with the slow clink of glasses and the kind of laughter that only comes from people who have weathered things together. Marco bought dried figs and a bar of soap that smelled of sage. Lawrence wrote in his battered notebook. Serge carved a small owl from driftwood and left it at the base of a pine tree near the chapel as an offering of thanks.

On their final morning, Serge and Michalis woke early and took the dinghy out to Vroulea, a little cove south of the Pelagia harbour, where the rocks sloped gently into turquoise. The sea was glass. When they slipped into the water, the cold gripped their lungs, then released them.

A moment later, a sea turtle appeared calm, ancient, curious. It glided near, looked at them with those dark, prehistoric eyes, then swam off, unbothered by the intruders in its world.

Back on board, wrapped in towels, Serge murmured, "We should come back every year."

Michalis nodded. "We owe this island something."

Kythera was truly a place that was hard to forget. Aphrodite had chosen well to land there.

As *Samantha* rounded the headland and headed north toward Poros, the cliffs of Kythera softened into haze behind them, and with them, a part of the voyage slipped gently into memory.

Part 1:
Summer's Promise

The final leg from Kythera to Poros was uneventful in the best possible way: a calm sea, a favourable wind, and the kind of companionable silence that exists only among close friends. *Samantha* glided past the coastlines of the Peloponnese, past islands like verses in a poem; Monemvasia, distant in the mist; Spetses, rising like a queen from the sea.

As they passed the curve of Spetses, Serge pointed out the Poseidonion Grand, the grande dame of hotels, all Belle Époque grace. "The waiters are as perfect as the cocktails," he said with a knowing smile. "Aimee would adore it."

Dokos followed, a quiet hump of green where goats roamed and clouds gathered briefly, then disappeared. They took watches in pairs, read weathered books, and talked in the evenings over bowls of chickpeas and fried peppers, voices trailing into the breeze.

On the second day, they caught a small tuna and cooked it on deck with lemon, oil, and salt. That night, they drank the last of Eleni's winter rakomelo, its cinnamon heat threading warmth through the night air. Laughter echoed across the sea. Lawrence remarked how strange it was how quickly one could feel changed at sea, as if something soft inside reassembled itself when far from land.

On the fourth morning, just as a blush of rose lit the horizon, they rounded the final headland. Poros rose from the water in sun-dappled tiers of white houses and terracotta roofs stacked along the hillside like amphitheatre seats awaiting a drama. The old clock tower glinted faintly above the strait, standing sentinel in the early light.

"Samantha," Marco whispered, guiding her with instinctual ease, "you're home."

They passed Frog Island a rocky outcrop shaped unmistakably like its namesake and raised a toast with the last of the white wine. It had become their ritual: passing the stone amphibian, laughter and cheers, someone tossing a coin into the sea for luck. Serge added a sprig of thyme to the water. "For the season ahead."

As they approached the jetty, figures came into view, three at first, then five, then more. Catherine's hair caught the wind like a banner. Aimee stood beside her, shading her eyes with one hand. Linda waved a cloth from the apothiki balcony. Caroline, unmistakable in orange linen, stood with Thanassis, whose strong arms were folded in quiet welcome.

The reunion was a joyful tangle of hugs, mock scolding, and real affection. James was swept into Linda's arms. Marco spun Catherine in a circle. Michalis, grinning, was handed a still-warm koulouri and a fig plucked from Aimee's basket. Serge simply touched his forehead to Thanassis's, a gesture they'd adopted one winter night, when words had failed them.

That afternoon, they gathered on the terrace of Villa Petrouni, the hills behind them humming their familiar chorus of pine and cicadas. The sea stretched below like hammered silver. A long table had been set: olives, bread, cheeses, and slow-roasted lamb that Michalis had organised with Eleni before they'd set sail. The whole retreat had been waiting, poised for this moment of return.

As the sun dipped toward the lemon trees, Catherine stood and raised her glass.

"To arrivals. To returns. And to everything this place has become."

She paused, soft-eyed. "Adeline would have loved this."

There was a hush, not sorrowful, but full.

"And," she added, smiling again, "to the rooms so close to finish."

Everyone laughed and cheered.

Part 2:
Summer's Promise –

The morning after the welcome feast, Aimee rose early. The cicadas had not yet begun their symphony, and jasmine drifted lazily through the shutters. She tied her hair with a ribbon and crossed the path to the guesthouse, where the last two rooms stood waiting like half-finished canvases.

The first room was bathed in gentle eastern light. Its palette was soft and grounded, faded pinks, terracotta shadows, the grey of ancient marble. Aimee had drawn inspiration from a sea lily frieze she once sketched at the Archaeological Museum in Athens. It stayed with her, its curls and lines a symbol of both fragility and endurance. A hand-embroidered bedspread, sewn by a woman in Galatas, covered the bed. Cushions bore delicate motifs stitched in soft gold thread. Above the writing desk, Aimee had painted a mural herself: a stylised wave with petals rising from it in memory, made visible.

The bathroom, tucked behind a sliding wooden door, featured rough-hewn stone basins and a mirror framed in driftwood, bleached by time. Michalis had installed the tiles, each one glazed in a different shade of blush and ochre, catching the sunlight like shells at low tide.

The second room, "the new style one," as Serge liked to call it, was a blend of minimalism and warmth. Serge and Marco had led the design, infusing it with quiet elegance: pale grey silk panels with embroidered Greek keys, polished wood floors, dark bronze fittings. In one corner stood a sculpture by a local artist, an abstract olive tree in silver wire, its roots sprawling into nothingness. "Hotel meets Hellenic," Serge had joked, but Aimee knew how much thought had gone into every detail. Even the wardrobe handles were shaped like stylised sea horses.

Linda added her signature: crisp white sheets and linen blinds that offered privacy without shutting out the light. Catherine had sourced the woven floor mats from a tiny Athenian market. And Caroline, ever unpredictable, had left a basket in each room with a handwritten note and a miniature bottle of homemade limoncello. *For the brave and weary traveller*, hers read.

By noon, the courtyard stirred to life. Hugo arrived last, carrying a wooden crate of almond blossoms, Adeline's final gift, still blooming into summer. He smiled more now, thinner, perhaps, and still quiet, but there was a lightness in his step. He had taken to trimming roses and baking koulourakia with monk-like dedication. His bread-making sessions with Pippi had become both ritual and joy, each attempt tastier than the last.

Aimee and Linda later found him beneath the pergola, where they were finalising guest bookings. The numbers were better than expected, a whole house for the next month. There was Manolo, an

Italian poet; Bart and Else, Dutch photographers; a family from Syros; and three young artists from Thessaloniki. The guestbook was now heavy with pages of handwritten messages, sketches, and watercolours. Echoes of presence.

"We'll have to start thinking about next year," Linda said.

"I think," Aimee replied, glancing at the blooming garden, "that this place is just beginning."

From the upper terrace, Thanassis called down, "There's a breeze coming. Should I put up the shades?"

Caroline appeared beside him, a long silk scarf tied around her head, cheeks flushed with either laughter or exertion. "Or we could just move inside and turn on the fan."

Instead, they stayed outside, passing around chilled glasses of ouzo, letting the breeze lift the corners of the tablecloth like wings. In the distance, Samantha was visible again, anchored just beyond the headland, bobbing gently like a contented sea creature, finally home.

Part 3:
Summer's Promise

That afternoon, in the shade of the almond trees, the courtyard buzzed with quiet preparation. Aimee helped Catherine string lanterns for the evening supper. Thanassis and James debated the best angle for the jasmine vines to climb the freshly painted wall. Caroline sat cross-legged, shelling almonds into a blue-glazed bowl, her bare feet resting on a cushion Hugo had embroidered with Adeline's initials.

Hugo, looking more at ease than he had in months, cleared his throat and tapped the table.

"I wanted to say something," he began. His voice was still a little fragile, like vellum drying in the sun.

Everyone turned to him with a circle of care and attention.

"There's a bakery in town," he said. "Just down from the square. You all know it. Mr. Stathis is retiring. He's looking for someone to take it on. I've been... thinking. I might buy in."

A quiet pause, and then James let out a soft whoop. "Hugo, that's brilliant."

"You'll be marvellous," Catherine said, already picturing the pastries. "Will you bake?"

"I'll help at the counter a few mornings a week," Hugo replied, smiling. "And I want to bring in young local talent kids who love baking, who need a chance.

Maybe help them start something of their own. Pippi promised to keep an eye on the figures."

Linda reached across the table and squeezed his hand. "She'd have loved that."

He nodded. "She would."

"And we'll help," Serge added. "Marco's already designing nautical-blue aprons. You'll have branding by Friday."

"And customers," Michalis said, "if your koulourakia are anything like the ones you made last week."

Hugo laughed then, a full, warm laugh. "I'll stick to Eleni's recipe, but thank you."

That evening, they gathered in the lounge, the one with Marco and Serge's wood burner. It was just cool enough to light, and Aimee did, sending gusts of heat up into the open night.

"It's our Greek eco-heater," Marco joked. "Heating us since Christmas."

They dined indoors at a long table draped in hand-stitched linen. Bougainvillea bloomed from the centre. Caroline had tucked handwritten name cards under each plate. "For once, not alphabetised," she grinned.

Pippi had returned from London in a flurry of sea breeze and hugs, carrying a bottle of London gin and a story about being mistaken for someone's aunt at Gatwick. She slipped back into the rhythm of the group effortlessly, warm and grounded. She and Hugo had been emailing bakery plans obsessively.

Later, over wine, the conversation turned to "drains and radiators", a phrase that had once come up and stayed.

"I lived with a drain," Aimee said. The silence that followed was not heavy, just true.

"We all did, in some way," Caroline murmured.

James raised his glass. "To the radiators, then."

"To warmth," said Lawrence. "And to choosing it."

"To all of you," Hugo whispered.

The next morning, before the sun climbed too high, they placed a plaque at the base of the almond trees.

Adeline – Curator of Beauty, Keeper of Grace.

Hugo stood beside it, holding Linda's hand as the breeze stirred the first petals into motion.

"She wanted you to keep dancing," Linda said gently.

"I think I will," he replied.

That afternoon, the courtyard filled again. Luggage wheels clicked over flagstones. New guests arrived. Catherine greeted them like old friends. Aimee handed out iced tea and paper fans. Linda double-checked bookings, and Michalis gave an orientation that was half practical, half stand-up comedy.

The small hotel was open truly open. And with it, something else had opened too: a future not imagined, but built. Together.

As twilight fell, Aimee and Catherine stood beneath the almond trees, arm in arm.

"We did it," Aimee said.

"No," Catherine replied, resting her head on her sister's shoulder. "We're just beginning."

And out on the water, the faint shape of Samantha rocked gently in the dusk, waiting for the following wind, the next journey, the next promise of summer.

Chapter:26
Engagement, New Beginnings, and a Garden in Bloom

It began as a whisper of an idea, just a small circle in the courtyard, a few flowers strung between lemon trees, and low music carried on the breeze. But as word spread, the circle grew.

Serge and Marco were the first to leap into action, sketching an impromptu plan involving paper lanterns, a string quartet from Nafplio they'd met on a past voyage, and of course a decadent cake from the local bakery made with figs, almonds, and whipped anise cream. Hugo arranged that last part with quiet joy.

The party was to mark the formal engagement of Catherine and Lawrence, a celebration of a love both steady and considered, weathered through years of long-distance negotiations, quiet decisions made in the half-light of winter, and finally, a shared dream here on Poros. They had once thought, perhaps, they were too old for such declarations. But now, beneath the almond tree, Adeline had chosen its pink-white blossoms catching the last golden light, and it all felt perfectly timed.

Catherine wore a dress the colour of summer dusk, her froth of pearls catching the fading light. Lawrence had borrowed a linen shirt from Michalis, one that fit in a way his London clothes never had. There were toasts many of them and speeches that wandered joyfully off-topic. Aimee spoke about learning to paint the light on water. Caroline made them laugh with tales of Lawrence's early cooking disasters. Thanassis presented them with a wreath of olive branches, and Eleni, in a rare moment of unguarded affection, kissed Catherine on both cheeks and said simply, *"You are our sister now."*

Guests filtered in from town: Anton arrived with his boat shoes still on, Kosmas brought wine and a local teacher of Byzantine music, and Anthi, the jeweller, presented Catherine with a small bronze charm shaped like the island. *"Your new compass,"* she said.

There was a feeling in the air that something had taken root, not just the engagement, but the quiet certainty that love, when planted well, will bloom.

Later, after the lanterns had been lit and the musicians had tucked into their own plates of lamb and rosemary potatoes, Aimee slipped into her studio to catch her breath. She paused at the open window, gazing out at the courtyard below. The laughter, the clink of glasses, the sound of Thanassis gently explaining to Caroline the difference between myrtle and wild oregano, it all drifted upward like a memory already in the making.

On her worktable sat a small, cloth-bound journal. It had belonged to Adeline. Hugo had found it beneath the cushion of her favourite chair and passed it to Aimee a few days earlier with quiet reverence. He hadn't opened it. *She'll know what to do,* he'd said.

Inside, the first page read, in Adeline's distinct, looping hand:

"I have always believed that true legacy is not found in museums, banks, or legal documents. It's found in the feeling someone leaves behind when they walk out of a room. My hope is to be remembered not for my things, but for the way I saw the world, a little cracked, but filled with light."

Aimee turned the pages slowly, her heart folding in and out with each carefully penned observation reflections on Hugo, Linda's kindness, the sound of figs falling on the roof at night. One entry, from just after the almond trees were planted, read:

"One day, I won't be here to see them bloom. But someone will. And that is enough."

The next morning, after a slow coffee on the veranda, Lawrence joined James and Michalis by the garden beds. Thanassis had mapped out the summer rotation, and they'd begun setting in lemon verbena and tall red basil, the soil already warm to the touch.

Pippi, freshly returned from London, came down the path with a notebook in hand and a hopeful gleam in her eye.

"We've had a dozen new enquiries," she called out, beaming. "One from a writer's retreat in Berlin that

385

wants to partner for residencies. Another from a group of landscape painters. And someone from the *Telegraph Travel* section is asking for an interview."

Michalis raised an eyebrow. "We're famous now?"

"Practically," she grinned. "But don't worry, I didn't mention the goat that keeps breaking into the storeroom."

Just then, Hugo emerged from the bakery, flour dusting his sleeves, a smudge on his cheek. He waved across the courtyard. He'd started working there three mornings a week, slowly learning the old recipes and rhythms of village life from the elderly owner, who was finally ready to retire.

"I'm going to need help," he called out to Linda, who was crossing the street with a woven shopping bag. "Teenagers who can knead dough, and not burn the sesame."

"You'll find them," she said, stepping up beside him.

"Or they're hiding," he chuckled, then added more quietly, "But I want to try. Adeline would have wanted it full of life."

Part 1:
Summer's Promise

A Late Summer Sail and a View to Forever

The breeze that morning was gentle, like the touch of an old friend. The Argolic Gulf glittered, and *Samantha* sat poised at anchor, her lines slack in the warm water, as if she too had been waiting for this moment. Marco and Serge stood at the stern, overseeing the final checks with the quiet rhythm of long familiarity.

Aimee was the last to arrive, sketchbook under one arm, straw hat in the other.

"You'll be pleased to know," she called up to Serge, "I've brought snacks this time."

"If it's oregano crisps again, I'm jumping overboard," came the reply, followed by laughter.

Lawrence and Catherine were already settled on the shaded deck cushions, arms brushing, wine cooling in a bucket nearby. Michalis untied the last rope, kissed Aimee's forehead as she climbed aboard, and the motor hummed softly to life. They were bound for a day at sea, no fixed agenda, only the quiet pull of summer's last call, and the need to mark it.

They glided past the curve of Poros Town, its pink and terracotta rooftops catching the morning light. Children waved from the quayside, and a few locals lifted coffee cups in greeting. Hugo was among them, apron still around his waist, standing outside the bakery. He waved broadly, holding up a loaf like a benediction.

As they passed Monastiri Bay, the engine was cut and the sails unfurled. The boat leaned gently, the sea catching her and carrying her forward with grace. Conversation drifted with the wind. Caroline and Thanassis were finishing the new lavender path, Linda's autumn bookings were discussed, and a spreadsheet printed in green ink had become the most talked-about item at the villa. Olive picking was being mooted as a tourist attraction.

Lunch was shared just east of Methana: feta, figs, and sardines grilled the night before. Aimee opened Adeline's small cloth-bound journal and read aloud a single line:

"Some journeys do not end. They become landscapes in the hearts of those who remember."

They raised glasses to Adeline, to Hugo, to almond trees in bloom, and to things that continue long after we expect them to.

In the afternoon, *Samantha* steered south toward the coast of Angistri. The water deepened in colour, but the sky held its calm. They paused outside the port of Methana, white houses climbing the hillside like scattered doves, the curved bay mirroring the shape of sleep. Serge suggested they stop.

"Not today," Marco smiled. "But soon."

They lingered near Vathi, where they had swum months before. The memory of the sea turtle returned, and James pointed toward a ripple on the surface. Michalis leaned back.

"This is what joy feels like," he said. "Not the big explosions. This. The quiet."

Aimee nodded. "Like finishing a painting and not wanting to sign it as if it belongs to the air."

By evening, *Samantha* was sailing the final leg home. The light bent golden across the deck. Catherine's hair lifted softly in the breeze. Lawrence stood beside her, watching Poros draw near. From this angle, Villa Petrouni and the guesthouse were just visible through the trees, small but complete, part of the island now.

"Poros off the port bow!" Serge called.

They gathered at the rail to watch it come into view, not just the place, but the people, the purpose, and the slow, steady love that had built it. Soon there would be rooms to prepare, bookings to confirm, and an autumn planting guide Thanassis had annotated with drawings of birds and herbs. But for now, they were simply here afloat, together, surrounded by sky.

Summer's Promise

An Evening to Carry Forward

Back on land, the light lingered that late summer gold that clung to the sea-facing walls of Villa Petrouni and turned the olive leaves to silver. Caroline and Lawrence hurried home, preparations to make—no need to rush. Pippi and Caroline had already worked their quiet magic.

The courtyard was not formal, but full of grace. Pippi arranged thyme and wild roses in mismatched glasses; Linda lit candles in old blue wine bottles she'd long refused to throw away. Serge and Marco moved through the space like theatre directors adjusting lanterns, debating the playlist, laughing over whether it was too French-English or too Greek.

Caroline arrived with Thanassis just before sunset. He'd spent the afternoon pressing herbs into the stone path near the almond trees, not from necessity, but because it brought him peace. She touched his arm and whispered something. He smiled in that rare way of his slow, luminous, real. She had brought lavender potted in hessian bags for the tables. "Waste not," she said. "Thanassis will plant them all by Thursday."

Lawrence stood near the steps, drink in hand. Catherine slipped her arm around his waist and raised her left hand to the lantern light. A ring glimmered not ostentatiously, but quietly perfect. She kissed him with the urgency of a love that had earned its stillness.

There were gasps, laughter, and applause, joy spilling into the night like wine over the lip of a glass.

Michalis kissed Aimee's hand and whispered, "See? More weddings."

"No more swimming proposals," she replied, mock stern. "Unless you want another sprained ankle."

James lifted a glass. "To love that finds us. To endings that bloom again."

After dinner, lamb, baked aubergine, and Caroline's accidental but delicious tzatziki, the courtyard quieted. Stars gathered overhead, casual and endless. Somewhere behind the house, Hugo baked almond crescents for the morning. He had stayed, found rhythm, even taught a local teenager how to shape dough with gentle hands. Linda often said Adeline would have been proud. And they all knew she was.

Aimee wandered to the almond grove, now fully planted and lit with handmade lanterns. She rested her fingers on the smooth trunk of the tree Adeline had gifted. At its base, a bronze plaque nestled in thyme read:

For the joy she gave, and the joy she wished for us all.

She heard footsteps. Catherine.

"You alright?"

"Yes," Aimee said. "More than alright."

They stood beneath the canopy of stars and petals, shoulder to shoulder, remembering everything; London winters, first sails, the heartbreaks that hollowed them, the community that restored them.

Later still, James and Linda walked down the slope past the fourno room, now strung with jasmine and warm fairy lights. The hotel was full. Guests painted, wrote, and cooked. Friendships formed. Stories began. The rhythm of the place had taken root.

"We've built something," James said quietly.

"We have," Linda replied. "And it's not just walls or bookings. It's real."

They stopped to listen. Laughter. Music. Clinking glasses.

Life. And love.

Epilogue

A Letter from Aimee, Poros, One Year Later

Dear friends,

I don't know if this will reach you. Perhaps it is just a note to myself, written in the early morning quiet while the shutters still hold the sun at bay and the swallows skim low over the garden.

A year has passed. A whole year since I first said yes to something I didn't quite understand. To Michalis. To this place. To the idea that maybe life wasn't finished with me yet.

I was so frightened when I arrived. You remember, don't you? Catherine had to almost drag me here. My bones felt brittle with disappointment, and I'd forgotten how to breathe correctly, that kind of breathing that comes when you're painting in the open air, or swimming beneath a vast blue sky, or laughing so hard your ribs ache. I'd stopped doing all of that.

Now I wake to the scent of lemon trees and coffee. I walk barefoot. I paint things that don't need to be understood, only felt. I love someone who sees me for what I am, not as what I once was, or tried to be.

There is a kind of grace in building something small and good. This place, this garden, these rooms we've shaped with our hands and our hopes, they matter. Not for how many stars they earn or what magazines might call it, but because people come here and remember who they are. They cry. They rest. They laugh. They dare to begin again.

Michalis just came in, carrying figs and bread. He's humming. I'll go join him in a moment.

But first, I wanted to write this.

To say thank you to all of you who held me through the fog. Who reminded me that joy is not a childish thing to be abandoned, it's a right, and a choice.

We're planning another sail soon. *Samantha* is being readied. I've packed sketchbooks and pencils and that ridiculous straw hat Marco insists I wear. I think we'll head for Kythera again. I want to see the cliffs in late spring, when the wildflowers push through cracks like declarations of stubborn hope.

Maybe that's what we all are. Wildflowers in strange places. Still blooming, despite it all.

With love,

Aimee

Acknowledgements

To the islands—for their light, their laughter, their lessons.

To those—real and imagined- who shaped this story in ways too subtle to name.

To those—who said "go," when I was afraid to leave.

And, to those—who said "stay," when I was tempted to run.

To the ones who always say "yes, please."
To the kind souls who meet ideas with light, not shadow.
Who answers, "Let's do it," before asking how.
Who bring casseroles and calm, champagne and cheer,
Who remind me — time and again — that love is a verb,
And found family is the finest kind.

This is for you.
Your faith, your fire, your quiet grace.
You are the true epidemic —
Of joy, of possibility, of saying *yes*.

My departed parents, David and Sheena, will forever be a joy and inspiration.

To my readers—Thank you for choosing to walk alongside these characters. Your presence means everything.

To my partner Mark and my son Chris, who are my greatest support and strength.

And finally, to life, messy, radiant, bewildering life, for always offering one more tide to follow.